UNKNOWN VARIANT

SARA GROVER

Unknown Variant

ISBN-13: 978-1-955937-62-7 (Paperback)
ISBN-13: 978-1-955937-61-0 (eBook)

Published by Defiance Press and Publishing, LLC

Bulk orders of this book may be obtained by contacting Defiance Press and Publishing, LLC. www.defiancepress.com.

Public Relations Dept. – Defiance Press & Publishing, LLC
281-581-9300
pr@defiancepress.com

Defiance Press & Publishing, LLC
281-581-9300
info@defiancepress.com

This book is dedicated to my friends and family who have supported me through my writing with feedback and encouragement.

PROLOGUE

BY THE YEAR 2152, HUMANITY had suffered from a plethora of maladies both environmental and biological. Over the past five generations, humans have been increasingly plagued by genetic defects dooming them to either develop serious diseases or be born with debilitating mental and physical handicaps. The oceans had risen, swallowing up coastal areas around the world and forcing billions to move inland. Precious farmland and pastures were lost in the flooding. Food became scarce and was rationed as billions of people crowded into already overpopulated areas.

The cities of the world plunged into chaos as people fought for what little space and resources remained. The poor became desperate; robbery and murder rates skyrocketed. The wealthy, who were unaccustomed to being denied their life of excess, lived in constant fear of the riotous general population and tried to use their otherwise useless money to lobby governments around the globe. With the threat of civilization unraveling entirely before their eyes, the leaders of the world congregated to make a decision that went against everything that humanity stood for. The task: to find a solution that would reverse the "de-evolution" of our species and lower the unsustainable population of approximately 9.5 billion.

The governments and the wealthy thought of these "inferior" people as a drain on the system. They simply cost too much to take care of, the wealthy claimed. They used up precious food, depleted scarce natural resources, and contributed little save for creating more children with more problems. It was decided that helping them to live was against nature, that it was reversing the very evolution of man by permitting such undesirable mutations to continue being passed down through the generations.

This plan was not shared openly with the general public, for it their true aim had been transparent, anarchy would likely have ensued. The first phase of the plan was to obtain blood samples from every single person. The samples were then sent to labs to decipher every individual's genome, and individuals who displayed any genetic markers for diseases or abnormalities received a tattoo that read "GI."

Those who received these tattoos had no clue what GI meant, nor did they know that there was anything "wrong" with them to be concerned about. In truth, the tattoo stood for "genetically inferior." They had been branded like cows for the slaughter.

Along with the tattoo, they each received an ID number. At first this seemed logical, like the old Social Security number system; the ID numbers were coded labels indicating a person's genetic follies. The numbers were just to keep count, but the letters were what mattered. The longer the ID, the more genetically inferior the person—H stood for hemophilia, SC for sickle cell anemia, MR for mentally retarded, and specific cancers were indicated by various abbreviations like BRSC, BRNC, LEU, etc. Anything that the elites deemed wrong with one's DNA had a code.

It took about four years to test and tattoo everyone. For babies born during this time frame and after the mandate, they were to be brought into the genetic testing centers no more than one month after birth. Their ID numbers went right on their birth certificates, and they received tattoos as well. They would grow up thinking this was always how it had been.

In 2157, those who had been tattooed found out what it was all for—and it wasn't to help them. Citizens who were severely disabled—anyone who couldn't walk, had been deemed mentally retarded or psychotic, or had cancer—were rounded up in night raids. Military and armed police in riot gear banged on their doors in the middle of the night and hauled them off in the back of large semi-trucks. Those poor souls were taken to military facilities and, as the governments put it, "put out of their misery—and ours." How they were murdered cannot be said for certain, as this information was classified and buried under heaps of bureaucracy. There are many rumors, but they are all too horrible to even imagine, never mind talk about.

Those who weren't "put out of their misery" were cut off from all medical care. The governments decided that it was a waste of money to prolong their lives. If they got sick and died, such was the natural order of things, and it should not be interfered with. Those tattooed that were left to live unaided had major or minor health issues or sometimes no obvious problems at all. Their "inferior" genetics caused conditions such as diabetes, obesity, autism, schizophrenia, dwarfism, a propensity to develop Alzheimer's disease, or just unknown changes in their DNA sequence that were deemed abnormal to the geneticist. If someone had a condition that required treatment or accommodation to lead a productive life, or if there was even a possibility they could develop such a condition, they were fully on their own. The best they could do was work to feed their families and hope they didn't get sick.

It didn't take long for people to start discriminating against those with tattoos, which quickly lead to segregation. Those of the GI population, even if they were educated or held positions of power, were fired. Schools stopped allowing GI children to attend, including universities, and thus the GI population that was left was forced into a life of poverty and servitude.

In the years that immediately followed the Cleansing, as it soon came to be called, the GI population that remained—which still greatly outnumbered that of the genetically "normal"—tried as best they could to carry on living, hoping that one day mankind would regain its humanity. People continued to marry and have children, though the rates of infant mortality skyrocketed due to the denial of medical care of any kind.

By 2190, GI communities around the world began stabilizing after the chaos left billions of people with their lives turned upside down. With a whole new generation of GI children raised to adulthood in this new society, people were becoming complacent; they didn't know of anything better than what they had. It was into this world I was born, nineteen years and eight months ago, on the night of September 22, 2195, in the midst of Hurricane Layla.

CHAPTER ONE

AS I REACH FOR MY purse, there's knocking at the door. "Just a minute!" I shout through the door. I can't let whatever creep lie behind that door in just yet. I scramble to open the zipper pocket in the lining, finally touching the syringe and vial. I set the goods down on the bed and tie off my left arm.

"Open the damned door already!" a man shouts at me through the door. I ignore him and draw a syringe-full from the vial and relax as the needle pierces my skin. I breathe a sigh of relief and fling open the door to see what I'm in for.

"About time there, little lady," says a balding man with a thick mustache and a creepy grin on his face. He stinks of booze, and at a quick glance I can see he doesn't have a tattoo on his wrist.

"Where's your receipt?" I inquire matter-of-factly.

"Wouldn't you like to know, sugar," answers the Normie pig.

I should probably clarify that for y'all: a Normie is a person of "normal" genetics, unlike myself, a GI—genetically inferior. Damn old Normie bastards are always showing up at my door to pay for forbidden fruit. I always seem to get a disproportionate number of old creeps, in particular.

"I don't have time for this shit," I mutter and pick up the phone by the bed to call Andromeda, the woman who runs this old crappy hotel. She gives us rooms to use, handles all the money up front, takes 25 percent, and pays you at the end of your shift.

"Hey, Andy, it's Layla. How much did this pig pay?"

"Fifty Ameros," she answers. I hang up and turn to the man in my room, who has now closed the door behind him.

"Fifty. You've got thirty minutes. It's 2:17. Go," I tell him.

At this point, it doesn't matter what he does as long as I'm relatively unharmed and get my pay at the end of the night. It only takes a couple of minutes for the haze to start kicking in. Then, it's all just an emotionless blur. I still have my wits about me somewhat, but I don't have to deal with the disgust and shame I would feel otherwise; there's only a peaceful numbness that takes over my body and mind.

I had to start doing haze to do my job. Being a prostitute is the best-paying gig a girl like me can get. I started working here when I was fifteen, and before that I worked at the fish cannery on the Wharf gutting fish all day. The job didn't pay well enough and wasn't worth the emotional toll it took on me. My dad died of pneumonia when I was fourteen, at which point I became the sole provider for my family. I'm the oldest of four kids; the youngest, my sister Daisy, is five years old now. My mom can't work because she has hemophilia; a cut on the job could kill her, as we GI folks don't get any medical care. So, because of all that crap, here I am.

I glance at the clock on the wall when, by chance, his ugly mug is out of my line of sight. My time on haze is my private time, at least in my head. I use the complete numbness to let my mind wander. It can be hard, though, with some of these pigs having their mouths and hands all over me, pushing me this way and that, and the annoying sounds that come from them would make me puke if I were sober. The sudden lack of jerking motions brings me back a bit as I realize that this pathetic excuse of a man is finished. I gaze up at the clock—2:26 a.m. I reach for my shirt when he grabs my wrist.

"I paid for thirty minutes," he says, squeezing my wrist tightly.

"Well you look done to me, so get out," I bark, yanking my wrist free.

"When I pay good money for your time, I expect to get every second of it. Or if not for myself, then maybe for some good buddies of mine until the clock runs out," he jeers.

"That's not how it works, asshole. Get out!" I protest. The pathetic bastard punches me hard, knocking me onto the bed. An explosion of pressure consumes the right side of my face. If not for the haze, I'm sure this would hurt pretty badly. I can't see straight, but I can hear the door open and see two figures stagger in.

"I paid good money for her. No point in wasting it," laughs the Normie pig who took his pleasures with me just moments ago.

"Well ain't she something!" exclaims one of the two new creeps. "You sure those are real, Trevor?"

"Felt real to me," replies the pig, now known as Trevor.

"Come on, Wally! You know these GI whores can't even get a boob job. Those are au natural!" the third man says, whose face is spinning around the more I try to focus. He walks over, crouches down on top of me, and starts groping my chest. He's stout and heavy, and probably in his fifties, but that's all I can make out. He stinks like hell, and he is speaking so closely to my face that I almost gag.

"I'm gonna have fun with you!" he says with breath that smells like a mix of rotting codfish, cigars, and horse shit. As he straddles me with all of his weight, Trevor and Wally pull at my arms, and I feel a burning sensation on my wrists. They're tying me to the bed, I realize, and I'm too dizzy and overpowered to fight back. *I'm helpless unless someone comes.* But I know that won't happen; sounds of screaming and moaning are considered normal here.

One by one, they violate me in ways I don't even want to remember as I lie helplessly tied to my bed like a prisoner. *I need more haze! I don't want to remember this!* I keep thinking to myself.

I have no idea how much time passes as they have their sick

ways with me, but the last thing I can remember is Trevor coming into my view once more as he stands over me.

"Know your place, you filthy whore," he whispers menacingly into my left ear as he places his hands around my neck.

I desperately gasp for air, and then there is just nothingness.

I start to move my head slowly and groan in both pain and relief as I feel my arms being set free from the ropes. Suddenly Andy is in my view, holding one hand on each side of my face, staring into my eyes.

"Layla, Layla! Can you hear me?" she says in a gentle yet frantic way. I nod slightly in reply. My neck is stiff and sore. Even the slight nod is painful, but I manage enough for her to notice. My wrists feel like they are on fire. My circulation must have been cut off for the most part for it to hurt so much as the blood returns to my extremities, awakening every screaming nerve and bringing it to my awareness.

"Girl, what the fuck happened to you? When you didn't come up at the end of your shift, I thought you fell asleep or something. I was going to bitch you out, but instead I find this!" Andy exclaims while gesturing around the room and to me on the bed. I want to explain what I remember, but my mouth is as dry as a tumbleweed. I mouth the word "water" as best I can, hoping she will understand.

"What you want, honey?" Andy asks gently. I try a few more exaggerated movements of my mouth and it finally dawns on her. "Oh! Water, of course. Coming right up." She rushes to the sink on the opposite wall facing the front door and comes back with a plastic cup. She props my head up with one hand and with the other helps me satiate my thirst. I gulp down the tepid tap water and let out a loud sigh of relief, which is significantly easier to do when your throat has some moisture.

Finally able to make clear vocalizations, I tell Andy to get me another glass. After I finish my second glass of that life-giving liquid, I ask her to get my purse. She picks it up from the corner of the room closest to the bathroom and sets it on the bed.

"Help me sit up."

"I think you need to lie down, sweetie. You need rest."

"What do you think I was doing for the past …"—I pause and look at the clock on the wall—"three hours!"

"Being choked till you pass out doesn't count as rest, Layla," she says in that tone of voice that reminds you of being scolded by your mother. Andy is basically like an aunt to most of the girls that work here. She can tell you what to do, but she's still someone you can talk to about anything.

Andy is definitely old enough to be my aunt or mom. Her mousy brown hair, which reaches to her shoulders, has some gray streaks in the bangs, but other than that she doesn't look a day over thirty. She doesn't have any kids of her own. Who can blame her? Having kids and being GI is bad no matter what the kid is like. If the kid is, by luck, a Normie, they're taken from you and given to Normies who couldn't conceive or want more kids. Babies born to GI parents are very rarely born Normies, so odds are, the kid is going to be GI just like you. Yeah, you raise them and love them, but you know their future is nothing to be excited for. All of us GIs live lives of servitude and die of disease because we aren't allowed medical attention, as it's deemed "a waste of resources on people who aren't going to make it anyway."

I love my family. I am thankful that they are in my life—with the exception of my father—and that I was given life, but I don't want to bring kids into this world either. Even though I have sex for a living, the odds of me ever getting pregnant are pretty much zero. My clients are "genetically normal," but the ones who show up at our doors at night are damn morons. They always have condoms on them because they think they can catch our genetic defects like some contagious disease. The real reason they need to carry them—and I think it is of the utmost importance for all involved—is that a Normie and a GI having a child together warrants a death sentence for all involved. Being a mixed breed is rough; they're immediately euthanized, and the mother and biological father are both sentenced to death without trial.

"I'll rest better if you can get my haze from my purse," I tell her. Andy nods and puts my purse in her lap, then starts digging through its contents.

"How the hell do you find anything in this mess? Wouldn't kill you to clean the thing out once in a while."

"It's in the side zipper pocket in the lining," I instruct her.

"Ah, here we are. You want me to prick ya?" Andy asks, pulling my syringe and vial out of my purse and tossing the bag on the floor.

"Well, I'm not really in much of a condition to do it myself, am I?" I say sarcastically. Andy pops off the cap of the syringe and sticks her tongue out at me. She draws a dose from the vial and sets the syringe on the bed while she ties off my arm. Once she finds a good vein in my left arm, as I've recently blown a few, relief floods my body. Haze brings a relaxing warmth and numbness as it travels through the bloodstream. It's like the feeling you get from drinking hot chocolate on a chilly day.

The haze takes away most of the pain, though I still feel some soreness. Now that I'm able to move about without feeling like I'm going to pass out from the pain, I manage to get up and take a brief shower to help me not look too horrible when I get home. I still look like shit, but at least not like death.

"Take a couple of nights off," Andy says as I'm gathering up my purse and hat.

"I can't afford to."

"After last night, you're going to give me that lame excuse? You are taking the next two nights off, period. No discussion," she lectures.

"Goddamn it, Andy! I got more than just my mouth to feed here."

"You won't be doing your family any good if you get yourself killed. Not to mention, most men won't want to pay for a girl who is all beat-up looking," she says, pointing to the bruises around my neck, wrists, and right cheek. "Go home, Layla, before your mom thinks you died or something." As I open my mouth to argue, she cuts me off. "Go, now," she commands, pointing at the door. I put my big sun hat on, sling my purse over my right shoulder, and head for the door.

When I get there, Andy stops me with a soft hug and hands me my pay for that nightmare of a night. "Take care now. And I don't want to see your ass here until Friday night! Now go on home."

Giving her a weak smile, I say, "See ya Friday," and walk out the door. It's probably about seven o'clock and people are already busy on the Wharf. The brothel is right at the edge of the Wharf, perfectly placed for horny bastards who come off the big shipping boats after being out for a few days at a time. The problem is that the GI men who work the ships don't get paid diddly-squat, so they hardly ever have money to burn on something as self-indulgent as a prostitute. It's usually just the ship owners and scumbag Normies who like to cheat on their wives that come our way.

Don't get me wrong; I like my job. It could be a hell of a lot worse. I get paid more than most people, and all I have to do, most of the time, is lie there and look pretty. To think of how much power my body has over some of these fools can be just as intoxicating as a shot of good moonshine. Most of the men are disgusting slobs, but on occasion I get a young, good-looking one. The ones near my age, the ones coming home from college on break to visit Mom and Dad who want to get a commitment-free fuck, like to drop by on their way in and out of town.

The best of all are the ones who come by just before they head off for their first year—virgins. Oh, how they crack me up! They don't want to go off to college a virgin, so they make it our jobs to teach them a thing or two. They are all sweaty, shaking, overly ex-cited, and nervous—so much so that they tend to go off in about ten seconds. I really try hard not to laugh at them, but sometimes I can't help it. I think the worst, though, was this poor kid who didn't even get it in before he ruined a perfectly good condom.

I like to think that if I were a Normie, I could have anything I want if I could stay how I look now—that is, save for the stupid GI tattoo on my wrist. Without that damn thing, I bet I could land myself a politician, a CEO, a doctor—you name it. Men are men, no matter how much money they have. They all can't help but stare when I walk by. I used to hate it, but I like it now. If I didn't have this damn tattoo, I just know I could hook myself a wealthy one and never have to worry about money again.

As I draw nearer to my home on Austin Avenue, I straighten the shoulder straps on my sundress, which have slipped during my walk home, and prepare to put on an "everything is totally fine" act for my mom. All the houses of New Houston are on stilts because of the flooding from storm surges every time a hurricane or good tropical storm comes through; that way, we don't have to rebuild every time. The buildings still take some good beatings from the wind and rain, though. No one bothers painting the houses around this part of town anymore, either. We are so close to Houston Bay that it's a futile endeavor. If you don't get a storm to mess it up, all the humidity making the wood swell up and the salty sea air will.

CHAPTER TWO

AS MY RIGHT FOOT HITS that first creaky step up to the front door, I hear little feet run across the floor and soon after the door flies open. My little sister, Daisy, jumps out the front door for me to catch her on my way up. I can't let her know I'm in pain because she will start asking questions and I will have to make up lies for her, and then my mom will start badgering me. I just make a grunting noise as I catch her and tell her it's because she's getting to be such a big girl.

I get to the top step with Daisy and let her down. "Alright, squirt, the ride's over. You're going to be too big for me to do that real soon at the rate you're growing!"

"I ain't big, I'm little!" she whines, her lower lip pursed out. "Mommy says I'm her little flower."

"Whatever you say," I tease as I muss up her hair.

"Hey! Stop that!" Daisy laughs. "I'm going to tell Mom on you!"

"Go ahead, see if I care," I reply nonchalantly.

I take my hat and boots off and set them by the door. As I get to the kitchen, I hear soft stockinged feet on the wood floor coming down the hall and stopping a few feet behind me. I've always had that sense of knowing when someone is watching me. Though I have my head stuck in the fridge, looking for the milk and enjoying the cold air, I know my mom is there watching me. "Hey, Mom," I say with my head still in the refrigerator.

"You're home awfully late today. Everything alright?" she asks. I can hear the concern in her voice, but I can't tell her the truth; she worries too much already.

"Everything is fine," I lie. "Me and some of the girls were just hanging out and chatting after our shifts and time just flew by. You don't have to worry about me. You know I can take care of myself."

"What happened to your neck?"

I grab the milk carton, step back, and close the refrigerator door. "Typical workplace hazard. Just some nasty hickeys, that's all. This one guy last night was a bit of a biter. No big deal," I say, taking a swig of milk from the carton.

"Well, just cover it up with a scarf or something later. I need you to go to the market for me."

"Okay, fine, but can I have a nap first?" I say while yawning. I put the milk back in the fridge and go to the bedroom before she can respond. I'm dead tired. Andy was right—spending three hours unconscious after being choked isn't really resting.

Our house is tiny, as are most houses in the GI part of town. The only homes smaller than our place are the tenements, run-down, smelly apartment buildings that house close to a hundred families each. There is a complex with eleven buildings like that just east of my place next to Gator Beach, which is covered in trash that washes in from Houston and, yes, gators. It's kind of a marshy area more than a beach, but it's got a decent view. From Gator Beach, you can see the remnants of the skyline of downtown Houston that haven't completely been swallowed by the ocean yet.

I get to our room, which three of us four kids share—Daisy sleeps with Mom—to see my bed is occupied. "Dylan! Get out of my bed, you twit; I'm tired. You've got your own damn bed," I order. He is on his stomach with his face in my pillow.

"But Mom just washed your sheets. They smell better," Dylan whines, his voice muffled by the pillow.

I snatch the pillow from under his head. "Your bed stinks because your smelly ass is always in it," I whack him on the back of the head with the pillow. "Now get your stinky ass outta my bed, Dylan!"

"Ugh! Fine! Jerkface!" Dylan groans as he rolls off my bed onto the floor.

Little brothers are annoying—especially teen brothers. All they do is eat, sleep, and smell like BO and farts. Dylan is thirteen and my other brother, Chase, is fifteen. Maybe if they weren't such insatiable pigs, then the money I make would go farther.

With Dylan out of my bed, I flop down on my mattress and fall asleep so fast that I can't even remember closing my eyes.

The wind whips my hair back as I take in deep breaths of the salty ocean air. A flock of brown pelicans is to my right gliding along the sea breeze, only flapping their wings once or twice to keep pace with me. Ahead of us I can see the glimmer of the Williams Tower, separated from its brothers of downtown. While the oceans gradually rose from the melting of the ice caps, Houston tried building sea walls to keep the water out, but storm surges still flooded the city time after time. They couldn't keep out the rising waters and eventually abandoned the city. Eventually, all of its splendors were swallowed by the sea, save the few skeletal skyscrapers that still manage to stand above the water.

The ocean is now 210 feet higher than it was at the turn of the twenty-first century. With such a drastic rise of the water, you would think nothing could still be left, but still the Williams Tower stands 740 feet above the waves. The other remaining sentinels of Houston are the JP Morgan Chase Tower and the Bank of America Center. Every time I look out to the ocean to watch the sunrise, the three sentinels glow like angels, remnants of kinder spirits of the distant past in which they were built.

As I soar toward the remains of the Houston skyline, the birds on my right break away and fly south. I watch them fly away as a heavy sadness surges through me like lead in my veins. I turn my attention back toward the sentinels, and I suddenly start to fall. I wave my arms and legs in futility as I fall faster and faster toward the water, screaming, but no sound comes out. Just as I'm about to plunge face-first into the sea, I sit up with a start, sweating and panting in my bed.

Now fully awake, I realize how much pain I'm in. The haze is wearing off, and I'm shaking and sweating buckets. Not only do I feel the pain from last night come back but the hellish effects of coming down from the haze as well. Once you start using haze, it becomes a major part of your life. It first came about from former doctors, those who were fired for being genetically inferior. It was made to act like the opiate painkillers used in the medical field, something to help ease the suffering of those in the GI community dealing with painful diseases. The drug was named "haze" for how it makes things look and feel: hazy. Soon after the news of this painkiller got around, others tried to replicate it to capitalize on the growing demand and it quickly became a commonplace street drug. It's so cheap and easy to get that most people I know outside of my family are on it.

I roll off of my bed and walk to my dresser to retrieve my stash that I hide under my underwear so that my brothers will never find it. I wish I could tell when I'm dreaming and wake myself up. I have that same dream almost every night. Every time, I fall face-first into the sea and wake up needing my haze fix. It's like my brain is telling me that I'm coming down, literally, and need to get high again. With everyone else in the house outside or playing in the living room, I have a bit of privacy to take care of business. When I don't have a room all to myself, I just act like I'm going to use the bathroom and do it there.

With my physical need for haze and a few hours of sleep taken care of, I can now be the dutiful daughter and big sister my family needs. I pull a clean, loose-fitting dress from my dresser, loop a light infinity scarf around my neck to hide my bruises, and head to the front of the house to get started on my domestic duties, albeit a very late start—12:37 in the afternoon, to be precise. In the living room, Chase and Dylan are playing chess while Daisy keeps bugging them to let her play.

"I want to be the pony!" Daisy pouts.

"You can't BE 'the pony,' Daisy, and it's called a knight," Chase says with a frustrated sigh.

"Look who finally crawled out of bed," Dylan chimes in.

"Well maybe if you had a job, you would know what being tired is like," I retort.

I wish those boys would get full-time jobs, but it's highly un-likely in their conditions. Chase is a genius at things like cards and chess, but he can't concentrate on the simplest of tasks without get-ting distracted. He has walked outside countless times half naked simply because he got distracted by sounds from outside while get-ting dressed. The only work he has done is seasonal and conditional. If the farm owners need extra help because there is a shortage of able-bodied prisoners, for example, they will hire Chase to help pick corn, tomatoes, or strawberries.

Dylan, on the other hand, has random seizures. If no one is around to hold him down and make sure he doesn't choke on his vomit, he's a goner. If a seizure happened while working in a fac-tory, on the docks, or in the desalination plant, who would help him? What if he fell and split his head open, or just fell into the water, and no one noticed? Mom is too fragile to work and Daisy is too young, leaving our survival 99.9 percent up to me.

"I would work if Mom would let me," Chase argues.

"Oh, I'm sure you would," I say sarcastically.

"Yeah, sure you would," mimics Daisy. She always likes to take my side when the boys and I exchange words, and I always take hers.

Mom pops her head into the living room from the kitchen. "Stop bickering with your brothers; I need you to head to the market. We're out of eggs, bread, and sugar. Could also use some meat around here."

"Yeah, Layla! We're starving here!" Dylan chimes in again.

"Gee, I wonder why? Pigs!" I jest.

"Pigs! Oink oink!" Daisy teases, putting her right index finger on her nose and pulling it up to look like a pig's snout while giving Dylan a squinty glare.

"Enough already. Layla, get the bags and go. Dylan, shut it, and don't do that to your face, Daisy, or it's going to stay that way someday," Mom chides. With that, I grab the canvas bags out of the small coat closet by the door, put on my boots and hat, and head out to take care of the shopping.

The weather this afternoon is typical—hot, heavy, and oppressive. The sun is high in the sky beating down on the coast, making the air laden with moisture, yet there isn't a cloud in the sky. The only times the weather is any different is when a storm comes off the ocean and a couple of months in the winter when the winds blow in from the north and bring in drier air. Otherwise, it's like breathing water when you're outside, and no matter how much you fan yourself or dump water on your head, it doesn't help to cool you off.

I start walking north up Austin Avenue from my house on my usual three-mile trek to the market. I wish I had some of those nice factory shoes the Normies wear, tennis shoes. They look a lot more comfortable and probably keep your feet cooler than leather boots. I would just go barefoot if I could, but it's too hazardous. The hot cement is enough to blister your feet, and if you ever need to defend yourself, it helps to have a good pair of shit-kickers to kick creeps in the balls with.

By the time I get to Lone Star Boulevard, I take off my scarf that I had put on for my mom's sake. I don't care if someone sees my bruises; it's too damn hot to wear more than I need to. It's probably two thirty-ish when I finally reach the south market entrance. The market is a huge space, always buzzing with people. It's one of the few places in New Houston where the two classes can commingle. Only a small section at the far north end of the market is for Normies only. That's where luxury items are sold, as well as the typical groceries so that the *really* snobby ones don't even have to see us at all if they don't want to.

The market is shaded under an enormous patchwork of colorful canopies to keep the vendors from baking to death in the sun while they work. There are few small permanent buildings in the market area leased to vendors who need refrigeration to keep their products fresh, like fish, meat, and dairy vendors. All the other vendors have booths or sectioned-off areas in which they operate their businesses.

You never want to buy the food that will spoil first since you have to walk home in the heat with it, so I always start by browsing the booths that sell clothes, hats, bread, grains, veggies, herbal remedies—those sorts of things. I make my first stop at Mr. Addelstone's booth. Mr. Addelstone sells his breads for a living, and they are superb. My favorite is his honey oat wheat bread with its rich dark color and just a little bit of sweetness.

"Good afternoon, Mr. Addelstone," I say in a chipper tone as I walk in. His little bake shop consists of half a dozen worn-down tables covered in baked goods and a counter for transactions.

"Well, if it isn't Ms. Mason. What can I do for you today, my dear?" he replies.

Mr. Addelstone used to work with my dad at the desalination plant, cleaning seaweed and dead fish out of the intake valves. His true passion has always been baking, and when his aging body couldn't take the hard days at the plant anymore, he set up shop here at the market. I used to be best friends with his daughter, Hazel;

we were as thick as thieves back in the day, pulling pranks on my brothers like digging up crawdads from the mud and putting them in Chase's boots. When I say we *were* best friends, it's not because we had a falling or anything like that. Hazel got really sick with the flu about nine years ago and died. That was the first time I saw someone I care about die. The pain I felt at the loss of my best friend felt like my heart just shriveled up and died; I just felt this emptiness in my chest that couldn't be filled. I've since moved on with my life, but I don't have friends anymore. I can't stand the idea of getting really close to someone just to have them suddenly leave me in the end.

"You have anything special today?" I ask.

"I've got a fresh batch of cornbread from this morning over there," he answers, pointing to the second table behind me.

I turn to walk to the table with the cornbread when I notice something on the table to my right, by the counter. "What kind of muffins are those?" My mouth is already watering at the sight of them.

"Those are my new banana pecan muffins," Mr. Addelstone boasts.

"How much?"

"Well … I was thinking five Ameros a dozen." He pauses and gives me a smile. "But for you, I could take three."

"You drive a hard bargain sir," I laugh. "Okay, so then I'll take a dozen of your amazing new muffins, two loaves of cornbread, three loaves of your honey oat wheat bread, a sack of sugar, and a pecan pie."

"Your brothers sure do eat a lot, don't they?'

"Yeah, I'll be lucky if all of this isn't gone within an hour of getting it home," I reply.

"Well then take an extra muffin, no charge," he insists. "Eat it before you get home and they will never know the difference." Mr. Addelstone puts the extra muffin in the bag with the rest of my order and gives me a wink.

"Thanks," I say, giving him a warm smile. He was like my second dad growing up. I miss having him around, but since Hazel died and then my dad four years later, I only see him at the market. "What do I owe you?"

"Thirteen fifty."

I dig my money out of the bottom of my purse, count out what I owe, and hand it to Mr. Addelstone. I gather up my bag full of baked goods and sling it over my left shoulder. Holding my empty canvas bags under my right arm, I bid Mr. Addelstone goodbye and head off to my next market stop.

After seeing Mr. Addelstone, I purchase spices and various vegetables from vendors around the market before making my most important stop: the herbalist. Herbal medicine is the best thing we GIs have. We are not allowed to attend schools, but we do pass down our knowledge the best we can in an attempt to preserve it. Among the GI community, many have second jobs that pay little or nothing but what can be given as a token of gratitude. The highest regarded of these amateur professionals are the midwives, the bonesetters, and the herbalist.

My personal favorite of our local herbalists is Kaya. Kaya is a wise older woman with short silvery hair that appears almost incandescent in contrast to her dark complexion. She knows all the local plants and what, if any, medicinal properties they have and how to prepare and use them, and she knows about the imported exotic plants as well. If I didn't need to make so much money, I would ask Kaya to be her apprentice. The ability to heal is invaluable here. If you haven't any money but know what plants you could use to eat and heal, I reckon you could survive okay.

"Good afternoon!" I greet her with one of my genuine smiles.

"Good afternoon to you too," bubbles Kaya. "My dear! What happened to your neck, child?" she inquires, grazing my neck with her slender, gentle fingers.

I shrug. "Just work."

"Well, I got just the thing to help get rid of those nasty bruises." Kaya holds up a small glass bottle. "St. John's wort oil ought to do the trick. Just rub a bit on those bruises three times a day, dear. Should help them clear up faster and make them less sore," she affirms.

"You know how to fix just about anything," I agree.

Kaya's face grows serious. "There is one thing I can't cure," she hints.

"What?" I ask in a hushed voice.

"Death."

I start laughing, thinking she's making one of her dramatic jokes, but when I look up at her, her expression is grave. She isn't smiling as she would if she were messing with me. She's just staring at me with a sad look on her face. "What? Stop looking at me like that!" I demand.

"Layla, I can help with your bruises, but someday one of those men could kill you. I can't cure that. No one can. You need to get out," she lectures, whispering so that no one around the market can eavesdrop on the conversation.

"You know I can't afford to do that. I've got my family to think about," I return.

"There are other jobs you could do, Layla. Even if you had to have more than one, at least you would be safer," Kaya pleads.

"I'm not having this conversation with you," I say, now in my normal voice to signify to her that our hush-hush exchange is over. "I came to do my shopping, not get a lecture, so if you don't mind, I have other items I need from you."

"Oh, but of course! What would you like to purchase, young lady?" Kaya declaims.

I ignore her outburst and place my order. "The oil you recommended, chaste berry seeds, betony tubers, horehound, balloon vine seeds, marigold, licorice root, and ginger. What do I owe you?"

"Forty," she answers. "You need to clean up your life, Layla.

Find a good man, let yourself be happy," Kaya tries to persuade me as I count out the cash and she fills my bag with my purchases.

"Yeah, right, a man. What the hell for? To tell me I'm pretty and load me down with kids that are just as screwed as we all are? I'll pass," I scoff.

Kaya gives me a pitying look and hands me my bag. I turn on my heels and leave without a wave or a goodbye. I don't need her goddamn pity or advice on how to run my life. If I need advice on medicines or tending to wounds, she's my go-to person, but I don't need advice on how to take care of myself. I've been doing that just fine for quite a while now, not to mention taking care of everyone else.

She wants me to find a *man*. I don't need a man to marry me and take care of me. Besides, I have had my fair share of men. A bunch of brainless jackasses, if you ask me. The only thing men are good for is sex. If it wasn't my source of income and I had no sexual needs, I could go my entire life without ever looking at another one.

I walk through the market at a brisk pace to the permanent buildings that line the western edge of the market, stopping by to see my dealer, Deacon, along the way. Deacon's front is a cigar and liquor shop, but everyone knows he sells haze. It's not legal, but no one cares. After dropping twenty-five at Deacon's, I put my haze in the bag with my herbs and spend up the last of my money I earned during the week on frozen chickens, pork chops, spareribs, rump roast, two gallons of milk, cheese, and three dozen eggs. I find myself wishing once again that I had all sisters; then I wouldn't have to spend so much damn money on food all the time. Another reason I don't need a man. Another gluttonous mouth to feed? No, thank you!

It's a good thing that the butcher sells a lot of frozen meats. You can buy it fresh, but unless you're a Normie, lucky enough to own a bike, or live really close to the market, it will start to spoil before you get home thanks to the heat here. To help keep the dairy cold, I rearrange my groceries in the bags so that I have some dairy in the bags of meat so that they stay cool. I load those two refreshingly cold bags onto each of my arms first so that the cold penetrating the bags will cool my skin. Then I arrange my three bags of produce, herbs, and bakery goods according to weight so that I can walk somewhat balanced instead of waddling around like a duck with a broken foot.

CHAPTER THREE

THE GROCERY BAGS CAN BE hard to carry because of how awkward and bulky they are, not because they are heavy. Just because I have a small frame doesn't make me some weakling, though people like to assume so. I hate when people stare at me and ask if I need help. I can take care of things just fine, and if I need help, I'll ask. I don't need advice on how to live my life, I don't need a man, and I don't need anyone's damn help. If there is one thing this fucked-up society has right, it's clinging to Darwin's idea of "survival of the fittest." Well, if I'm anything, it's a survivor. Most people here, if they get sick, they're goners. I've had quite a few illnesses as a young child, and I am still here. I had plenty of problems with mucous infections in my lungs and a couple of cases of the flu, and I am still alive and kickin'. No matter what, I always seem to survive.

A stream of thoughts continues winding through my mind of how sick I am of people's concern and pity as I awkwardly trudge along the west edge of the market. I can swear I keep seeing someone just dodging out of view every time I stop to rest or look behind me. I'm getting a creepy feeling like someone is following me, the one where the hairs on the back of your neck stand up and you know it is not because it's cold. I stand still for a moment, looking around to see if I can spot the mysterious person, but instead, I hear something else. My stomach decides to interrupt my vigilance with annoying churning and low-pitched grumbles. I then remember the thirteenth muffin that Mr. Addelstone had given to me—just for me. I maneuver myself to the outside of the market, along the sidewalk on Market Street out of the way of all the foot traffic of busy shoppers, and carefully unload my bags at my sides. I crouch down, balancing on the front of my feet, and search through my bag of baked goods. When I find the package of muffins I pull one out, leaving the rest in the bag, and crumple the paper at the opening shut.

I haven't eaten anything in a while, unless you count the milk from this morning. I really should try to remember to eat more, but I just have too many things on my mind to notice my hunger. I'm always focusing on feeding everyone else in my family, making sure they have what they need. I always survive; it's them who I worry about. Haze also helps suppress your appetite, so most of the time I never even feel hungry when I should.

Since Mr. Addelstone was so kind as to give me something just for me and my stomach has my attention for once, I figure it would be ungrateful of me not to eat it. I survey my surroundings. I don't see anyone coming up the sidewalk, so I shift my weight back and sit on my butt on the ground. It looks almost too pretty to eat as I carefully remove the muffin from its paper cup. The pecans have that lustrous candied glaze, making it look like a porcelain trinket instead of something to eat. Unlike a trinket, it smells divine, with just a hint of cinnamon to it.

I give in to my desire and pull a corner off the muffin and neatly place it into my already watering mouth. As I close my lips, the sweet flavor makes my tongue tingle with delight and I close my eyes, letting out a slight moan. The pecans, brown sugar, cinnamon, banana, and other subtle flavors take over my senses as I savor that first piece. I wish I didn't have to swallow it so that I could taste it forever. When at last my mouth is so full of saliva that I think I might choke, I decide to swallow that first bite. My self-control is gone at this point, and I eat up the remainder of my banana pecan muffin as fast as a jackrabbit running from a brush fire. If anyone is watching, I hope the loser is jealous of how awesome my muffin was.

I finish licking the crumbs off my fingers, not wanting to waste a bit of that delicious treat, and as I look up from my low vantage point on the ground, I suddenly notice the significance of my location. I was so distracted by my hunger and then delight in that muffin that I failed to notice what lie just across the street from me—the GI cemetery. A huge plot of land, yet it's insanely overcrowded, as we GIs tend to die a lot more often. Only some of the very first buried there have their own patch of grass and headstone. Everyone else gets entombed in gray cement walls that house cremated bodies like papers in a filing cabinet.

I always know it's there, but I rarely think about it anymore. Thinking about it fills me with sorrow and anger, which is weakness, and I can't afford to be weak. If I weren't too caught up in my pathetic emotions and hunger, I would have taken my usual route through to the south end of the market to head home. Instead, I sit here, staring west across Market Street to where my father lies for eternity in a plastic bag in one of tens of thousands of tiny sealed drawers in massive cement walls. A small metal plate with the inscription of a name and the dates of birth and death are all that mark where what used to be a loved one is interred. Unless you know exactly where someone is, you will probably never find them. People have tried to make a directory for the cemetery before, but the number of dead is just too high and rises faster than anyone can keep up with.

I don't know how long I've been sitting here staring across the street—ten minutes, maybe, debating whether to go to see my dad or get the groceries home. It's been almost three years since I've been to the cemetery. We used to go every year as a family on the anniversary of his death, but I've made excuses lately. Too tired from work, not feeling well, misplaced my boots. The truth is, I don't want anyone to see me cry. I'm supposed to be the supporter of this family now, the strong one. I don't like people seeing me cry, ever. I'd rather be angry and screaming than crying. Crying is a weak reaction to pain that makes me feel helpless and makes it hard to breathe.

Maybe just a quick visit by myself will be okay, as long as no one else is near the wall holding his remains. Just a quick visit to say hi. I feel stupid about wishing he could hear me or know I'm there. I know he can't, but I can't help but wishing that he could. Going to talk to my dad is completely illogical, but it comforts me. I know I'm just talking to myself and imagining what he would say back. Heaven was just a figment of humanity's imagination. Sure, belief in such things may make you feel better about knowing you and everyone you love will die one day, but it also makes people do crazy things, like killing innocent people for not believing the same myths they do. When physicists proved that the universe was able to have come into being without the intervention of some all-powerful god, the world's religions fell apart.

The small minority of people who still practice religion claim the loss of it was the cause of humanity's downfall. I think it just pulled back the curtain, so to speak. You should be a good person for the sake of being good, not because you think you will be rewarded for eternity. Still, I visit my dad's final resting place anyway, knowing he is gone forever and that my feeling of his presence is only my imagination. I admit, it would be amazing if it were real and if my dad were able to hear me talk to him. What I wouldn't give for my dad to be an angel watching over and protecting me somehow, to be with him again someday.

I stand up, brush the crumbs off my lap, and load my bags back onto my arms. I'm almost halfway across the street when a sudden unseen force shoves me forward and into the gutter.

I feel a heaviness on my back that steals the air from my lungs.

The loud buzz of a vehicle speeding by just inches from my feet startles me out of my temporary stupor. I blink my eyes rapidly, trying to shake off my disorientation, and curl my fingers under my palms to push myself up off the ground. The ground refuses to move away from my body, no matter how much I will it to do so. My awareness turns to my ears, and I hear a muffled male voice, but I can't make out any words. I feel the heaving of his chest against my back as he takes in rapid breaths. This unknown man unceremoniously flips me onto my back, and now I can hear him shouting at me.

"Are you fucking crazy?! You trying to get yourself killed?" yells the man, his face still a blur to me. I try to make my mouth move to make words, but I just make unintelligible noises. I stare up at him, confused, as he starts waving his fingers back and forth in my face. I want to ask him what in the hell he is talking about. *I was crossing the street just fine until he tackled me.*

The man ceases the insane waving of his fingers in my face, crouches down beside me, and proceeds to lift me from the gutter to the brown grass of the cemetery. As I lie here, staring up at the cloudless, hazy sky, I hear the crunch of his feet walking away and then return, dropping things on the ground around me with several small thuds. "Well, it looks like most of your groceries are done for," the mystery man declares.

I sit up in sudden alarm to see what he is talking about, but as soon as I do the world is spinning, and nausea grips my stomach. I close my eyes tightly and lay my head back on the ground, trying not to puke. I figure it's best just to talk to this man while laying down; I don't want to risk throwing up all over myself and then having to walk home like that.

"Who are you? Why did you tackle me? What do you want from me?" I inquire in a weak voice as fast as I can manage. If I were not dizzy and could stand up, I'd be screaming in his face. I want answers. I want this vulnerable, helpless feeling to go away. "I don't have any more money, so you tackled the wrong girl," I continue.

I feel his hand grip my own in a comforting grasp, and he begins to speak in a calming tone, "My name is Adonis. You were crossing the street with a car speeding toward you that you seemed oblivious to."

"You're crazy! There wasn't any car on the road. I would have seen it," I protest. I maybe heard a buzzing after I fell, but I never actually saw a car. It just sounded like the fuzziness I hear when I'm spacing out or coming off a high. *Am I losing my mind? Is my drug use making me permanently hazy to the point that I'm not seeing cars coming at me?*

"You seemed kind of out of it and not paying attention. I shouted at you, but you didn't respond. So, I did all I could think of, which was to push you out of the way of the car. And I don't want any money from you," he laughs.

I groan as I slowly roll to my side so I could get up gently in hopes of not puking. When I'm able to push myself up into a reclined sitting position, my heart sinks. My bags are strewn about the brown grass, milk soaking through one, smashed eggs oozing out of another. My bag from Mr. Addelstone's is now a bag of crumbs. *All of that money, wasted. How can I go home with no money and no food?* On top of all that, I realize that one of my bags is unaccounted for. I don't see my bag from Deacon among the wreckage. If I need any of these bags to survive right now, it's that one.

"Here, put this on your cheek," this man, Adonis, instructs.

He hands me a still-intact frozen pork chop. I take the slab of meat from his hand and spot my missing bag. "Hey! Don't go through my stuff!" I demand.

"Calm down. I'm just trying to see if there is anything useful in here."

"I'm fine, just give me my bag."

"That shit isn't good for you, you know," Adonis chides, showing me my bottle of haze like one shows a kid a toy that was just taken away after they misbehaved.

"I didn't ask for your advice, and I don't need it. So, if you would be so kind as to help me up so I can gather what I have left and go home," I snap.

"How far do you live from here?"

"Couple of miles—not far at all. I don't need you to walk me home."

"Who said anything about walking?" he laughs.

He walks in front of me and offers me his hand. I grip it firmly as he pulls me to my feet. For the first time, I see him clearly. He's about five or six inches taller than me, wearing casual long shorts and a loose-fitting T-shirt. His eyes are piercing, yet gentle with a deep hazel color, and his skin is slightly tanned. "I'll give you a ride," he says with a stunning smile on his face as he lets go of my hand.

"You have a car? Like … your own car?" I ask in disbelief.

"Yeah, it's parked up by the Wharf," Adonis replies as if it's no big deal.

"Oh no. No, no, no, no!" I start repeating as I back away from him. He starts moving toward me, and I start to panic. "You're one of *them*? I don't need any trouble." This comment makes him stop and stare at me in confusion.

"What are you going on about? I'm just offering you a ride home," he says with what I bet is feigned confusion in his voice.

"Yeah sure, you want to give me a ride," I jeer. "You want this"— I gesture to my body—"then you're gonna have to pay like all the others down at Andy's. I'm not gonna let some Normie pick me up in a car and get raped," I hiss.

As I'm glaring at him, I notice a hurt look cross his face. He reminds me of a kid who just saw their puppy get run over. He takes in a deep breath and straightens himself. "You think I'm going to rape you?" he repeats in disgust. I cross my arms and keep staring him down. He turns away from me, running his hands through his hair before turning back to face me. "I just saved your life, you psycho!"

"I don't need your saving

Adonis throws his hands up in frustration and turns his back to me again with a loud sigh. "Listen, I just want to give you a ride home, to be nice, okay? You hit your head; your groceries are trashed. I won't even look at you if you don't want me to, okay?" he implores.

My head does hurt pretty badly, and it's hot as hell out here. *If he tries anything, I'll kick his balls in.* "Fine," I concede, accepting his offer with a plan of action in mind.

"Just stay here, I'll be back in less than five minutes," Adonis says. He backs slowly away from me and then turns and runs in the direction of the market.

This guy is nuts! I watch him run across the street toward the market. He looks pretty close to my age, maybe a couple of years older. The craziest thing about him is that he's a damn Normie! Why would he want to help me? If there had been a car, which I don't recall there being one, why bother to push me out of the way? Since when do they care if we live or die? If I got flattened like an armadillo on a scorching summer highway, not one Normie would give two shits about it.

This guy—Adonis, as he claims—is a square peg, to say the least. I'm usually really good at pigeon-holing people right off the bat. I can tell just by looking at them if they are decent or a total scumbag. I've never been wrong, by the way—ever. Even if everyone else thinks someone is nice, I know before everyone else does what a piece of shit they are. In the end, I always end up saying, "Told you so!" But with this guy, I just don't know. *He should be a jerk, but he's not, and he has a damn car. Why does he care whether I get run over or not?* Then he says he doesn't want to screw me. *Yeah, right—they all do.* If he weren't a Normie, maybe I would peg him as a decent guy, but I just don't know what to think of Adonis.

I reach up mindlessly to wipe what I think is sweat off my forehead, but it's hot and sticky, plastering my dark-brown hair to my

face. Looking at the back of my hand afterward, I can see blood. It doesn't hurt much. I examine my forehead with my fingers and find the source of the blood, a nasty cut above my right eyebrow. "Stupid jerk," I mutter. I rip a small piece off the end of my dress to apply some pressure to the cut on my forehead when I hear the soft thud of a door.

I look up from my spot on the grass and there Adonis stands at the edge of the sidewalk in front of a silver-colored car. I never even heard him coming. Stupid electric cars are so damn quiet now, they could drive right into your front door and you would never hear them. "I'm glad you stuck around," Adonis says, slightly panting. He's probably still catching his breath from running to get his car.

I start to stand up, holding my makeshift bandage to my forehead with one hand and picking up the remnants of one of my produce bags, which now looks more like a bad salad and mashed potatoes. "Where should I put this?" I ask, holding the bag away from my body so as not to drip its smashed contents all over my boots.

"Just toss it in the trunk," he answers.

"I'm sorry, where?"

"The trunk." He pushes a button on a little remote and the back of the car opens up with a soft clicking sound. The door to the trunk is so seamless with the rest of the car's body that I didn't think one existed until he opened it with his little remote.

"You're not afraid of getting your fancy car all dirty?" I ask in a slightly mocking tone as I load a bag into his pristine black-upholstered trunk.

"I'll have it cleaned later—no big deal. Nothing compared to the bodies," he says flatly.

I stop dead still, my heart feeling like it is going to come out of my mouth. *I knew there was something wrong with this guy! He doesn't want to rape me;*

he wants to kill me and shove me in the trunk!

"Actually, come to think of it, I really don't need a ride. You're too kind," I insist. I start backing slowly away toward the cemetery. "I'll just go now." I'm no more than six feet away from the trunk when I feel him come up from behind me and grab my arm.

"Boo!" he whispers.

I almost jump out of my boots. "I'm just screwing with you. You should have seen the look on your face," he laughs.

"Yeah, ha, ha! Trying to scare a girl to death—very classy." I say, trying not to sound frazzled.

"Well, sorry," he says, drawing out his words. "Just trying to lighten the mood a bit."

Adonis walks from the back of the car to the passenger side door and opens it with one hand, and his other arm gestures toward the open door. "I'll take care of the rest of your stuff."

I look at him, bemused, unsure of what to do. I've never actually been in a car before. I've been in the back of an old truck and on a bus, but never inside an actual car.

"You sure?" I ask nervously. "I don't want to mess anything up."

"Yes, I'm sure," Adonis confirms, still holding his arm out, gesturing me to the door. "Now are you going to get in, or do I have to stand like this till my arm falls off?" he jokes.

I let out a slight forced laugh and slowly make my way to the open passenger door. I bend down to look inside, and I'm awestruck. The seats are deep and made of a soft white leather, way fancier than any chair I have ever seen in the public buildings, which are pretty damn fancy looking. I straighten back up and look at him, my mouth slightly agape. "You're really sure?"

"Just get in," he replies, enunciating each word. I slowly crouch down, trying to figure out how I'm going to get in without looking foolish. It's so low to the ground that I'm afraid that I will fall on my ass in the attempt. "Look." He grabs my right hand and puts it on the roof. "Hold your hand here, place your left foot inside the door, and swing your left side in and sit down." Before I can respond, he gives me a small push and my butt lands in the seat of the car as my right

leg still hangs outside the door. "Pull your foot in," Adonis instructs. I pull my foot in, and the door makes a soft thud that shakes the car as it closes.

CHAPTER FOUR

AS I SIT IN ALONE in the car, waiting as Adonis finishes putting my mangled groceries in the trunk, I think, *This must be how it feels to be abducted by a UFO.* It is the most foreign thing I have ever experienced. The only vehicle I've ever been inside of was a bus, and it's nothing like this. The feel of the soft leather, the coolness of the air, the smell. I can't compare the way it smells in here to anything I've smelled before. Whatever the scent is, it's relaxing and almost makes me feel safe. I know I have to be on my guard with this guy, though, no matter how nice his car smells. He's just too nice—and weird. No Normie is this nice. Not to a girl like me, not to a GI.

I feel the car shake a bit. *He must have closed the trunk.* Any moment that door will open and there he will sit, next to me. My guts feel all knotted up inside as I wait nervously for him to return. *What will happen when he gets in here? You'll be fine, you're always fine,* I try to reassure myself and take a deep breath, attempting to calm myself. The door opens on my exhalation.

Adonis gets into the car in—what seems to me—a weird manner, but what do I know about getting into cars? He slowly stretches his right leg in all the way to the far end of the seat and then his nicely shaped ass, which I can't help but now notice, quickly follows, causing his seat to release air in a hissing sound as the car shakes a great deal. "Where to, Miss …" Adonis starts. "Hmm. I haven't even asked your name yet."

"Layla," I respond quietly.

"Layla," he says slowly. He pauses for a moment as if he's deep in thought about something. "Where to, Miss Layla?"

"Home."

"And where is home?"

A feeling of embarrassment suddenly envelops me like a thick fog. I don't want him to see where I live. His damn car is nicer than any home I've ever seen; I can't even begin to imagine how nice his house is. "You don't need to take me all the way, you know. Just drop me off at Bluebonnet and Austin," I insist.

"Nonsense. I'm taking you home." His voice is firm but gentle.

I don't understand why I feel so embarrassed. *I don't know this guy; I don't need to impress him.* I nervously brush my hair out of my face, trying to think of a good excuse as to why he shouldn't take me to my house.

"You're still bleeding," he says softly. "Let me take care of that." He grabs my face and starts to study the cut above my eyebrow. My breath catches in my chest. His eyes are hypnotic. The atmosphere between us feels electric. *Is he going to kiss me? I might just explode if he kisses me right now.* He lets go and reaches for something in his door pocket.

"I'm fine, really. It's just a cut."

He pays no attention to my comment. "This might sting a little," he says as he wipes my cut with a wet piece of cotton.

I cringe slightly, hissing through my clenched teeth.

After cleaning the cut, he places a small bandage on it and sits back, looking at my cut. "There," he declares. "All better."

Not going to kiss my boo-boo? I can't help but feel a little disappointed yet relieved at the same time. "You didn't have to do that," I say, my cheeks feeling warm. If one could die from embarrassment, I would be a corpse right now!

"I don't want you bleeding all over my car," he chuckles.

I reciprocate with a light laugh and look at him to say thank you, but the words escape me. I'm like a deer in headlights—he's just heart-stopping and stunning. His eyes, a dazzling deep green with gold flecks and blue around the pupils. His jawline, strong and masculine, yet still soft and inviting as it leads to his lips, which are full, but not to the point of looking feminine. His hair is a chestnut brown with just a hint of red that hangs in a slight curve at his bangs, which are a bit longer than the rest of his hair.

He is goddamn hot—and I only use the word "god" as a force of habit. I don't believe he exists, but the expression still seems to get the point across. I don't believe that I've ever felt this attracted to someone before; he is just breathtakingly sexy. *If only the GI guys I know looked this hot.* Yeah, some of them are kind of cute, like the boy five houses down the street, but he's a bit of a douchebag. Why is it that all the good-looking ones always have to be douches? It's like they think because they aren't hideous that they can treat you however they want and that you will still want them or some shit like that. Not me. If a guy plays with my feelings, he gets a knee to the nuts. Not like any decent guy would want anything to do with me anyway, what with me screwing random guys for a living. Who wants to be with someone who has sex with other people all day? I can also be a bit of a bitch at times, too, so my romantic prospects are pretty much nonexistent.

He starts waving his hand in my face. "Hello in there. Layla?" I hear him say. I blink rapidly, suddenly realizing I must look like a spaced-out idiot.

"Sorry," I say, looking down at my hands. "I was just going to thank you—for cleaning up my cut, that is. You still don't need to take me all the way home, though," I explain.

"But I want to. It's the least I can do. Just tell me the address."

"I don't want you to know where I live, okay?"

"Why? You think I'm going to stalk you or something?" He sounds taken aback, offended.

"No, it's not that, it's just . . . look at you and look at me, okay? Your car is the nicest thing I've ever been in. I don't want you to see where I live because I'm embarrassed. Okay?" I rant while staring at my fidgeting hands the entire time.

"You don't need to be embarrassed. It's not like I expected you to live in a mansion. I know I'm out of my element over here. I'm not going to judge you because your house isn't nice," he tries to assure me.

"Why are you being so nice to me? I don't get you! Why would a guy like you even care if I got run over by a car, or got home okay?"

"So, you think you got us all figured out, don't you? All us 'Normies' are all alike, huh? Just a bunch of privileged assholes who don't care about anyone but themselves, take what they want, and enjoy watching the sick suffer and die?" he rebukes.

"I've dealt with enough of you to say that is a fair summary," I return, crossing my arms and glaring at him.

"Then I guess you're just like every GI then, right? Stupid, drug-addicted, law-breaking scum that just waste oxygen?"

I move my face forward, right up to his, so that our noses almost touch. "Fuck you!" I snarl. I reach my hand for the door, but when I pull the handle, it won't move. "Let me out!"

"Not until you calm down," he says.

"So, you're holding me captive now? First you shove me into the gutter, and now I'm your prisoner?"

"I pushed you to save you! Why can't you just let me take you home?"

I still myself for a moment, trying to get my bearing on the situation. "Why? You never answered why. Why did you save me?" I demand. I stare at him intently, wishing I could see what the hell is going through his crazy head.

"I'm not like everyone else, okay? I don't believe what all the other 'Normies' do." He puts up his hands and does air quotes while he speaks in an obnoxiously sarcastic voice.

"What does that mean?" I ask.

"Ever since I was little, I wanted to be a doctor; that's what I studied in school. I read a lot of books as a kid out of curiosity about the practice of medicine before the Cleansing. I think it should still be that way. If you can figure out why someone is getting sick, then you should fix it, not doom them to die so that it just goes away over time. Everyone should be able to see a doctor. Making people suffer from preventable or treatable conditions and letting premature babies die is just inhumane to me. So, when I see a person I can help, that's what I do," Adonis expounds.

I sit silently, trying to process all that he just said.

"Just let me take you home, okay?" he sighs.

Either he's a good actor or an okay guy; I still can't tell, but I'm tired and he's hot, so I give up. "Okay," I answer with a smile.

"Address?"

"235 Austin Avenue."

Adonis pushes a button by the steering wheel and the car quietly starts. There's only a slightly audible hum to let you know it's on. That, and the clock in car lights up. 5:05. "Oh my god! It's already after five?" I gasp.

"Don't worry, I'll get you home in a jiffy," Adonis replies.

"No, don't rush. I just didn't know it had gotten so late." I've never been in a car before, and I am nervous enough as it is. I don't want him driving fast.

"Okay, we'll take the long way. Just put your seat belt on."

"My what?" I ask, looking around me.

"Seat belt," Adonis says, reaching across me, pulling a strap down from over my right shoulder, and securing it across my waist. I shiver slightly at his grazing touch. *I hope he didn't notice. That would be embarrassing.*

He lightly touches some buttons on a panel between our seats and the car seamlessly starts moving. It's quiet between us for about two minutes when Adonis breaks the awkward silence. "So … you work at Andy's, huh?"

"Yeah," I answer quietly, my voice laced with shame. I really don't want to talk about my work with some guy I just met, a good-looking one at that. A guy like him would never want to be with some cheap piece of trash like me. Why can't I just accept that and stop feeling so weird about being near him?

"At least it pays well, right?" he asks awkwardly.

My god does this guy suck at choosing topics for small talk. "Puts food on the table," I respond.

"A lot of food, from the looks of it," he says with a forced awkward laugh.

"My brothers are pigs. All they do is eat."

"Brothers? How many?"

"Two, and a little sister."

"What about your parents?"

"My dad died a while back; I was going to visit him when you tackled me," I reveal.

"I'm sorry. What happened, if you don't mind my asking?"

"Pneumonia. He got very weak, didn't want to eat anything, and then just stopped breathing," I confide, the hurt of the memory starting to creep up into my throat. We come to a stop sign, and he turns toward me as I sit totally still, staring at my feet.

"You okay?" Adonis asks gently, putting his right hand on my shoulder.

"I'm fine," I claim, nodding my head.

"You still have your mom, right?"

"Yeah, I still have my mom," I answer, giving a small smile at the thought of her.

"Let's go on that then. No more sad stuff," he proposes. "Why don't you tell me about your mom?"

"Why don't you tell me something about *you?*" I inquire. *I'd rather not talk about my life. It's hard and filled with stress. I'm not interesting enough to talk long about. He is the confusing one. I want to know more about him. Like maybe how old he is, or his favorite season. Anything, really.*

"Me? My life is boring. I'm more interested in you," he says.

"Okay," I start and then pause a moment. "My mom's name is Diane. She stays at home with the boys and Daisy. She can't work— has hemophilia. One work accident or bad cut and she would bleed out."

"I said no more sad stuff," he reminds me gently.

"It's not sad, just a fact. My life isn't sunshine and rainbows," I counter.

"What if it could be?"

"What do you mean by that?" I ask incredulously.

"Well, maybe not *totally* sunshine and rainbows, but maybe a little sunshine."

"Stop being weird. What are you trying to say?"

"Well, recently, as in just three days ago, a job position has opened up at my house," he hints.

"Yeah, so what?"

"So, we are in need of a new housekeeper, as poor old Rebecca has gone home to her family to die in peace."

"That's awful!" I exclaim.

"It is. I miss her already. She was a great lady. Was there as far back as I can remember."

"I still don't see what any of this has to do with me."

"Well, we need a new housekeeper. Would you like a new job?" he proposes.

"I doubt your family will pay me anything close to what I make already. I've got others to think about, not just myself," I contend.

"What do you make now?"

"I don't see how that is any of your business."

Yeah, how much do I make. Ha! Talk about a backhanded way of

asking "How many guys do you screw a night?" I don't like thinking about it myself. Hell, most of the time I'm not thinking at all; I
just exist.

"They will probably pay you a hundred a week, but I could make
up the rest of it and bring it to your family. You would have a place
to live, clothes, food," he starts.

"What makes you think I want to be a housekeeper for some rich
people?" I interrupt.

"If you can make the same money, why not? It's safer than what
you're doing. Doubt you're gonna drown in a mop bucket on the
job," Adonis replies, punctuating his statement with a laugh at his
own joke.

"What makes you think I am just so vulnerable that I can't handle myself? Huh?"

"Do you think that no one can see your bruises? I just finished
school to begin a residency at the hospital here. I think I can tell
when someone has been physically abused."

I feel sick to my stomach suddenly. *Is it that obvious to everyone
that saw me? Did they all know what had happened?*

"Well, you're wrong, Dr. Obvious. It's just hickeys. Sometimes
you just get a biter," I lie.

"You're such a liar. Those marks are spaced like a man's hands.
You were choked."

"So, what if I was? Big deal. Every job has its hazards. Mine
pays more to compensate for it," I say nonchalantly.

"Just consider it, alright?"

"I don't need your charity; I'm fine."

"It's not charity. It's an opportunity. Just think about it, please,"
he maintains.

The car is slowing to a stop, and Adonis puts it in park in front
of my pathetic little house. "I get that you care about all people
and what not, but why me? Why not expound your philanthropy on
someone else?" I ask.

"I don't know," he shrugs. "Do you believe in fate?"

"Nope."

"Well, I do."

Adonis gets out of the car, walks around to the passenger's side, and opens my door, offering me a hand up. I take it and thank him as he helps me to the sidewalk. With a push of the button on the remote, the trunk opens. I walk to the back of the car to get my bags out, but he beats me to it. I gather the remnants of my groceries into my arms and head for my front steps. Before stepping on that first creaky step, which will announce my return, I turn to face Adonis, who is standing by his car.

"Thanks for the ride," I say with a shy smile.

"Anytime," he replies, getting into his car.

I watch him drive off, let out a quiet sigh, and walk up to the door.

CHAPTER FIVE

I OPEN THE FRONT DOOR and start carrying the bags in and place them on the floor. I hear the scampering of Daisy's little feet coming from the kitchen to greet me.

"You're home!" Daisy cheers as she comes around the corner. She gasps when she sees the bags and asks quietly, "What happened to the food?"

"I had a bit of an accident. We'll be fine, I promise," I assure her.

"What are we going to eat, though?"

I pick up one of the produce bags and give it a little shake. "Tossed salad, of course!" I joke. "Some food made it. We can have some smashed muffins for breakfast, and I'll just ask my boss for a loan in the morning. No big deal, you'll see," I affirm. "Now how about you be my little helper and help me unpack and we'll see what we have to work with?"

"Okay," Daisy agrees.

I get a colander out of the cupboard and place it in the sink. "Okay, so if it's vegetables and they aren't too smashed, put them in the colander and we're gonna rinse 'em off. Okay?"

"Got it." Daisy nods, trying to act serious about her assigned task.

I grab the bag from Kaya's first as we start going through the bags because I don't want Daisy getting into whatever is left in there. Since most of the herbal remedies need to be smashed up anyway, there isn't much of a loss with those. However, the bottle of the oil Kaya gave me for my bruises got smashed along with six bottles of haze I got from my dealer, which sucks. I take the remaining bottles and slide them in my dress pockets while Daisy is distracted working on her bag. I put the herbs up in the medicine cupboard, out of the reach of her little hands, and move on to the next bag when Chase walks into the kitchen.

"What the hell happened?!" Chase exclaims.

"Layla had an accident," Daisy chimes in.

"I can see that. What are we going eat? We're gonna starve," he whines.

"Oh, shut up. You're so damn dramatic," I say.

"MOM!!" Chase screams.

"Mom's napping, stupid," Daisy scolds him.

"Mom, get in here! Layla ruined all the food," he continues.

I put down the bag from the bakery, walk up to Chase, and slap him upside the head. "Shut the hell up, you idiot. Daisy said mom's sleeping."

"Ow!" Chase exclaims, rubbing where I smacked him. "Asshole!"

Daisy runs up and kicks him in the shin for his comment as my mom comes into the kitchen.

"Daisy! Don't kick your brother," my mom chides. "Now what in the world is going on in here?"

"Layla ruined all the food, and she hit me, and—" Chase starts, but my mom cuts him off.

"Get your butt out of here and go to your room, Chase," she commands.

"But—" he tries to argue.

"Go, now!"

Chase sulks off toward the bedroom and moments later the door slams loudly. My mom turns to look at me, concern written all over her face. "What happened to you?"

"I'm fine, just a mishap on my way home from the market. Some stuff made it. We've got a couple of pork chops that survived, fresh breadcrumbs, squished muffins, herbs, and salad," I say, trying to lighten her mood.

"I didn't ask what happened to the food; I asked what happened to you."

"Yeah, what happened, Layla?" Daisy echoes with concern.

"Daisy, Mommy needs to talk with Layla alone. Go to our room, please," my mom says with that calm but stern voice that every child knows means that there's no negotiating.

"Yes, ma'am," Daisy says quietly, leaving the room and hanging her head.

My mother and I stand there while we wait to hear the other bedroom door close so we know we have privacy. "Okay, now what happened?" she asks.

"It was just a freak accident," I reply casually. "I was walking along Market Street with all the stuff, and I thought I'd stop by to see Dad and then this guy pushed me. He said there was a car, but I never saw one. It was just crazy."

"Who pushed you?"

"Just some guy. He said there was a car coming and that he pushed me out of the way, but that caused all the groceries to get all smashed to shit."

My mom lets out a distressed sigh.

"Don't worry; it'll be fine. I'll go and talk to Andy in the morning, ask if she can loan me a little for groceries. Wouldn't be the first time," I reassure her.

"Salad, huh?" my mom laughs.

"Sure, why not? The boys could use more veggies."

"I think I can handle that. Everything's already been cut up from your little accident."

"Yup, no knives necessary."

"I'll fix dinner, then. You get yourself washed up," she insists.

I give her a light hug and a kiss on the forehead and leave the kitchen.

As I reach the door to my room, I can hear the boys whispering. Dylan must have already been in there, being lazy when I got home, and now he's gossiping with Chase. When I open the door, the boys immediately start badgering me with questions and comments. I ignore them as I get some clean clothes and my syringe stealthily from my dresser.

I place my clean clothes on the sink counter and close the bathroom door. Of course, one of the boys left the seat up, like usual, so I have to put it down so I can use it as a chair. I take my haze bottles out of my pocket and place them on top of my clean clothes and get out my syringe. Sitting on the toilet I take a hit of haze, a piss, and then jump in the shower. As the shower steams up the room, I brush the knots out of my hair before stepping into the hot mist.

Shower time is relaxing, but it never lasts long. Five people and one bathroom means that I'm lucky if my only true private time at home lasts fifteen minutes until someone comes pounding on the door saying they have to pee. I hum as I scrub myself down, taking care around the cut on my forehead. The cascading water on my scalp from the shower head is so relaxing, it almost puts me to sleep. It's like hundreds of little fingers massaging my head. I could wash my hair forever if it didn't keep falling out and getting stuck in my butt crack all the time.

I'm all rinsed and just standing there for a few minutes under the water when I hear a light knock on the door and a little voice. "Layla, Mom said dinner's ready," Daisy calls from behind the door.

I turn off the shower. "Tell her I'll be out in a couple of minutes," I call back.

I twist my hair to wring it out, grab a towel from the rack, and wrap it up. I take the second towel to dry myself off before stepping onto the floor, as wet floors don't dry well with the humidity here and we don't need anyone slipping, especially not Mom. I crack open the window above the shower to let the moisture out and step out to get dressed. I pull on my shorts and tank top, roll my haze up in my dirty dress, put my stuff away, and head to the kitchen. Everyone is sitting at our little table eating "salad" and drinking water.

"Saved you a seat next to me," Daisy says with her mouth full.

I sit next to her and take in the image of our meal for the night. It actually doesn't look half bad: smashed up lettuce, carrots, some small tomatoes that survived, and some of the smashed bread broken up as croutons.

"Looks great, Mom," I say while loading my plate.

"Taste horrible," Dylan mutters.

"You know, you should be more thankful, Dylan. It's not like you're the one bringing home the bacon," I chide.

"Hell, if only there were bacon in this house," grumbles Chase.

"Can it, you two," orders Mom.

"I'll fix it tomorrow, stupids."

"What you gonna do, Layla? Kiss some guys, have them buy you more groceries?" Chase jeers. The table shakes, and a pained look crosses his stupid face.

"Go to bed, now!" Mom yells.

"Boys give you food for kisses?" Daisy asks.

"No, sweetie. Your brother is just being a jerk. Don't pay him any attention," Mom assures her.

I stare down at my plate, my face hot with anger. *Fucking bastard.* He only knows what I do because one of his friends went to Andy's once to hook up with Beth. Little shit saw me in the front office and then told Chase all about it. If my mom hadn't already kicked him good and sent him away, I might have punched his stupid face in. My mom and I don't want Daisy to know what I do. She is too young for that kind of information, and she looks up to me. I don't want her to end up doing what I do for a living. She's too sweet and loving to end up like me.

Dylan decides to use his brain for once and politely excuses himself from the table after finishing his food without further complaint. I eat quickly, clear the table, and send Daisy off to brush her teeth and get ready for bed.

"Chase will be sleeping on the couch tonight," Mom informs me as I do the dishes. "What he said is unacceptable, and I'm not going have you two in a room together overnight. I don't want to have to bury one of you or clean up all the blood."

"Thanks, Mom."

I could kill that little shit right now. I know it's stressful for her when we get into it, but he asks for it.

"I'll tell him to hit the couch while you're brushing up. Go on now."

I put the last plate onto the rack to dry and head off to get ready for bed. After washing up, I go to the bedroom and Dylan is already pretending to be asleep. Since he has the bed above me, he can't see anything I'm doing once I'm in my bed. I sneak a dose of haze to my bed, shoot up to help me calm down, close my eyes, and wait for sleep to come and put this shitty day behind me.

CHAPTER SIX

I START TO STIR IN my bed—not from dreams of falling but because of a pleasant scent invading my nose. It's comforting. I roll onto my left side, squish my face into my pillow, and take a deep breath. I reach my right arm underneath to hug my pillow when I feel something stiff and folded. I grab the strangely placed object and pull it out from under my pillow and lie on my back. It's a note, folded in half twice, and the front reads "Open me."

I prop myself up on my elbows and sit up, turning the note over and over in my hands to make sure it's real and that I'm not dreaming. I bring it to my nose and smell it. It smells amazing. *That must be what woke me up.* The scent is familiar, yet I cannot remember what it is. I keep sniffing it, trying to trigger my memory, when it dawns on me. "Adonis!" I whisper. I fumble to unfold it, wondering what in the world it says, never mind how the hell it got under my pillow.

Layla,

I'll be coming by to get you around 6:30 tonight. Hopefully, your brothers saved you some breakfast.

Adonis

P.S. You look so cute when you're sleeping.

I feel my face flush with embarrassment. *What was he doing here? Why is he "coming to get me" tonight? Is he still here?* My mind races a mile a minute with the possibilities brought on by this creepy note under my pillow that, for some strange reason, I also like. I fold up the note, close it in my hand, and swiftly make for the bedroom door. As I open it, I hear the others chattering away contentedly in the living room. I walk cautiously down the hall, hoping he isn't still here. I notice a different aroma as I approach; it has a meaty, greasy smell to it. It smells heavenly.

"Layla!" Daisy beams, coming up to hug me as I walk slowly into the living room.

"Hey," I reply, giving her a light squeeze back. "What's that smell?"

"Your boss came by this morning with, like, half a cow and some bacon, that's what," Dylan interjects.

"What?" I ask, clearly confused. "Andy? Andy doesn't have that kind of money."

"No, not Andy—your new boyfriend," Chase chimes in.

"Adonis? He isn't my boss or my boyfriend!" I snap.

"Layla, come get some bacon before the boys eat your share!" Mom calls from the kitchen.

I use that cue as an excuse to get away from the kids and satiate my hunger for both food and answers. I walk across the kitchen to the table to see a single plate piled with bacon and fried eggs. My mouth drops open a bit at the sight. I've only had bacon once in my life on Thanksgiving a few years ago. Some of our neighbors put money together to have a big dinner as a group, and they put bacon on the turkey. If there were a heaven, it would be full of bacon.

I pull out my chair without saying a word and sit down. I stare at the plate for only a moment before I start devouring its contents. My head is full of questions, but I figure they can wait until I take advantage of the unexpected feast before me. The food is a bit cold, but the fact that they actually saved it for me is unprecedented. Those boys must have pigged out to their heart's content in order to not have eaten my share by now.

I eat so much that at some point I feel like I may puke it all up. *I doubt it would taste as good coming back up as it did going down.* I finish clearing my plate and my mom grabs it from me and puts it in the sink. I let out a loud belch, clear my throat, and start badgering her with questions. "Why was that boy here?" I inquire.

"That boy," Mom starts, "that sweet, sweet boy came by with food early this morning for us. He said it was an apology for knocking you down and ruining all the food you bought from the market."

"It's one thing to replace what I had, but this is ridiculous," I contend. I walk over to the small chest freezer in the corner by the sink and open it. "This"—I gesture to the contents of the freezer— "is, like, half a damn cow! And *bacon?* And the note, and this crap about being my new boss ..." I continue.

"Layla, sweetie, he was being nice," she assures me.

"No. 'Nice' is giving someone a bit of cash and saying 'Hey, sorry for tackling you like a crazy person,' or just replacing what got destroyed. This is just creepy. It's too much."

"I swear, child, that storm was born in you, not the other way around. You need to mind your emotions better. He told me all about what happened, and you should be thankful, not angry and suspicious," she lectures.

"I knew he was lying when he said he just wanted to drive me home. 'Not a stalker,' my ass. Only a stalker comes to your house when you're sleeping, drops off more gifts than Santa on Christmas Eve, and slips a note under your pillow! And you still haven't told me what this shit is with him 'being my boss' that the boys are jabbering on about now, and why is he saying in this note that he is picking me up tonight? How the hell does he even know I can read? I could be illiterate, for all he knows!" I rant.

"Layla Suzanne Mason."

"What?" I whine.

"That boy, Adonis, is offering you a job."

"I don't want it!"

"Technically, his father is offering you a job, and you better listen here. You don't turn down a politician when they offer you something decent in this world. The last thing you want to do is offend them," she cautions.

"Politician? What in the world are you talking about? Adonis is a doctor."

"Do you know who his father is?"

"No, and I don't care," I emphasize.

"His father …" She pauses and puts her hands on my shoulders. "Is Donovan Caraway."

"Senator Donovan Caraway?" I ask, feeling a cold chill run through my whole being.

"Yes, and you don't say no to him if you know what's good for you, and for us," she warns.

"That son of a bitch!" I yell, slamming my fist on the table. "If I would have known that, I would have pushed even more to keep him away from me. Damn snake! Acting all nice just to trap me into cleaning up the senator's shit!"

"Layla, he's a nice boy. Maybe his father is a horrible person, but that's not his fault," she reasons.

"He's got you fooled already."

"He's offering to give us food and two hundred extra a week of his *own money* in addition to what his parents will pay you," she coaxes.

I roll my eyes. *I can't believe that she believes this bullshit!*

"You'll have food, shelter, clothes, and we'll have all we need here too. And you can visit us when they give you some time off. It works out for everyone," she continues.

"Really, Mom? Really? Who's going to do all the work around here? Who's going to keep an eye on Daisy when you don't feel well? The boys?" I counter.

"Daisy is getting older; she'll be fine. I'll be fine. You need to grab this opportunity."

"Opportunity implies a choice. I'm not really being given one, am I?" I scoff.

"Layla, growing up means you sometimes have to choose to do things you don't like in order to get by."

"You think I like what I do?" I shout. "I hate it! I feel disgusting and trashy and empty inside! But I do it for you guys, because no one else works around here!"

"Well, I don't want you to feel like you have to do that anymore, Layla," she quavers. I can see the tears welling up in her eyes. "I never wanted you to do it, but you have such a goddamn hard head. You could have just stayed at the cannery, and we would have been okay, but you wanted more than just okay. The boys would have adjusted eventually."

"Don't you start crying on me," I tell her as I start to feel my own tears coming.

"Then take the job, Layla! I don't want you selling yourself to those horrible men. Do you know how hard it is for me to see you every day, knowing what you were doing the night before? It kills me! To know that some monster has been defiling my sweet baby girl just kills me," she cries.

"What are you going to tell Daisy?" I ask. I wipe a tear from under my right eye before it can fall.

Mom grabs a paper towel and blows her nose. "That you're going to be living somewhere else, but that you will come and visit, and that you will always be her big sister no matter what."

"So that's it, huh?" I sniff. I stand up from my chair to leave.

Mom stands as well, placing her hands on my shoulders and looking me straight in the face. "You have a chance. You have a chance to take care of yourself, and us, without putting yourself in danger every day. Sure, we'll miss each other, but we'll still be together from time to time. You're all grown up now, my little prairie chicken. It's time for you to roam. Just remember that you can always come back to your booming grounds," she reassures me with a warm smile.

I wipe my nose and give her a long hug. When we release from our embrace, I take a step back and shift my hair to one side, trying to regain my composure. "How much should I pack?"

"Probably just a few dresses for your time off, underwear, socks, and pajamas. They should be providing work clothes," she advises. "Maybe take a few pictures with you so you don't forget what we look like."

"Okay, Mom."

As I walk out of the kitchen, the living room is empty but I can hear some noise out back. *The kids probably went outside to play and to get away from the tension.* I continue slowly back to my room and slump down on my bed. I then remember that I still have the note clutched in my hand; I'm so tense that I haven't opened my fist. I throw the note at the wall and start to cry. Throwing that note isn't a sufficient expression

of just how pissed off and sad I am in addition to everything else I can't describe. I wish I had something to break, but I don't have the luxury of owning things that I can just smash and easily replace.

I don't want to leave my home. I don't want to clean up after rich assholes for a living, but I don't want to have to keep fucking gross creeps forever, either. Why is life so hell-bent against me being happy? And working for Senator Caraway, no less, that piece of slime! Cow chips are better people than he is.

Senator Caraway is the one who drafted and pushed the bill that got rid of safety regulations in the workplace for GIs. The fat-cat business guys loved it and threw loads of money behind the campaign; after all, money not spent on ensuring workplace safety meant more money for the business owners and their stockholders. So what if people get an arm cut off in a ventilation fan while working on it, or if they fall off a rickety catwalk with no rails? Workers are disposable to them! One dies? Just hire a new one. The only medical attention those workers get is if they have organs that can be harvested. Normies get the only real medical care. It's pretty much cosmetic or stuff caused by stupidity that ends them up in the hospital, like boob jobs, nose jobs, drunken car crashes, bad lungs from smoking, bad livers from drinking too much, drug overdoses, domestic abuse, etc. So, if a Normie needs new lungs or a new liver, freshly dead GIs on a work site are necessary.

Not only did Caraway push that bill, but he has a few other atrocious ones on his record as well. The one I find most appalling is the treatment of GI prisoners. We pretty much have no real rights to begin with. We can't vote. If we commit a crime or get accused of one, we're basically guilty until proven innocent. GIs will rot in prison until they get sick and die for minor crimes like petty theft and be executed for crimes of rape, murder, assault—of Normies that is. No one cares what happens to us. The executed and those who die of illness will also have their organs harvested. Hell, sometimes they may even be executed for that purpose alone. Now the law states, by Caraway's doing, that everyone who gets arrested has a blood sample collected and gets put on an organ donation registry. If someone rich or powerful needs another liver and you happen to be a match, kiss your life goodbye. They have no qualms about killing you to save themselves.

Senator Caraway is also a well-known alcoholic and is rumored to be on his fourth liver. He has no personal reservations about killing others to save his own ass. He is lower than whale shit on the sea floor—and now I have to live in his home and cater to his wants and needs. Worst of all, Adonis is his son.

I resign myself to my fate and grab a canvas bag. I don't own any real luggage, just canvas or plastic bags. I clear my underwear drawer out into the bag, haze and all, save for one bottle that I quickly self-medicate with. I next gather some dresses, a couple of pairs of shorts, my hairbrush and toothbrush, and put the bag at the foot of my bed. I flop on my back onto my bed with my arms stretched out wide and my legs spread, looking like a big *X*, and let out a loud sigh.

Fate—ha! Yesterday that jackass asked me if I believed in fate. Well, whether I believe in it or not, it looks like I have one now, and I'm fucking pissed off at it.

CHAPTER SEVEN

I STAY IN MY ROOM for the remainder of the morning just staring at the bottom of Dylan's bunk and thinking. *What's going to happen to me now? Am I just going to spend the rest of my life serving some corrupt asshole?* I know I don't want kids or anything like that, but I don't want to clean toilets until I die either. Maybe I'd like to find a guy one day—not that I need one—just for company. Then there is the young doctor, Adonis Caraway. *He's handsome, no doubt about it, but he is such a jackass, trapping me like this. Even if I do want him and he wants me, we can't be together.* It's bad enough when a GI and a Normie get caught together, but the son of a senator? That would be a huge disaster. They would probably string us both up for the public to watch instead of humanely putting a bullet through my brain. *I wish he were hideous; it would be easier for me to hate him.* I want to hate him so much more than I do, but those eyes and his smell just turn my insides to jelly.

Who am I kidding, though? A guy like him would never want any more from me than an easy lay. Yeah, I have an objectively attractive body, but things like that fade over time. My personality sucks, my lips are too small, my eyes are too big, and my curly hair gets puffy with the humidity and always does this stupid thing where one side flips out and the other flips in. On top of that, I'm uneducated—you know, since we aren't allowed to attend schools. What little I do know, my mom taught me, like her mom taught her. Sure, I can read and do some simple math so I can get by in the market and manage time at work, but what little I know of any other subjects is from digging old textbooks out of the dump across the street from my house. Yeah, I live across from the dump. Fitting, isn't it? Sometimes I find some interesting stuff, though. I've found books on flowers, a few story books, and old history books with pictures and maps of what the world used to look like. I'm by no means what a Normie would consider smart. Adonis is a doctor, and I'm just some dirty GI whore who lives next to the dump. We're about as compatible as a toaster and a full bathtub.

This GI stuff is total bullshit. They don't even know what's supposedly wrong with me. When they profile your DNA when you're a baby, they tell your parents that you're going to get this disease or that disease, if you're mental, if you're a carrier for a condition to give your kids, if you'll be crippled, etc. With mine, the results were "unknown genetic variation." Yeah, that's really something! *Unknown variation.* That doesn't necessarily mean something is wrong with me; they just don't understand it, and therefore, they don't like it. Scientists used to like to figure out the unknowns, but now they just do what they know to keep the Normies happy and the GIs segregated. I sometimes wish that I had been labeled a Normie, but then I would have been taken from my parents and adopted by some rich jerks.

There's nothing I can do about any of it, so why bother thinking about it? I am forever labeled as "genetically inferior" by this stupid tattoo and doomed to a life of cleaning up after despicable people like Senator Caraway.

Around noon I go to the kitchen for lunch and indulge on bread and cheeses. Yeah, all brought by Adonis—"the nice boy," as my mom likes to say. He really knows how to lay it on thick to get a fragile lady to give up her daughter to be a slave.

After lunch, I decide to take Daisy with me for a walk down to Gator Beach and look out on the ocean. The "beach" has more seaweed and trash than sand, but if you can ignore all that, and the noise from the desalination plant, it's nice. It has a decent view. I stand with Daisy on the edge of the water and point out to Old Houston.

"Can you believe they used to send people into space and talk with them from there?" I ask her.

"I wish they still did," she replies.

"It would be pretty cool, huh?"

"Yeah, it would! To have people fly up like birds to the moon."

"I wish I could fly up there," I sigh.

"But then you would be on the moon and not here," Daisy surmises.

"True, I might miss it here a little bit," I concede. I crouch down on my knees to get on her level. "You know I'm leaving, right?"

"Yeah, Mama told me." She nods and starts to pout.

"I don't want to go, but Mom says I have to."

"Can I come, too?" she begs, jumping up and down with her hands clasped.

"No, squirt, you gotta stay here and take care of Mom and those idiot brothers of ours," I laugh.

"You're going to come and visit a lot, though, right?" she asks. She's starting to purse out her lips, and I see her little eyes beginning to well up.

"Yeah, all the time! I promise," I say, trying to not only reassure her but myself as well.

"You better bring me presents when you come back."

"I'll try to get you an amazing one for your birthday," I promise her.

"Can I get give you a present?" Daisy asks.

"Where are you going to get me a present from?" I inquire. She points out at the water. "You're gonna jump in the ocean and find me one? I think a gator or a shark might get you first," I joke. I grab her and pretend like I'm a gator trying to eat her and make munching sounds. She laughs every time I do that to her.

"No, silly, just watch!" she calls. Daisy runs toward the sea as the waves are pulling out and I run after her when I see her bend down and start searching the muddy sand. When the next wave comes in, she runs back toward me and then out again. She does this about five or six times and then comes back to me with something in her hands.

"Here, so you can fly home," she says, putting two shells in my hands.

I start tearing up. The shells are what they call "angel wings." They are delicate white clam shells that have grooves that look like feathers and taper off at the ends like wings. "Oh, they're perfect," I quaver. I wipe away the tears that are on the verge of spilling over my bottom eyelids and down my face. "Thank you, Daisy. I'll keep them with me all the time so that I can fly home whenever I can."

I pull her in for a big hug and hold her for a long time. I'm going to miss my little parrot and shadow, always following me around at home. When I pull away from the embrace, I stoop down and motion for her to climb up on my back. I walk back home, for the last time, carrying Daisy piggyback style with the shells carefully tucked in my right hand.

When we get to the front step, I let Daisy down and she runs up and goes inside. It's nearly four o'clock, probably. *Only a few hours left until my life changes forever.* I let out a long sigh, slowly walk in, and flop down on the couch.

"You want to help me make dinner?" Mom calls from the kitchen.

"Sure," I reply as I get up and walk to her. "What do you want to make?"

"I don't know. We have all this meat; I don't even recognize most of the cuts. I haven't a clue where to start," she says, throwing her arms up in the air.

"Just pick something. I can throw it in the frying pan, and we'll be good," I suggest.

"You're going to throw a whole roast in a frying pan?" she teases.

"No," I chuckle. "Just give me some steaks or something. I'll bread it up, chicken fry it, maybe mash some potatoes. Easy peasy," I say. "You gotta start teaching Daisy to help you out, Mom."

"She'll start learning soon enough."

"You sure you can handle this all when I'm gone?"

"No, I'm not sure. You can never be sure, but I'll do my best. That's all I can do," she confides.

I kiss her cheek. "Well, until then, do you wanna tag team this?" I say with a competitive edge in my voice, challenging her.

"You bet! Dibs on breading," she calls.

"Okay, fine, but you better be able to keep up," I tease.

Mom does all the egg breaking and breads the meat. As soon as the steaks are prepped, they go to me to fry. We always make competitions in the kitchen when we can. Competition makes the mundane task of day-to-day life somewhat enjoyable. We compete to see if I can fry faster than she can bread, who can crack eggs for cake batter faster, who can peel more potatoes in five minutes—stuff like that. You can't do it half-assed, either, or it doesn't count. You can't have eggshells in the bowl, partially peeled potatoes, or half-breaded meat. The meats have to have a nice, even coating and no bald spots.

After we finish frying up the steaks and peeling the potatoes to boil and mash, we clean up the dishes and get the table ready for dinner. As for the competition results, I can still fry faster than she can bread, but she is faster than a bullet at peeling potatoes. She never gets a nick or anything; I suppose she can't take a risk like that with her hemophilia. She wears a little protective leather glove that covers her fingers but leaves her palms bare to protect herself from cutting her fingers in the kitchen. It's kind of an unfair advantage, but I let her have that one.

We call the kids in for dinner and sit down for our last normal family dinner. The boys are quiet at the table for what seems like the first time since Dad died. They aren't complaining one bit that I'm about to leave, but I know they must care on some level—at least I hope they do. They stuff their faces and drink their milk while making their usual rude noises. One thing I won't miss is the belching contests they have at dinner, that's for sure. Those bozos can go on forever doing that. My mom chooses to ignore their behavior, but it bugs the hell out of me.

I'm trying to finish up my potatoes when the knock I have been dreading comes on the front door.

Chase runs to the front door and flings it open. "Hey!" he greets my captor enthusiastically. "Can I see your car?"

"Yeah, just don't start it or break anything," Adonis replies with a carefree air.

"Cool!" Chase exclaims. "Come on, Dylan, come check it out!" Dylan is already putting his boots on before Chase can finish his sentence and Daisy follows suit.

I hunch forward in my seat, which faces away from the living room, and resume slowly eating the rest of my dinner. My mom shoots a look at me as if she's disappointed I didn't jump up to meet him. She pushes out her chair and goes to the front door.

"Don't just stand there. Come on in and have a seat on the couch," Mom says warmly. I can hear him walking across the floor. *I wish he would just fall right through it.* I start fidgeting with my food, making little doodles in my mashed potatoes with my fork. I don't want to get up from the table and have to get in his stupid fancy car to go to his stupid fancier house. I can hear my mom making small talk with him in the living room, and I know they'll run out of things to talk about eventually.

My mom speaks a little louder than the rest of the conversation but acts as if she's still talking to him. "I'm sure Layla would love to come out here and chat once she finishes her dinner and puts the dishes in the sink." she insists.

"Yeah, I'm coming! Just give me a minute!" I holler. I shovel my last bit of potatoes into my mouth, push in my chair, and place the dishes in the sink. I take a deep breath through my nose and walk into the living room. They both stand up as I enter.

"Sweetie, I was just telling Adonis that you're already all packed," Mom says.

"Yeah, I guess," I mumble, looking down at my feet.

"Would you like me to carry your bags?" Adonis asks.

Like I'm going to fall for that chivalry bullshit.

"No, I can get it myself," I say stubbornly. Without ever looking at Adonis, I leave the living room to get my bags. Only two canvas bags contain my worldly possessions. The bare necessities, a couple of pictures, and Daisy's angel wings are all I have. I sit on the edge of my bed for a moment, wondering if I will ever get to sleep in it again, then I stand up and pat the sheets straight. When I'm satisfied with the tidiness of the bed, I let my hands linger on it, taking in one last feel of my soft place to fall. I sigh and pick up my bags, leaving my childhood room and old life behind me. I shuffle slowly back to the living room, where my mom and Adonis are still making awkward small talk.

"You're all ready to go?" Adonis asks.

"Yeah," I reply sullenly.

Adonis heads for the door. I follow behind him, and behind me my mother gently holds her hand on my shoulder. The kids are still ogling at the car when we get outside. They stop suddenly in surprise when Adonis pops the concealed trunk with his remote. With that simple movement, the emotion of the moment quickly shifts. Daisy comes running toward me from the car.

"Don't go, Layla, don't go!" Daisy bawls. I put my bags down and scoop her up into a tight hug. She almost gags me with how tightly her arms constrict around my neck.

"I'll come back to visit soon; I promise. I got those wings, re-member?" I assure her. My mom comes up behind Daisy, hanging on to the front of me by my neck, and envelops both of us.

"Layla will be back, sweetie," Mom soothes her. She pulls Daisy off of my neck but then she just clings on to my waist instead. Mom hugs me, rocking slightly from side to side like a mother soothing a baby. "Be brave, my little chick. I love you," she whispers close to my ear.

I'm already crying at this point, and I hate it. *I need to be strong for them.* She releases me, and I sniff back the contents of my runny nose and wipe under my eyes with the back of my thumb. "I love you, too, Mom." I pause and look her in the eyes. "I'll be back real soon, I promise."

Mom smiles and then calls out to the boys, running around the car. "Boys! Come and say bye to your sister," she hollers out, the Southern twang strong in her voice as it always is when she has to round them up. Chase and Dylan come up and give me weak hugs, say goodbye, and go inside.

Stupid brats probably don't even care that I'm leaving. My new job means that they get more food to stuff their faces with, and I won't be there to smack them when they deserve it, but whatever. I bend down to pick up my bags, but they're gone. I look around my general vicinity for them to no avail.

"I already put them in the car," Adonis interjects. I must not have noticed him taking them; I was too busy with my emotional exchanges. I bend down to Daisy's level, giving her a kiss on the forehead. "This isn't goodbye forever. See you soon, squirt." I give her head a little rub, messing up her hair a bit to get a smile out of her. I give my mom one last quick hug and "I love you" before stepping out into the street. Adonis goes around to the passenger side and opens the door for me. I awkwardly get in, he closes the door, and all is silent for a short moment.

Adonis opens his door and gets into the car, quietly and without shaking the car like the last time. I don't look at him; I just stare at my feet and give him the cold shoulder. He starts the car and we start to move slowly. At the end of the street, he turns around and drives back by my house. He rolls down my window so I can wave goodbye to my family as he drives away. Now out of direct sight of my family, I crane my head over my right shoulder, looking back helplessly.

He puts my window back up, and an oppressive silence befalls the space between us. After a few minutes of silence, Adonis clears his throat, trying to get my attention, but I continue to ignore him.

"Are you even going to look at me?" he whispers imploringly. I just sit there, looking out my window, and continue my silence. "I'm sorry I sprung this on you like that," he adds.

Hearing his pathetic apology makes me seethe with anger. "Sorry? You're *sorry*? I'm sorry, but I don't believe that at all!" I snap at him.

"You have every right to be angry with me, but just let me explain," he begs.

"Damn right I'm angry!" I yell, cutting him off. "Using your father's position to trap me into working for you! You're just as bad as he is! Why me? Huh? Why? You see that sad scene back there? That's my fucking family! You think you can just waltz in with food and promises of more and money and then just take me away?" I rant.

Adonis hits the breaks quickly, and I lurch forward. "I didn't know what else to do, okay!" he confesses. He turns to me as I try to recover from the surprising stop of the car.

I gather my wits and continue my inquisition. "What else to do about what? I never even knew you before yesterday, and I wish I'd never met you," I seethe.

"I didn't want to lose you," he reveals.

"Lose me? You never had me! And what the fuck is that supposed to mean? You are insane, you know that? Batshit crazy!"

"I was browsing the market with the intent of finding someone new to take poor Rebecca's place."

"So, you were shopping for a new slave to work to death? How nice!"

"It's not slavery," he defends. "I saw you at the herbalist, and I started to follow you."

"I knew someone was following me. I always can tell. You're a damn creep!"

"I can't explain it, okay?! When I saw you, I knew I wanted you around me, and this was the only way I could make it happen!"

"You don't want to be around me, okay? I'm not smart, I'm not rich, I'm not a Normie, I'm nothing. I fuck pathetic losers for a living, you idiot," I contend.

"Not anymore," he counters meekly.

"Yeah, thanks so much for *saving* me," I say sarcastically.

"When you started crossing the street, you weren't paying attention. There was a car coming at you quickly, and you never even looked. I ran at you as fast as I could to push you out of the way."

"I'd have been better off dead," I assert. "So what did you do then, after dropping me off at home?"

"I told my father that I met a young strong girl at the market today that would be perfect for the job. You are strong. The way you carried all those bags alone, and you're tough! I tackled you in the street, and you sprang right back," he explains.

"So you tell Daddy you found someone, and then that's it, huh? Daddy gets what he wants, and so do you?"

"I'm sorry I used my father's influence to force you into this, but I had no other option."

"Yes, you did. Leaving me alone would have been a perfect option, you idiot!" I interrupt. "You want to get me killed, don't you? You can't be with me. For one, I hate you, and two, it's against the law. They would put me in prison and throw away the key. You're a selfish prick!" I revile.

"I said I'm sorry!"

"Well, it's not good enough now, is it? You're what? Twenty-two? Twenty-three? A new hotshot doctor. Get yourself some Normie bimbo."

"Twenty-two, and I don't want them. I'm not like them!" he insists.

"Well, I have to agree with part of that. Your DNA results must have been screwed up, because you're screwed in the head. You should have been a GI, or you got dropped on your head as an infant," I continue to insult him. "Now are you going to drive this thing or not?" I demand.

Adonis puts the car in drive and then pulls it over to the side of the road, putting it in park.

"What are you doing? Are you going to let me go back home?"

"No—I can't. My family is expecting you."

"Then what are you doing?" I ask, starting to feel uneasy.

Adonis turns to look at me, and I look away. I hear him unbuckle his seat belt and the sound of it retracting. Now his hand is on my shoulder. I scoot up closer against the door. "Layla, please, listen to me," he pleads.

"I don't care what you have to say," I sneer.

He keeps encroaching on my personal space, and I can't shrink away any more than I already have. He gets his arm behind my back and hooks his hand around my right shoulder. I just want to disappear. I don't want this jerk touching me, no matter how hot he is. Sure, I've had plenty of jerks touch me, and worse, but none of them had done to me what he has. He has taken me from my home, my family, my life. I'm so tense I think I might just implode.

In a swift movement, he pulls his arm toward his body, still gripping my arm, and forces my body to turn toward his. He brings me toward him and puts his face right against mine, kissing me roughly. I jerk away quickly, pull back my arm, and slap him right in the face.

"You sick freak!" I scream. "How dare you!" My slap sends him fleeing back to his side of the car like a kicked puppy. The look of stunned surprise and hurt that he wears on his face is pathetic.

"I'm s-s-s-sorry," he stutters, quickly putting his seat belt back on. Driving again, he looks straight ahead at the road as if I don't exist next to him.

The silence is tense for the next few uncomfortable minutes before he speaks again. "When we get to the GI Divide checkpoint, just let me handle it. I have the papers signed by my father granting you permission to cross on official business," he informs me.

"Or I could just scream and tell them that I've been kidnapped by a psycho!" I snap, emphasizing the last word.

He tightens his grip on the steering wheel, clenching his jaw. "I'm sorry, I don't know what came over me. Can we just forget it happened?" he implores.

"That's not something I'm likely to forget."

"When we get to the house, you will have your own room, your own space; you'll hardly have to see me."

"Sounds splendid!"

Moments later, Adonis slows the car to a stop. There's a gate up ahead with a small guard shack. Adonis rolls down his window and pulls a folded paper out of his pocket.

"Good evening, sir," says the gate guard. "Why aren't you using the usual express lane, sir?"

"I have a GI passenger with me. I have her work papers here," Adonis says, handing the folded paper to the guard.

The guard steps back from the window, unfolds the papers, and starts reading it to himself. Then he bends down to level with the window and speaks across toward me. "Is your name Layla Mason?"

"Yes," I answer.

"ID number?"

"UV095612."

"Says here you're to be working at the Caraway estate as a housekeeper. Is that correct?" he continues.

"Yes, sir," I answer in my fake polite voice.

"Everything looks in order," the guard says. He hands the paper back to Adonis. "Have a nice night, sir."

"You too," Adonis replies. The guard goes back to the shack and raises the gate arm to let the car through.

The GI Divide is a wonderful little barrier that cities erected to keep the GIs out of the Normies' sight and keep the trouble and riff-raff out of their neighborhoods. Normies can go wherever they want, but we can't cross "the Divide" unless we have official business. The other side of the line has the schools, Normie neighborhoods, hospitals, parks—you know, all the nice things that we aren't allowed to go to. I've never crossed the Divide before.

I just want this damn ride to be over with already. "How much further from the Divide is the house?" I ask.

"About fifteen more minutes."

I sigh, not wanting to spend another fifteen seconds in this car. I turn to my window and just stare out, looking at the sky as the sun descends toward the horizon. The sun will soon be setting on this horrible day, leading way to a miserable and lonely night.

I watch the sky for a good while when I notice large houses begin to get in the way of my view. *These houses look too big to be real.* You could probably fit a dozen families or more in one of them. It makes me feel so small, so insignificant—like an ant. *I don't belong in a place like this.* I feel so poor and so low that I want to cry, but I can't let this bastard see me cry again—never. I swallow hard and start staring back down at my feet.

"Nervous?" Adonis asks quietly.

"No. Not at all," I lie.

The car slows down and continues up a long drive. We're moving toward a mansion looming against the backdrop of the ocean as the setting sun in the west casts an eerie orange-red glow on the façade.

CHAPTER EIGHT

THE CAR STOPS AT THE top of the long winding drive, and in front of me is the biggest house I could ever imagine. It has two large sections that split off from the looming double doors at the front entrance. Surrounding the drive and the front of the house is a lush green lawn interspersed with large palm trees, strange sculptures, and flower beds. I feel so out of place, like I'm on a different planet. I'm sure that the moon would feel more natural to me than this place.

I hear Adonis exit the car. He moves around toward the back of the car, retrieves my bags, and then opens my door. I get out warily, unsure of how to exist in such a place. I grab my bags from him and stand there for a moment, just staring at the walk that leads from the drive to the front door.

Adonis clears his throat. "Well, this is it. Come on." He walks a few paces toward the door and stops to look back at me. I just stand there in stunned, terrified silence. He walks back toward me and reaches out to grab my hand.

I pull back and stand up tall. "Don't touch me. I don't need anyone holding my hand," I mutter.

"Then move it, or I'll carry you."

I take in a deep breath, hold my head high, and start slowly walking toward the door. As the path gets closer to the door, there is a network of small waterfalls and ponds filled with the strangest fish I have ever seen. They are large with big mouths, but I've never seen anything like them at the market. I stop for a moment, staring at the darkening water as the sunlight wanes toward the horizon. I look at my reflection on the water. My forehead still bears the cut from the day before and my necklace of bruises from my last night at work is still obvious. *I look like gutter trash.*

"Those are koi," Adonis says. I jump slightly, startled out of my trance.

"What?" I ask, not hearing what he's saying, just jarred by the sound of his speaking.

"The fish, they're called koi."

"Oh, that's nice," I reply nonchalantly, pretending not to care.

I turn my attention back to the task at hand: getting to that door. I'm probably five feet from it when it suddenly opens, casting a bright light behind the person who is standing in the doorway but not illuminating them, causing them to look like a shadowy phantom.

"What took you so long, Adonis?" a woman calls out.

"Traffic," he answers.

"Well, come in," the woman replies.

Adonis walks toward the door and across the threshold. I hesitantly follow a few feet behind him, trying to avoid making eye contact with the woman. As I enter the house, I freeze in awe. Before me, toward the back of the large entry area, is a staircase that branches off in opposite directions at a landing. The stairs are carpeted in a deep burgundy color, and the handrails are exquisitely carved and highly polished. On the high ceiling hangs an enormous crystal chandelier sparkling in perfection as if not a single mote of dust has ever touched it. The floor on which I stand leads off in either direction for quite a distance, tiled with a shining white material. I don't want to move any further, fearing I will contaminate the immaculate space before me. After a few moments, which must have been awkward for the woman as she watches me stand there in silence, she speaks to me.

"You must be Layla," she says spuriously. I just nod in the affirmative. "My name is Margaret Caraway, but you may address me as Mrs. Caraway or ma'am."

"Yes, ma'am," I say and nod again.

"Very good," Mrs. Caraway says, clasping her hands in front of her with a single clap. "Adonis, if you would show Layla to her quarters. I'll fetch Lucinda to acquaint her with the rules and her duties." She immediately turns to walk away noisily in her tall pointed shoes down the southern wing of the house.

I watch her walking for a few moments, haunted by the echoes her shoes make with each step. She is probably shorter than me without the shoes, blonde, with dead-looking blue-gray eyes and a face that looks like it's being pulled back and secured with clothespins. *Adonis looks nothing like her at all.* I then turn my attention to the hallway leading to the left, toward the north wing of the house. The large entryway leads off to a large carpeted room filled with plush yet ancient-looking chairs and couches with coffee tables and lamps placed around the room. The hall then goes on to pass numerous doors.

"Follow me," Adonis beckons in a very formal, authoritative tone. I start walking a few paces behind him, briefly examining the pictures and paintings on the walls as I go. "Your room will be next to Lucinda's and Phillip's."

"Who is Phillip?"

"Our chef," he answers without missing a beat. He is now acting like the typical prim and proper Normie asshat. "You guys are near the kitchen and utility room downstairs. You'll primarily stay in the north wing, which also contains the dining room, library, natatorium, and drawing room. The south wing is mostly for my father's work purposes," he explains as we walk.

"Nata-what?" I ask.

"Natatorium. Swimming pool."

Talk about pretentious! Just call a spade a damn shovel! Nata-torium ... for fuck's sake!

"If you have all these amazing things, then why do you bother ever leaving?" I ask.

"It gets lonely," he answers quietly with a shrug.

We are almost to the far end of the hall when I see a set of glass double doors to my right. I stop and look out curiously at the dark shapes I see outside. It's already too dark to make anything out clearly, but they look like large animals. Adonis must have noticed I stopped following him and come up to me as I gaze outside. "That goes to the garden."

"You keep animals in your garden?" I ask, clearly confused.

"Oh! No, no, no," he laughs. "Those are just topiary." He looks at me, still seeing the confusion on my face. "A fancy word for shrubs that you trim into shapes. You know, like elephants, birds—any shape you want, really."

"Oh" is all I can manage to reply, and I start walking down the hall that now bends to the left.

"You don't even know where you're going," Adonis says, walking swiftly to close the gap between us. He slows once he catches up to me and walks beside me.

"Well, I know it has to be this way," I assert. We continue walking for another two minutes probably, in which we pass the game room and the theater. Up ahead at the end of the hall is a large door and to the left of that, the biggest kitchen I could have ever imagined. Across the hall from the kitchen are five normal-sized doors. This is where we stop.

"The doors on the very end of the group are the bathrooms. One for Phillip, one for you and Lucinda. The bedrooms are these three in the middle." Adonis then steps toward the door nearest to the bathroom and the dining room and opens the door. "This"—he gestures with his arm—"is your room."

Compared to the rest of the house my room looks miserable, but compared to my family's house, it is slightly better. *It's at least my own room. I don't have to share it.* The floors have carpet, too, which I've never had the luxury to walk on barefoot before. All we had were splintery old wood floors. *It isn't very big, but it's sufficient.* There's a worn-down old dresser along the wall that you see as you open the door. In the back left corner is a bed just big enough for one person, but the mattress is thick and looks comfortable. Next to the bed is a small side table with an alarm clock, and the wall that runs parallel to the hall has a fairly large closet. Large to me, anyway, though I'm sure it doesn't compare to those of Adonis and his family.

I walk slowly into the room and place my bags down by the bed. I then walk over to the dresser and stare back at my reflection in the mirror above it. *Even this basic room is too fancy for the likes of me. I don't belong here, like a lone weed in a flower bed.*

Adonis sneaks up on me while I'm not paying attention and puts his hand on my shoulder. I look back at him in the mirror. "I know it's a lot to take in, but you'll get used to it," he says, trying to reassure me.

"I doubt it," I reply.

"Well," he starts, "I've got to go and get ready for my shift at the hospital. I'll see you around."

He gives my shoulder a slight squeeze and leaves. There I stand alone in this strange place. All I have from my former life is on my back and in two small bags. I let out a quiet sigh and decide it would be wise to start unpacking, as I'm sure they will have me tending to their every whim starting bright and early tomorrow. I unpack my bag with my few dresses and hang them in the closet next to the long gray dresses which I assume are my working clothes. It just looks sad and lonesome. *Such a large colorless space, and the only thing I have to put in it are five sun dresses.* I put my socks and underwear in the top drawer, as I tend to do, and then find my stash at the bottom of the bag along with my pictures and Daisy's seashells.

I pick up the first picture, one of my dad and me when I was maybe three years old. I was riding on his shoulders down at Gator Beach. The day was bright, as most days here are, and so were our smiles. I take the picture and sit down on the bed. I place it beside me and take off my boots as to not dirty the sheets. I wonder, *What he would think of me now? The things I've done with my life since he left?* I can't help but feel that he would be ashamed of me. Especially now, working for the likes of Senator Caraway, whom my dad had always despised. I wish he were still alive; then none of this would be happening.

I stand up from the bed and walk to the dresser, propping the photo up against the mirror. I take the other two pictures I have with me, of my mom and me and the other of all us kids together, and put those next to Dad. The only things left are the shells and my haze. I place the shells in front of my picture of my dad and put them facing out, touching at the hinge, so that they looked just like their name-sake—angel wings.

I stare at the five bottles and syringe left in the bag. That's all I have. *What am I going to do when this runs out?* Withdrawal is a painful bitch; the shaking, fever, vomiting. I realize I'm going to have to ration it out the best I can, only using it when I feel like I'm going to be sick. It's not like I can just leave here and go to the market to meet up with Deacon. *I'm stuck here like a damn prisoner.* I put the bottles in my top drawer and go to lie down on the bed. It's softer than anything I have ever lain on before, but I'd still rather have my old bed. I take a deep breath and close my eyes, weary from all that has happened during the day, when a knock comes at my door.

"Come in," I call. In walks a thin woman with long salt-and-pepper hair pulled back into a bun. Her skin is a dark tan color and shows slight wrinkles around her brown eyes. She looks very tired, but kind. *Finally, a real person to talk to in this place.* I get up from my bed to greet her politely.

"You must be Lucinda. I'm Layla," I say, trying to sound confident as I introduce myself.

"Yes, I'm Lucinda, but we have no time for pleasantries," she states curtly. "You will start working before the rooster's crow in the morning, so you need to listen carefully to everything I have to say."

"Okay, I'm listening," I respond, wanting so badly to roll my eyes at her uptight attitude.

"You will be up every day by five in the morning and be ready to work by five thirty. Unless instructed otherwise, the first thing you will do is take care of laundry in the utility room. That includes starching, ironing, folding, and handwashing when called for," Lucinda goes on.

"Umm," I start to interrupt. "I don't know how to use a washing machine or iron. We just handwashed everything with a board and hung it out," I confess.

"I figured that much," she sighs. "I'll show you how in the morning. Hopefully you learn quickly, because I can't be around to hold your hand. We eat our meals in the kitchen after the family has finished. After that, you will be doing the dishes. You can do that, right?"

"Yes," I reply, feeling a bit embarrassed.

"When you are not doing laundry, dishes, or having mealtime, you will be doing general upkeep of the north wing. I mainly take care of the south wing, but since Rebecca left, I have had to do it all myself. The north wing consists of the family's bedrooms upstairs, the halls, bathrooms, drawing room, et cetera. If something looks like it needs dusting or polishing, don't ask, just do it. The carpets are to be vacuumed weekly unless there is a mess—then do it immediately—and the tile floors are to be swept and mopped every three days."

I feel kind of dizzy with all the things she's listing off so quickly; it feels like my brain is going to explode. I hope I can remember it all. "Is that all?" I ask hesitantly.

"No. There are still the rules."

"Rules?"

"Yes. The basic rules for us are simple to remember unless you are just plain stupid. One, when addressing any of the masters of the house, you will start with either 'sir' or 'ma'am.' Two, do not speak unless asking a pertinent question or you have been given permission to speak. Three, never argue when given an order. Four, don't try to steal anything. The most important rule of all, five—never, ever interrupt the senator when he is working. Ever."

"Sounds simple enough," I reply, trying to sound confident.

"Your time to yourself is from nine in the evening until you wake up in the morning, so use that time wisely. Make sure you are well rested. Also, you are free to use the restroom when you need to, but don't make a habit of going excessively to try to avoid work," she concludes.

I look at the small digital clock on my side table; it's already past nine thirty. With my orientation over, Lucinda bids me goodnight and leaves my room. My head is so overloaded with information that I have no qualms about getting into my pajamas and ending this nightmare of a day. I take my socks off and feel the soft carpet between my toes; I've never felt something so soft on my feet. It feels better than digging my feet into the warm wet sand at the beach. I curl my toes into the plush fibers. I lie on the floor on my stomach and smell it, run my hands through it, and quickly fall fast asleep.

That night I sleep a deep, dreamless sleep, or if I did dream I don't remember it. The alarm on my small clock next to the bed goes off promptly at 5:00 a.m. I roll over, half awake, and turn it off. Only when I sit up do I realize that I wasn't where I had fallen asleep. "What the hell?" I whisper to myself.

I could have sworn I fell asleep on the carpet. How did I get in the bed? Maybe I did that thing where I moved and don't remember because I was so tired. Or maybe I just dreamed that I fell asleep on the floor. I shake my head to try to clear my confusion and grogginess. Now slightly more alert, I realize that I really, really have to pee. I get up to go to the bathroom, and something different on my dresser catches my attention.

What the hell is that? There is a piece of paper on my dresser that wasn't there when I fell asleep. I fumble with it a bit as I try to open it, my fingers still acting like they are asleep. Getting it open, I see what it is. I can't believe this is happening again. "What is with this guy?" I say out loud as I read the note.

Layla,

I thought I'd check up on you when I got home. I put you in bed. Why in the world would you sleep on the floor? Did I mention how sweet you look when you're sleeping?

Adonis

I fold the note back up, return it to the dresser, and leave for the bathroom. As I walk in, I realize that I haven't actually looked inside there yet. It's not very big, merely adequate. It has two standing showers, a toilet, and a sink with a mirrored cupboard above it. While relieving myself, I decide that I should shower while I have the chance. I look in the cupboard under the sink and find some towels and soap and then jump in the shower. I know I have to be brief, because I don't know if Lucinda will need the bathroom anytime soon or not. I wash up quickly, wrap a towel around my hair and my body, brush my teeth, and go back to my room to get ready for my first day.

The work clothes in the closet are so depressing. It's all gray dresses that hang down to the middle of my shins with mid-length sleeves. It's a bit too snug around my chest, but it is high collared, so everything should stay covered up. I check the clock to make sure I won't be late, and at 5:25 I leave for the utility room. When I open the door, Lucinda is already there waiting for me.

The room is dimly lit with a concrete floor, loud, hot, and smells like soap. Against the back wall are what I assume to be the washing machines, two large silver boxes with windows in the front. In the far left corner is a large water heater, which probably accounts for why it's so damn hot in here, and a cleaning supply closet. There are laundry baskets stacked on the floor by the machines, some full, some empty, and a large table in the middle of the room with an ironing board next to it.

"You ready, kid?" Lucinda asks.

"I think so," I reply nervously.

"Okay, the first thing you need to do when you get dirty clothes and linens is to sort them by color and wash settings. The instructions for how to wash things are on the tags in the clothes. There are also reminders on the washer that tell you how to do it.

"For example"—she picks up a random shirt—"this shirt is not really dark, so I'd classify this as 'colors.' Regular colors can go on normal cycle with warm or cold water, depending on how dirty they are," she explains. "Each load of laundry gets one cap full of detergent, which is on top of the machine. Once they finish, they go into the dryer unless it is a 'delicate'—those have to be air-dried—then you put it on a hanger on the rack by the door."

Lucinda goes on and on about the ins and outs of separating washes, pretreating stains, which clothes should be starched and ironed, and which just need folding. I think my head is going to explode. *How in the hell can washing clothes be so complicated?* At home, all we did was use soap, water, and a scrub board, and then we hung them out to dry. Then she goes on to tell me how to tell which clothes belonged to whom for when I would have to deliver the clean clothes to their owners. There are four people in the Caraway family: the senator, Margaret (Mrs. Caraway), Adonis, and Brenda. Brenda, I'm told, is the youngest child, just seventeen years old, and still attends the school here in the city with all the other Normie kids.

Lucinda supervises me putting in my first load of laundry to make sure I understand what I'm doing. Once that is in, she leaves to attend to her duties in the south wing. I'm left alone in a hot room with the sounds of a machine sloshing around and the job of folding the clean clothes that didn't get folded the day before. At least this is something I know how to do for sure. I fold pants, skirts, dresses, shirts, and roll socks without trouble. The only trouble I have is in my head when it comes to touching strange people's underwear. I know it's clean, but that's not the point. Just knowing where it's been—on their naked asses!—weirds me out. I have to hum and sing to distract myself so I can do the job. The worst is when I know it is Adonis's that I am touching. He has these undershorts with various colors and patterns. My face flushes every time I have to fold another pair.

I wish I could just get him out of my head, but it's impossible. *I'm living in his house, and I am folding his damn underwear.* Not only that, but he is constantly being a weirdo and leaving notes for me when I'm asleep, watching me sleep and moving me around. I just don't know what to do with these awkward emotions. Part of me wants to kill him, and another wants to be with him. It doesn't make any sense. He just confuses the hell out of me. *It would be much easier if he weren't so damn good-looking and pleasant smelling.* Usually I would have no problem hating someone if I decided to, but I can't with him. I want to hate him, especially for what he did, trapping me into working and living here, but I just can't.

I put the first load in the dryer, start a new one, and go through four baskets of folding before Lucinda comes back and tells me to come to the kitchen to eat breakfast. The kitchen is gigantic, with multiple ovens, a walk-in freezer, a large island in the center, and a small table in one corner for us. The small table is where we, "the help," eat. Lucinda first introduces me to Phillip, the chef. He is a cheerful, slightly rotund man who appears to be in his late thirties.

"Good morning! You must be our new cohort. Layla, right?" beams Phillip.

"Good morning," I return cheerfully. "You are correct."

"Well, have a seat, dear, and eat up."

On the plates set on the table are blueberry pancakes with syrup and a pitcher of milk. *Heck, if this is what the servants get, I wonder what the Caraways eat! Probably stuff even better than what I had yesterday with all that bacon.* Lucinda joins me a few minutes later and eats her breakfast swiftly before leaving to go back to the south wing. I mop up the syrup on my plate with my fingers and lick them clean before bringing my plate to the sink and starting on the dishes. While doing the dishes, I start shaking—the first sign of withdrawal. It's only a slight trembling of my hands, but I come pretty close to dropping a plate.

"Are you okay there?" Phillip asks, noticing my quick save of the falling plate.

"Yeah, I'm fine. Just a bit nervous I guess," I lie.

"You'll be alright. Just don't go walking around the other parts of the house in those boots."

"Why not?"

"Well, for starters, they're dirty, and secondly, they will make too much noise on the tiles. I would suggest just wearing socks when you're not in the utility room or kitchen areas until you can afford to buy some tennis shoes," he instructs.

I look down at my boots. They aren't dirty, per say, just seasoned, worn in. The idea of having tennis shoes is somewhat appealing, but I think I like my boots a little more. I'm used to them to the point that they are almost a part of me. I finish the dishes and excuse myself from the kitchen. Instead of returning immediately to the utility room, I go to my room and close the door, bracing myself against the wall.

I can't hold off anymore; I know the shaking is just going to get worse and be obvious to anyone who sees me. I pull my haze out of my dresser and give in to my body's needs. At this rate, I'll be out in a week or less. I feel completely powerless against my own body. I wish I could will myself not to need it anymore, but I can't. I've been using it for so many years that it's like my blood; I need it running through my veins in order to live. After I take care of myself, I go to the bathroom and splash my face in the sink to try to bring myself back into the real world.

I return to my work in the utility room and continue putting in new loads of laundry when other ones finish, folding and ironing in between. I finish around nine thirty, according to the old clock on the wall. I take another bathroom break and then resign myself to the fact that I now have to go upstairs and drop all of this off. I'll have to make several trips up and down those intimidating stairs, and I'm already sweaty from being in that hot utility room all morning.

I decide on the method of bringing all of the baskets up to the top of the stairs first and then dropping them off one by one from there instead of bringing one up, dropping it off, and then coming back down and over and over again. *If I'm going to do this for the rest of my life, I may as well make it as easy as I can.* I take off my boots in the utility room, put one basket on top of another, and start walking down the hall. I just hope no one comes down the hall in the opposite direction, because I can't see a thing in front of me. I navigate the hall by counting the doors, luckily never running into anyone, and bring the baskets up the stairs to the left. All the Caraway's bedrooms are upstairs and to the left fork of the staircase except Adonis's.

Apparently, he decided to move rooms when he got back from college a few months ago because of his unpredictable work schedule at the hospital. He sleeps weird hours and doesn't want to get woken up by everyone else going about their day. The rooms off from the right fork are only guest rooms, with the exception of his. *I'll deal with his crap last, as everything else goes to the other side of the house.* My first trip contains the laundry of the senator and his wife. I knock first to make sure no one is in and then enter cautiously.

That bedroom is bigger than my whole damn house. It has large glass double doors leading out to a balcony with a decent view of Dixie Beach. I would be lying if I said that I don't feel especially bitter at this moment. *Who needs this much space? It's just obnoxious!* I feel the powerful urge to snoop around, see if they have a safe full of money and jewels in there or something, but I stifle my urge, knowing that if I get caught doing something like that it will not be a good outcome for me. I don't know what would happen, but I don't want to find out, either.

I make their stupid oversized bed and stack their folded laundry in neat piles on top of it, then take my empty baskets and return to pick up the rest. I have three baskets left, but I really don't want to make a third trip, so I take a risk and pile up all three and carefully navigate the hall. When I get to the entry area—or "foyer," as they like it to be called—I put it all down to catch my breath. *One basket to the left for Brenda and two to the right for Adonis.* I let out an audible sigh and take care of Brenda's less than modest clothes, which are so skimpy and lacking in fabric that they all can fit in one basket. Now I'm faced with the one room I do yet don't want to go in.

My palms are sweating as I stop in front of his bedroom door. Unlike the other rooms, whose occupants were up and about their day, Adonis is supposed to be in there, sleeping. *Should I knock?* If he is sleeping, then I would wake him. It would be rude just to walk in, though. I go back and forth in my mind trying to figure out how I'm going to do this. I finally decide to go in very quietly and just put the clothes on top of his dresser or whatever has room since he is in his bed and I can't put it there. *What if he sleeps naked?* The embarrassing thought suddenly comes to mind, and I get even more anxious. From what I can tell he has a nice body and all, but I don't want to see it. That's a lie; I do, I just *can't* see him naked. I don't want to like him, and I know if I see him naked, or close to it, that it's going to be impossible not to. I take a couple of deep breaths to try to calm my nerves, which doesn't help much. My heart is beating so loud that I'm sure he'll hear it and wake up. I open the door as quietly as possible and go in.

Compared to the rest of this house, Adonis's room is modest. It also has a balcony, but the curtains are closed, so I can't tell how big it is or what kind of view it has. All the furniture is a matching set made of a dark wood. At the back of the room is an opening into a bathroom and to the right is another door, which I'm guessing leads to his closet. Situated against the right-hand wall is a bed that sticks out into the center of the room. Lying there asleep, curled up on his side, is Adonis. I feel weak in the knees at the sight of him. His bare torso is sticking out over the covers. I put down the baskets quietly before I drop them and just watch him.

He has done that to me twice, so I think I'm entitled to watch him sleeping too. His mouth is open a little bit, and his chestnut hair is sticking up here and there. I watch silently as his chest moves with his breathing. Like I suspected, he looks pretty good under those clothes. His chest and abdominal muscles are sharply defined, as are his arms. He is paler without clothes, though. His arms are much more tanned than the rest of him. *He is more bearable to be around when he is asleep. When he's awake he does and says stupid things that mess up my life, but like this, he's perfect.*

CHAPTER NINE

I WATCH HIM FOR A short while and then quietly take care of what I came here for. The only space that seems big enough for me to put his clothes is his desk. I start piling laundry on the desk when I take notice of a book left on the desk chair. It's an anatomy book. *Probably one of his books from school, or to help with being a new doctor.* I open it and start flipping through the pages, pausing here and there to examine illustrations of body parts. I wish I'd had the chance to have gone to school. I can read, but this stuff has really complicated words that I can't pronounce for the life of me. I'm looking at a picture of the structure of the human brain when I'm startled out of my wits.

"I could get used to this," Adonis murmurs suddenly.

I jump and drop the book. It hits the floor with a loud thud, and he starts laughing. "I … I was just bringing your laundry, and I got curious. Sorry," I stammer. I turn around to face him and see him sitting on the edge of his bed stretching, only wearing underwear. I look away quickly, and my face feels like it's on fire. If you could die from embarrassment, I would be dead right now.

"Don't like the view?" he asks.

SARA GROVER

"What?" I asked, confused. "Your curtains are closed; I can't see anything."

"Not that view. Me," he says, laughing.

My face is flushing even more now. I just want to run, but my feet won't move. I don't respond to his question. I don't know how.

"Did you get my note?"

"Yeah, I got your creepy note."

"Creepy?" he asks with disbelief.

"Yeah. Who the hell watches people sleep?" I say rhetorically.

"You, obviously, by how embarrassed you look," he teases.

"It's payback—that's all. You did it to me, so that means I can do it to you. See how you like it."

"Well, I for one, like it," he ripostes.

"Well, I don't. It's weird. Stop doing it."

"It's my house. I'll do as I please," he declaims pompously.

"I just came to drop off your clothes. Now that you're up, I'll just make the bed and get out of here."

"Not yet. I've got something for you," he says with a sly smile.

"Whatever it is, I don't want it."

"I'm pretty sure you do. Your stash is running low. You don't want to go through all those withdrawal symptoms, do you?"

"How do you know how much I have?" I ask.

"I may have looked."

"You went through my things!" I say, trying to keep my voice down but also sound severe.

"Like I said, it's my house. I'll do as I please."

"You'd have to go through my underwear to get to that, you creep!"

"Like you didn't have your hands all over mine this morning," he says cheekily.

"Doing laundry is different! Not like I wanted to touch your nasty underwear," I mutter crossly.

He has such a big smile on his face that it is making me angrier at

92

him. *He is enjoying all of this. Enjoying embarrassing me and push-ing my buttons.* The more vulnerable he makes me feel, the more I want the floor to develop a gaping hole and swallow me up.

"All joking aside, you're going to want it. It'll help you wean off the haze without getting sick," Adonis says, no longer laughing at me.

"Why didn't you just leave it in my room, then?" I ask, my arms defensively crossed.

"Because you have to do something for me first." That playful tone is back in his voice. He pulls a plastic bag out of his bedside table and holds it up so I can see. "These are kava leaves. You chew them when you start to crave it and eventually you won't need it or the haze anymore."

"Can't you just get me more haze instead?" I ask. "I don't want to chew some nasty-looking leaves."

"In case you don't remember, haze is technically illegal, and there's no way would I go and buy drugs for you."

"Fine, then, give me the stupid leaves."

"Not yet. You gotta give me something first," he teases.

"I don't have anything but your stupid laundry to give you."

"If you want it, you've got to give me a kiss." He puckers his lips into a comical kissy face.

"What? No way!" I object.

"Yes, way. Unless you'd rather deal with all the shaking, sweat-ing, and throwing your guts up."

"Fine by me."

"Why are you so difficult? I know you like me." That last part sounded boastful.

"No, you're just crazy."

"Crazy for you. Come on, just one little kiss," he says, making a stupid puckering face again, this time smacking his lips and making an exaggerated kissing sound.

I make an irritated sigh, "Fine." I walk over to him from the desk. He is at least a head taller than me. I look up, close my eyes, and plant a quick peck on his cheek and back away. "There."

"Oh no, no, no," he says, wagging his finger at me like I'm some misbehaving child. "On the lips or no deal."

"You're infuriating!" I snap at him.

"So are you. I mean, really, this isn't that hard," he retorts. I go in quickly, standing on my toes, and give him a peck on the lips, then jump back before anything else can happen.

"You call that a kiss?" he teases. "I thought you did this kind of thing for a living. I don't see how you made any money like that."

I just want to slap him around and scream. *I know what he's trying to do. Tease and poke at me until I prove him wrong. Going and bringing up my past to get me all worked up.*

"You want to see a kiss, huh?"

I walk back up to him and push him hard so that he falls onto his bed. I climb on top of him and lay an intense kiss on him. I mean *really* kissing him for a good thirty seconds or so before needing to breathe. When I open my eyes, I see him staring back into mine and breathing heavily. He's a pretty damn good kisser, and his gorgeous eyes … it's like he's staring into my soul. *Oh, fuck it!* I throw caution to the wind and go in for another kiss.

His strong arms wrap around me and he rolls us over, pinning me under him. He initiates a luscious kiss, and my hands can't help but caress his bare back and arms. He smells amazing, but not like cologne or anything; it's just his natural scent. He moves his lips down to my neck, and I let out a soft sigh as I run my fingers through the hair on the back of his head. I have had sex more times than I can count, but I've never felt this much intensity with a man. And we aren't even having sex, just kissing and touching!

"I knew you liked me," he whispers in my ear.

"Oh, shut up," I say, pulling him back to my lips.

His hands wander, exploring my body, and mine explore his. He starts to run his hand up my dress along my leg. As he reaches my panties, he runs his fingers along where they meet my thighs, and I have to push away. It's not him that makes me need to stop; it's my fucked-up past.

"What? What did I do?" Adonis asks, clearly shocked by my sudden retreating.

"We can't do this, Adonis! You know we can't. I could go to prison! You would ruin your career. We just can't," I explain as an excuse, albeit a good one.

"No one will know. It will be our little secret."

"There's more to it than that, okay? Even if we didn't get caught, I just can't," I insist.

"Why not? Was it something I did?" he asks, sounding hurt.

"No, it's me, okay? I know that sounds like crap, but it's the truth."

"What about you could be so horrible?"

"I've been lying to myself since I've met you. Yes, I like you. I don't want to, but I do. That is why I can't have sex with you."

"So, you can't have sex with me ... because you like me? How is that supposed to make any sense?" he asks incredulously.

"Every time I have ever had sex, it meant nothing. I was just some object to be bought. I felt nothing; I never felt love or anything like that. I'm afraid that if we had sex that I wouldn't feel anything for you," I reveal.

"Layla, I don't just want to have sex with you. I want to make love to you. I love you," he professes.

"You don't even know me!" I almost shout.

"Because you won't let me! Let me know you."

"How can I let you know me when I don't know myself?" I say solemnly. "Listen, I need to get back downstairs before lunch, or someone might get suspicious. I'll see you around." I kiss him on the cheek. "Thanks for the leaves," I whisper, and then I walk out of the room.

I close the door to Adonis's room behind me and let out a large sigh. *I have to compose myself before anyone else sees me.* I run my fingers through my hair to straighten it out and take a series of deep breaths to calm myself. I just can't wipe the smile off my face, though. After a moment or two, I proceed back to the downstairs north wing to find something to do to distract myself until lunch.

I return to the utility room, confident there's something there that needs doing. I finished with the laundry earlier, so I grab a duster and go around dusting anything I can see with any speck on it to help pass the time and look busy. The whole time, I can't stop thinking about what just happened with Adonis. I still can't stop smiling. If someone were watching, they would probably think that I'm crazy and love to dust things. The truth is that I think I'm falling in love for the first time. I've never really had a boyfriend or anything like that. I thought I did one time, but I was just being used, like always.

When I was thirteen years old and worked in the fish cannery, I had my first intimate encounter. I worked an early shift, gutting and cutting up the fish that came off the ships before dawn. We had just gotten a new shift manager, Gavin, fresh out of business school. Like managers before him, he walked up and down the line periodically to make sure we were productive and on task. I, as well as the other workers, would always get nervous when he did this, afraid of being yelled at for something.

He was a tall and intimidating man. When he would walk by me, I would tense up. He walked by my work area much more than the previous shift managers did, which made me even more paranoid. I felt he was constantly watching me, waiting for me to screw up and so he'd have an excuse to fire me. It was ten minutes before the end of my shift one day about a month after he started there when he called me into his office over the intercom. Everyone looked at me like I was a dead girl walking. I was filled with anxiety. I went over my work day in my mind time and time again, trying to figure out what it was that I must have done to cause this. *Never has anyone been called into the manager's office and not been fired,* I thought to myself. What was I going to tell my parents? I was so scared that I thought I would throw up and faint for sure.

I left the factory floor, washed my hands, and approached his office door. My hand was shaking as I reached for the doorknob. I drew my hand back before touching it, afraid of what was waiting for me behind that door; I just knew I was going to be yelled at and fired. I went for the knob again and it rattled loudly in my shaking hand.

"Come in, Layla," Gavin said from behind the door.

I swallowed hard and hesitantly opened the door to that unforgiving place. There sat Gavin, behind his desk with a serious look on his face. At least he was sitting. If he were standing, I probably would have fainted. He must have been at least six feet tall or more.

"Take a seat," he commanded.

I nodded slowly and sat in the chair in front of his desk, facing his imposing presence. I was thirteen but felt like a toddler in comparison to him. I was like a scared little girl afraid of an imminent whipping.

"Do you know why I called you in here?" Gavin asked.

I shook my head as I stared down at my hands in my lap, too nervous to look at him.

"I've been watching you for a while, Layla, and I have to say, I'm very impressed with you," he said in a softer voice than usual.

I raised my head slightly to look at him, confused by this compliment. He had a slight smile, and his dark-brown eyes were looking straight at mine. "Impressed, sir? May I ask impressed with what?" I asked meekly.

"With you."

I looked back down at my hands. His gaze was too intense for me to handle for long. My palms were sweating, and I had them clasped together so hard they were starting to go numb. "I don't understand, sir."

"I'm impressed by you. You are quite a lovely girl, you know."

I just sat there in silence. I had no idea how to respond. He was a good-looking man, but he was at least ten years older than I was.

I heard Gavin get up from his chair. My stomach tightened with anxiety, and then I felt his hands on my shoulders. I shrank down in my chair, scared out of my mind and confused by what was going on.

"How would you like it if I moved you off of cleaning fish and onto the canning line?" Gavin asked, still holding my shoulders in his massive hands.

"I ... I guess that would be okay," I stammered in response.

"A lovely girl like you shouldn't be having to get covered in blood and entrails all day long," he said matter-of-factly.

I didn't have a response for that either. I just felt awkward and scared; I'd never been in such a strange predicament in my life. I almost would have rather been fired. At least then I would know how to feel.

Gavin then started to massage my shoulders slowly. His hands were so strong that it hurt a bit. "Why are you so tense, Layla?"

"I don't know what I'm supposed to do right now," I managed to get out.

"Have you ever kissed a boy, Layla?" he asked softly.

I shook my head. I had never been kissed by anyone but my parents, in the loving family way. I didn't have much interest in boys at the time. I spent my free time at the beach or reading books I found at the dump. He wasn't a boy, either; he was a man. *Will he fire me if I refuse him?* I wondered.

"A pretty thing like you? Really?" He sounded genuinely surprised. "I can fix that for you," he whispered in my ear. His massive hands stopped massaging my shoulders and started to slide down to my chest. I started shaking uncontrollably as he began fondling my breasts. I didn't know how to feel, overwhelmed by an intense mix of emotions and confusion that made me feel like I would just explode to smithereens. "Don't be nervous."

Gavin let go of me, got his chair from behind his desk, and placed it beside mine. He then took the liberty of turning my chair toward him, with me still in, so that I had to face him. I stared at the floor, not knowing what I should do. "Look at me," he said.

I kept looking at the floor, unable to move. He waited a moment for me to respond and then put his hand under my chin to force my head up to look at him. He pulled his chair closer to me so that my tensed-up legs were situated between his. I was sweating profusely and shaking like a leaf; I couldn't have stopped it if I wanted to. He put his hands on my thighs, leaned toward me, and pressed his face into mine. I kept my lips sealed tight. He pulled back and sighed. "If you want that job on the canning line, you're going to have to loosen up. Don't be afraid of me. I'm not going to hurt you. Just relax," he instructed calmly.

In truth, the idea of working on the canning line was a relief. It wasn't nearly as disgusting as the work I already did every day; I constantly had the smell of fish on my hands no matter how much I washed them. The blood and guts just stick under your nails and in every pore of your skin. Canning was a lot easier, mainly just operating the machines, and it paid a little bit more. I took a deep breath and let out a long exhale, trying to relax a bit. If this was what it took to move up in the world, I figured I might as well learn to do it. *It could be a lot worse. He could be really ugly and old,* I thought.

"Good girl. Let's try this again." He leaned into me again and his big soft lips touched mine. I tried to relax a bit, and when I did, he started sticking his tongue in my mouth. I started gagging and he backed away. "You'll learn to like it," Gavin assured me.

Gavin came toward me again, this time moving his head down toward my neck. He kissed my neck softly with one hand behind my head, the other rubbing my thigh. I felt so strange, a mix of fear and pleasure overtaking me. It was the most foreign thing I had ever felt. He got up again and went to lock his office door. He then sat down on the rug near the door and patted the spot beside him. "Sit over here," he said softly.

I slowly got up and crossed the office to the rug. I stood there awkwardly for a moment and then sat down on my knees. He scooted closer and then leaned into me, kissing me again, gradually pushing me further and further back. I felt like I was going to fall. He put his hand behind my back and then lifted me a bit so I could pull my legs out from under me and avoid falling on my head. He had me lying on the floor of his office and straddled me, kissing and touching my body.

The sensations I felt from his touching made my body feel like it was filled with electricity, and I started to reciprocate his actions. I kissed him back, trying my best to mimic what he had done. I let my hands touch his body. He was strong, and his dark skin was slightly moist with perspiration. He sat up for a moment and removed his shirt. His chest was toned and completely hairless. He bent down over me again and I touched it. It was smooth and firm.

Gavin then ran his hands under my shirt and bra and fondled my breasts. I let out a quiet sigh, but he heard it. He got up and pulled my boots off, then my pants. Goosebumps spread all over my legs as he touched them. I was breathing heavily and so was he. I didn't know what was happening, but I was starting to like it. He got up and went to get something out of his desk. When he returned to the rug and took off his pants, he laid back on top of me. I felt his genitals against my leg through his underwear and started to get nervous again; I'd never seen a man's privates before. He continued kissing and caressing me, pressing his crotch against my leg.

He sat up, panting, and pulled off my underwear. I felt vulnerable and afraid in that moment. *What is he going to do me?*

"What are you doing?" I asked in a shrill panicked voice.

"Shhh." His hand ran up the inside of my leg and touched my privates. I tensed up and started hyperventilating. He sat up again and tore open a small foil square before he pulled his penis out of his underwear. I stared in fright at the thing. It looked so disgusting, covered in bulging veins and rigid. He rolled the contents of the foil square over it and laid back on top of me. I wanted to run, but I couldn't with him on top of me. He was too strong, and I couldn't run out of his office half naked. He ran his hand along my stomach and then downward.

"Shhh, don't be scared," he whispered. He grazed my privates with his hand and then wedged it between my legs. Prying my legs apart, he then angled his body between them. The next moment I felt an extreme pressure and pain shoot through my body. I let out a gasp of pain and he placed a hand over my mouth.

"Shhh, it's okay," he whispered. He reached over and grabbed my panties and shoved them in my mouth. "Don't scream. Just bite on that."

I wanted to spit it out, but then he started thrusting his body, causing me to clench down in pain. Soon the pain ebbed and I felt a strange sense of pleasure tingling through my body. I spat my underwear from my mouth. I was breathing heavily as he kept thrusting into my body. My toes started to curl, and my lower back started to arch. An intense rush flooded me and I gripped his back, digging in my nails. He tensed up and lowered himself against me, breathing heavily. When he withdrew from me, we kissed so long that I was out of air and gasping when he stopped. A wide smile was on his face when he looked down at me. "That was amazing, wasn't it?" he asked.

"Yeah," I said breathlessly. *That's what I'm supposed to think, right?*

"Go on and get dressed and head home. I'll see you tomorrow on the canning line," he said with a smile.

He got up and helped me to my feet. We put our clothes back on, and I walked up to him and squeezed his hand before leaving. As I walked home, I felt a slew of emotions, but the most prominent was love. I felt so close to Gavin after that encounter. He thought I was beautiful; our bodies had been joined together as one. I couldn't wait until work the next day when I got to see him again. I had never felt more alive before than in that moment.

Our sexual encounters became a daily thing at the end of my shift. I looked forward to it and craved him when I wasn't near him. We went on like that for almost a year when my dad got sick. As much as I was in love with Gavin, I had to be there for my father. I stayed home for weeks to help my mom take care of him and my siblings.

When my dad died, I broke down and ran away from my house. I couldn't handle my grief. I felt like a giant hole had been cut out of me, and an emptiness filled my chest. I ran crying to the cannery. I needed him. I needed him to make me feel whole again. I ran to his office and flung my arms around him. I squeezed him tight against me to feel his warmth, to not feel alone.

"What's the matter?" he asked, concerned by my sudden appearance.

"My dad," I sobbed.

"Is he getting worse?"

"No," I began, my chest heaving with my erratic breaths. "He's dead!" I began crying uncontrollably.

Gavin patted my back and shushed me, trying to calm me down. It didn't work, though; I was in so much emotional pain that I physically hurt. I let go of him suddenly and ran to the trash can and threw up. I felt like my insides were being twisted and squeezed. When I finished retching into the trash can, I wiped my mouth on my sleeve and went back over to Gavin, hugging him tightly.

"You're the only man that loves me that I have left," I said quietly.

I felt Gavin get tense, yet his arms grew lax around me. A sudden new pain hit me that felt like a boulder had dropped in my stomach.

"You love me, right?" I asked.

"Listen, Layla," he started in a voice that sounded full of pity.

He was supposed to say "yes." At his words, I let go of him and slowly backed away, staring at him with tears and hurt in my eyes. "Do you love me?" I demanded.

"Layla, please, let's talk about this," Gavin pleaded.

"Yes, or no?" I yelled at him, more tears welling up in my eyes. "Answer me!"

"You're a great girl, but no. I don't love you. It's just sex."

I walked up to him, reached up, and slapped him with all the strength my pain and anger could muster. "You bastard! You fucking bastard!" I screamed. "You used me, you sick son of a bitch! I hope you fucking die! I never want to see you again, ever! If I do, I'll kill you! I quit!"

I ran out of his office and away from the cannery. I just ran and ran, not caring where I ended up. I just wanted to die right then. I had nothing. My father was gone, Gavin had used me—I couldn't take the overwhelming pain. From that point on, I never opened my heart to anyone. I quit my job at the cannery and started having meaningless sex for a living. Sex was "just sex," right? Love had nothing to do with it. I would just use them like Gavin had used me. Sex meant nothing.

The memory of what Gavin did to me destroyed my ability to love. After him, I've never felt any emotion during sex other than disgust. The idea of having sex with Adonis makes me afraid—afraid that I will have that empty feeling inside when I'm with him just like I have with every other man I've had sex with. I don't want to feel that way about Adonis. Maybe at first I did because I was afraid of getting close to someone again, afraid of letting myself be vulnerable again. But now, I don't want to ruin what we have with sex.

Lucinda walks by me as I'm cleaning and beckons me to come to lunch. With her snapping me out of my thoughts, I realize just how hungry I am. I'm more than glad to stop the mindless chores that allowed my brain to wander into the dark reaches of my past. *Food should be a good distraction.* I stop my dusting and follow behind her to the kitchen.

Unfortunately, lunch isn't as good of a distraction as I'd hoped. My brain just keeps going a million miles a minute as I eat my lunch. It baffles me that only three days ago I was living with my family and working at Andy's. Now, I'm living as a servant in a senator's mansion and falling in love with his son. *Life is strange.* If someone had told me that this would be happening to me a few days ago, I would have never believed it. The strangest part of all is that some of this just feels *right* in some crazy way—with Adonis, at least. No matter how much I want to fight it, I just can't. He just feels right, even though the laws say he shouldn't.

After I finish my lunch, I do the dishes as I'm supposed to, this time without shaking. *If I do start shaking, I have those leaves Adonis gave me.* I start to wonder what kind of person I will be when I am finally free of the haze. Will I be a better person? Worse? The same? So much has changed already that I have a hard time believing any of it is real.

I continue my day's duties after lunch and a short break. The early afternoon consists of sweeping and mopping the entry area, and around four in the afternoon I meet Brenda—well, kind of. She comes through the front door as the floor I just mopped is still drying. She is pretty tall for a girl, I guess, and has long blonde hair, the same dead eyes as her mother, and is as skinny as a rail. Her clothes are trashier than some of the things the girls and I would wear at Andy's; her denim skirt is so short you can almost see her underwear, and her pink tube top exposes most of her midsection. She comes sauntering in the door with annoying high-heeled shoes just like her mother's and tracks dirt on the wet floor, leaving little muddy spots as she walks.

She doesn't even bother trying to be polite to me. She gives me a quick look and then proceeds up the stairs. After a few steps, she turns toward me and gives me a disgusted look. "Don't just stand there, you idiot. Clean it up."

I bite hard into my lower lip to keep myself from saying anything I'll end up regretting. I just nod and mop back over where she walked. After she goes upstairs out of sight, I give the middle finger to where she stood. *What an arrogant little bitch! I just want to punch her stupid face in.* A decent person would say, "Oh, I'm sorry about messing up the floor," or something like that. Not this girl. *Screwing things up for me on purpose and then ordering me around like a dog to clean it up. I don't understand how Adonis is related to these people. He is nothing like them—as he said.*

I take one of the leaves out of the bag Adonis gave me and put it in my mouth. If it is anything like haze, then it will help me calm down and be little less pissed off, I reason. It tastes horrible, but it has a very relaxing effect.

The rest of my first day is relatively uneventful. I dust, sweep, mop, wash windows and mirrors, and clean dishes. I have to clean up after Brenda once again, who walked out of the natatorium soaking wet in her tiny bathing suit, leaving a trail of water behind her all down the hall. By the time nine o'clock comes, I am more than ready to hit the hay.

Since I have the leaves now for when I run out of haze, I figure I might as well use some haze now, as it helps me to sleep better. I finish off the bottle I had used earlier in the day and feel a sense of calm and numbness wash over me. Unlike the night before when I fell asleep on the floor, I get under the covers of my bed properly this time. They're sort of slippery, but it feels good. It's a great bed compared to what I had at home, but at the same time it's lonely having a room all to myself now; I don't have the noises of my siblings breathing and snoring in the background.

All that can be heard now is silence, which soon induces my slumbering.

CHAPTER TEN

THE WIND WHIPS AT MY face, but it is a rare and refreshing sea breeze. As I stare out into the water, I can barely make out Old Houston. The sky is gray with overcast and slightly hazy. I dig my feet into the warm sand and squish it between my toes. As I watch the waves move in and out, an object catches my eye. It's glittering in the sand, just at the edge of the water line as the waves recede. I start walking toward the curious object, wanting to pick it up and see what it is, but as I go to retrieve it before the next wave tries to wash it away, I hear a low growl to my right.

Coming toward me from the direction of the desalination plant is a congregation of alligators. They are the biggest I have ever seen and are acting strangely. They usually don't bother you if you stay away from their nest and territory, and they rarely ever advance on a person without being provoked or feeling threatened. These gators, which look at least ten feet long, are slowly advancing on me, gnashing their jaws and making low growls. I walk backward as fast as I can toward the water to grab the object, not having a chance to look at it yet. I don't want to let them out of my sight for a moment in fear that they will suddenly be much closer the next time that I look.

Now directly facing them, I start moving backward again when

I hear another unwelcome warning. A chorus of rattling erupts close behind me. I turn my head quickly to look at the source, but I already know what it is. The sound is unmistakable—rattlesnakes. Not just a few but dozens, all slithering across the sand toward me, shaking their malicious instruments. I'm being chased into a trap like a rat with nowhere to run. If I run into the sea, I'll be at an even bigger disadvantage than I am right now. Gators can swim faster than I can and can death roll me in no time flat. I try to recede as far from the beasts as possible, clutching the unknown object to my chest. *This is it. I'm dead meat. There's no escaping this situation.* If I try to run through the snakes, I will be bitten for sure and will have to suffer a long and agonizing death. The gators will surely chew me to bits, but at least it would be faster.

As the circle of carnivorous and venomous predators tightens around me, I take the only chance I have to find out what it is I'm holding. I move my hands slightly from where they are pressed against my chest in fear and open my hands. It's a necklace. A dainty gold chain with a heart-shaped pendant—a locket, to be precise. As I prepare for my imminent demise, my heart also aches for who-ever lost this token of love to the sea. My fingers fumble as I try to open it. I want to know at least one more thing before I blink out of existence. My fingers keep slipping as I try to grip the edges of the opening, but I finally dig my thumbnail into the crack of the locket and pry it open.

A single picture stares back at me of a young man with dark hair and kind eyes. It's the last face I will ever see, and I know that I have seen it before, but I can't place it in my mind. The vicious reptiles draw nearer still as one snake makes a close strike near my foot. I clutch the locket in my hands and pull it to my lips, kissing it and my life goodbye.

I thrash violently and shoot up from the bed, screaming like a maniac. "Hey! Shh! You're okay, you're okay," I hear a voice coo. Someone is sitting at the foot of my bed. I go to scream in terror again, but my voice is muffled by a large hand. "Layla, stop! It's me, Adonis," he whispers loudly.

I cease my screaming and brace my arms on my bed, trying to calm my breathing. He grabs me, and as I feel his tight embrace I realize I'm safe. It was just a nightmare, but by far the worst I can remember. *I'm used to the falling dreams, but this one just felt so real.* I have a hard time trying to shake that feeling of entrapment and panic. He keeps shushing me and telling me that I'm okay over and over again, never relinquishing his hold on me.

"What time is it?" I whisper.

"A little after three."

"What are you doing here? You should be getting to bed." I realize I'm scolding him like I would one of my siblings if they were up and about in the middle of the night.

"I'm a creep who likes to watch you sleep, remember?"

"I'm sorry I called you that," I say, feeling ashamed. His weird tendency is admittedly comforting after a dream like that.

"Don't worry about it. I kind of deserved it," he replies with a slight laugh.

"I'm kind of glad you were watching me tonight."

"You were tossing and turning pretty badly. Must have been a nasty nightmare."

"Yeah, it was, but I'm fine now. You're here," I say softly. My head is still beside his as he holds me and rubs my back soothingly.

"I have today off, you know," Adonis says as he pulls back to look at me, releasing me from his comforting arms.

"Really?"

"Yup."

"Well, what in the world will you do with yourself all day? Follow me around the house?" I ask playfully.

"No, silly. I thought I might do some shopping later after I get some rest. That's part of the reason I came to see you," he says.

I reach over and turn on the lamp next to my bed to the first setting, lighting the room just enough for us to see each other but not brightly enough to draw attention. I look at his face intently. He has a little bit of beard stubble, which gives him a rugged look. His eyes are red with exhaustion yet vivid with emotion.

"You're going to take me shopping?" I ask incredulously.

"No, can't do that. But I can bring something back for you."

"Did you come to my room at three in the morning just to ask for a shopping request?" I deadpan.

"Not request—to get your measurements. I want to get you some new shoes that you can wear around the house. That way you don't have to walk around in your socks all the time when you're working."

"Tennis shoes?"

"Uh-huh."

He pulls a flexible white measuring tape out of the pocket of his green scrubs. He obviously hasn't changed since he got home. *It's sexy to see him as a doctor.* Those scrubs look like comfy, loose-fitting pajamas, but he pulls it off with style. He pulls the blankets off of my legs and I try to pull them back up, giggling like a little girl during the struggle.

"Give me your feet," he laughs.

"You have to promise first that you won't tickle me."

"Okay, I'll try not to, but accidents happen," he replies in a sing-song tone.

I give him a playful pretend-angry glare and pull my legs out from under my blankets. He swiftly grabs my right foot up into his hands, knocking me off balance, and I fall onto my back on the bed, giggling like a little kid. He holds my foot in his warm hands and looks at it, then puts his measuring tape at the back of my heel and stretches it to the top of my big toe.

"Keep your foot straight. Stop curling it," he says seriously, as if he has to concentrate hard on such a silly thing. "Hmm, just as I thought," Adonis whispers. He lets my foot down, and I sit back up.

"What? What's what you thought?" I ask in sudden alarm.

"Your feet."

"What about them?"

"You have ..." he starts. He clasps my hands in his and stares me straight in the eyes. "You have donecpede," he says solemnly, as if I were one of his patients and he just diagnosed me with something fatal.

"What is that? Is it serious?" I'm starting to feel a bit of panic.

"Oh yes, very, very serious. Feet that are perfectly nine inches long is a dead giveaway. There is just no cure for your sexy feet!" He breaks character as a grin spreads across his face.

"You idiot." I playfully hit him in the arm. "You had me seriously scared that something was wrong with me," I try scolding him, but I can't stop laughing.

"Well, the lack of a pair of size six tennis shoes is a problem. I'll fix that this afternoon. As for the other problem, it must be treated right away."

He grabs my foot again and starts tickling me. I try to kick my feet away as I laugh, but I also kind of like it. I try attacking back, going for his rib cage, a common place to be ticklish, but my advance causes him to retreat from my feet. As we sit on the bed, our laughter slowly lulls to an awkward silence. To end the silence, I put my hands gently on his face and kiss him. He doesn't hesitate to kiss me back, and in no time we are all over each other.

That dream was too weird of a coincidence. The only face I saw in that dream was his, and in a locket, no less. He was here when I woke up. It's like it's meant to be, like fate—something I told him I don't believe in. I didn't then, but I do now. He just knew it before I did, that we were supposed to be together. *To hell with the laws. We'll find a way, somehow, some place.*

"Adonis?"

"Yeah?"

"You knew all along, didn't you?"

"Knew what?"

I hesitate a moment, fearing that once the words leave my mouth, it will be a mistake that I can't take back and I'll look like an idiot. "That we were supposed to be together. You asked me if I believed in fate, remember?" I almost whisper.

"I remember that. I knew. I knew it the moment I saw you." He smiles.

"Do you remember how I told you yesterday that I couldn't be with you in that way because I was afraid that it would mean nothing to me?"

"How could a man forget such rejection?" he answers, the disappointment obvious in his tone.

"I don't want to feel that way anymore." I pause for a moment, wondering if I'm going to end up scaring him away. "If I tell you something about me—something bad—I need to know that you won't just run away."

If he does, I may as well give up forever on love ever happening for me. If he can't see past my fucked-up past, then no one can.

"Layla, nothing you can say could make me run away," he assures me.

I take in a deep breath. "Okay. My first time that I had …" I pause for a moment. "Sex, I was very young."

"That's it?" Adonis ask, raising his eyebrows in disbelief.

"No. It was with my boss at the cannery. He told me how beautiful and amazing I was. I fell in love with him only to find out that he never loved me at all. He used me, and it broke me inside. When my dad died, I told him that he was the only man left that loved me, and then he told me that he didn't. He said it was just sex. I need to know, for sure, that you actually love me. That you're not just saying these things to get me to sleep with you and then abandon me when I need you."

I continue without any more pauses, telling him about what Gavin did to me. I finish my story and look him in the eyes expectantly. He's silent, staring at me with a blank expression. My heart sinks like an anchor to the bottom of the deepest chasm in the ocean. He reaches up and puts a hand on my shoulder; a sorrowful look adorns his face.

"Layla," he says softly. "I'm so sorry that happened to you. I can understand why you would be afraid to let me get close to you, but believe me when I say this: I will never, ever abandon you. I know it's crazy, but like you said before, we're supposed to be together, and I love you. I'm not just saying that to get you to have sex with me. I say it because I mean it. I don't know how or why, but I am crazy in love with you. Crazy enough to tackle you in the street, saving your life, and then pretty much forcing you into working here just so that I can be around you," he declares.

As he's speaking, my eyes start to water. If what he's saying is the truth, then I need nothing else in the world but him. I lean in and kiss him softly as a tear tumbles down my cheek. *He is it for me.* I can feel it in every fiber of my being. My reservations disappear, and the walls around my heart fall to ruins as I feel a lightness come over me. It almost feels like the sensation I have in my dreams when I fly with the birds.

"You're such a kind person, Adonis. I don't understand how these horrible people are your family. I'm just glad that you didn't end up like them, and that you're here with me," I say, hugging him again.

"You're not the only one with secrets, Layla."

"What are you talking about?"

I hope he doesn't have a past like mine. I love him, but I don't know if I can handle knowing he was hurt too.

"My family is not what it is portrayed to be in public. Stupid campaigns and publicity try to make us out to be some perfect little family, acting like she never existed," he says bitterly.

"She? Who?" I ask.

"My mother. My real mother."

"So, Margaret isn't your mom? I have to say I'm a bit relieved. She's so phony and cold."

"No, Maggie isn't my mother. She's just a heartless bitch," he snarls.

"What happened to your mom?" I ask gently, hoping to soothe him. I don't like the anger I see in his face; I want to make it go away.

"She died when I was very young. Hell, I can't even really remember her anymore."

"I'm sorry, Adonis." I lean in and hug him tightly.

"Don't be. You didn't cause her death. I'm fine. It was a long time ago," he insists, trying to keep his composure, though I can tell he is hurting.

"So, Brenda's your half-sister, huh?"

"Yeah," he answers. "Shortly after my mother died, my father was on the prowl for a new woman. He married Maggie shortly after sailing to victory on sympathy votes. My father was supposed to go do some campaign speech in Dallas but wasn't feeling up to it, so my mother went on his behalf. She was shot," he says in a flat, matter-of-fact tone. I grab his hand and squeeze it gently. He looks at our hands, gives a weak smile, and then continues.

"Her being there to speak was an unannounced change of plans. That shooter didn't come for her; he came for my father. Since he didn't show, she was the next best thing. She died because of his stupid campaign, and he didn't even have the decency to take the time to mourn her. He just moved on. He sailed to an easy victory for his seat in the House of Representatives on people's sympathy for his lost wife. Then he turns around and marries the Ice Queen four months after the election," he rants.

"Adonis, you don't need to tell me all of this if it's going to cause you so much pain," I propose.

"No. You should know. Hell, the whole world should know, but they just forget it ever happened!" He sniffs. "I was only three years old, and that bitch was no substitute for my mother. She just ignored me and had the nanny take care of me all the time. Then when she got pregnant with Brenda, it was like my mom had never even existed. All pictures of my mother were taken down and put in a closet. The pictures didn't fit into her 'perfect little family,' and it's not like my father cared. Whatever she wants, she gets. I'm not like any of them. If I'm like anyone, it's my real mother—Daphne. From what little I can remember, she was kind and smiled a lot. I get my brown hair from her. She's probably the only real person I've ever known before meeting you."

"I'm sorry you lost your mom," I say, attempting to comfort him.

"Don't be. It's fine—really. Now we just know each other better," he reasons. "Anyway," he begins, indicating he's changing the topic, "being that it's Saturday, the rest of them will be gone for most of the day. My father will probably be out golfing, and the witches of the house will likely be at the mall or spa all day. You should have less to do today. When you finish up your morning work, come up and see me, okay?"

I answer him with a slight nod of my head. I glance at my clock; it's already after four o'clock. *I might be able to manage an hour more of sleep before having to get up again if I go to bed now.*

Adonis gives me a light kiss and leaves to go to bed in his own room, and I waste no time in turning out my lamp and falling back asleep.

CHAPTER ELEVEN

5:30 IN THE MORNING COMES way too quickly. I slap my alarm clock to shut it up and get up to get ready for the day. Weekend laundry is a little bit different, I discover. All the linens come down the laundry chute on the weekends—load after a load of towels and bed sheets, but at least they're easy to fold. Breakfast today is waffles, which are pretty damn tasty. Then it's back to work again, dishes, mopping, vacuuming, and dusting.

This house is so huge that it usually feels empty even when they're all home, but with everyone gone after breakfast time, it really just feels like a huge void. Every little noise I make echoes and makes me feel so alone. I know that I'm not technically alone; I've got Lucinda and Phillip, and Adonis is upstairs sleeping, but I still feel such an emptiness around and inside me. The one silver lining to being so alone is I can maybe check some things out without anyone asking what I'm doing.

If the whole family were to be gone for days, I would take the risk of going for a swim. I haven't been swimming in forever, not since before my dad died. He used to take me swimming in the ocean; I wouldn't get in that water otherwise. He made me feel safe out there. He would say, "If a shark or gator comes near you, I'll punch them in the eye and they'll swim away crying to their mamas." I know now that if something like that actually happened, we would probably end up hurt or dead, but somehow he had a way of making me feel better about taking that risk.

I quietly prop open the door to the natatorium to take a quick peek. I never imagined that such a large room could be behind such a small unsuspecting door. A large pool, at least one hundred meters long, lies in the center of the room. The ceiling reaches all the way to the top of the house. *No wonder there aren't as many rooms upstairs as you would suspect. All that space is being taken up by the ceilings of rooms like this.* At one end is a tall ladder and two platforms for jumping off, and in the back corner is a bubbling hot tub. A strong chemical scent burns my nostrils a bit. The water is crystal clear and looks inviting. *Such a huge pool and yet not a person in it.* It's just such a waste that these people have all these wonderful things, and yet they hardly ever use them. If this pool were in the GI sector, it would be full in the winter.

The water is so tempting that I at least have to touch it. I quietly go inside and walk up to the edge of the water. As I stare at the water, a clear reflection of myself looks back at me, periodically interrupted by ripples. *There can't be any harm in just putting my feet in, right?* I sit down on the smooth pavement and remove my socks, setting them behind me, then scoot up to the edge of the pool and gently ease one of my feet down toward the water. As my big toe touches it, I flinch back reflexively. It's a bit cold, which is surprising. Any of the bodies of water I've encountered were at least lukewarm, being that it is so hot most of the year. Even the water coming out of the tap is warm. This pool, though, being inside a huge air-conditioned house, is cold and refreshing in comparison.

I go to ease my foot back toward the water, now knowing what to expect. I fight the urge to retract my foot back and plunge both feet in quickly. A small shriek escapes my mouth as my senses are shocked by the temperature difference. The huge room echoes my noise back at me with an eerie repetition. I hold my feet in until they adjust to the change and sit for a while, kicking my feet back and forth in the water. *If only I could be living in a house like this as a Normie and not a servant ... I would be in this pool every day.* It's unfair how just a few people have everything and anything they could want, and so many don't have enough to eat.

"What are you doing in here?!" I hear Lucinda blurt out from behind me. I jump up, startled, and turn around. "You better get out of here. What if one of them saw you? Do you want to get beat? Don't come back in here, ever," Lucinda warns me sternly.

"I was just looking around," I whine.

"You're not supposed to be looking around. If you're going to be stupid enough to do that, don't be stupid enough to leave the door cracked open. Now get to the kitchen and get your lunch before Phillip eats it for you."

I put my socks back on and leave without arguing any further. I don't understand what the big deal is. It's not like anyone else was using the pool. I hear Lucinda following me down the hall and when I get into the kitchen, she starts in on me again.

"If you finish your work, you can go to your room or take a walk in the garden or walk around the beach, but you don't *ever* use that pool, or any of the other recreational rooms, for that matter. Those are for the Caraways only. You understand?" she barks.

"Why didn't you tell me that with the rest of the rules?" I sass.

"I figured that would be obvious! We aren't allowed to eat where they eat, so why would we be allowed to have fun where they do?"

"It's not like anyone was using it. It was just my feet," I counter.

"The last servant that got caught enjoying that pool was beaten and fired. Do you want that to happen? I don't think so!"

"Okay, okay! Fine, I'm sorry! I won't do it again. You happy now?" I concede. I just want her to shut up and stop lecturing me like a damn child with their hand caught in the cookie jar.

"You'd better not. You're lucky it was me who found you."

"Okay, already. Are you done?" I ask impatiently. Without saying another word, Lucinda leaves the kitchen.

I eat my lunch of grilled cheese and tomato soup while fuming about what just happened. *Are they really stupid enough to think my feet in the pool is going to contaminate it or something? All these wonderful things around them that they hardly use, yet no one else can use them when they're not. It's so immature and selfish. Toddlers share better than these people, with the exception being Adonis. I'm sure that if he had found me, it wouldn't have been a big deal. I need to see him soon. It's half past noon already and I just barely sat down to eat.* I eat my lunch quickly, but slowly enough to enjoy the spices in the soup, take care of the stupid dishes, and then slip away to go upstairs.

I knock lightly on Adonis's bedroom door, but he doesn't open it or say anything. I look down the hall in both directions to make sure no one else is there, and I walk in. His bed is empty. *Where can he be? He told me to meet him here. Why would he tell me to meet him here and not be here? Maybe he went down to get something to eat and I missed him in the hall?*

On his bedside table I see a small rectangular box with a hinged lid on it. I don't recall seeing it there the other day. He's snooped through my stuff before, so I see no betrayal in snooping through his things.

I sit down on his bed and take the light box in my lap. I open the top and stare at the contents in awe: a pair of white and purple tennis shoes. He said he was going to buy them later, but he must have gone in the morning, wanting to surprise me. The shoes have a weird new smell to them that is not at all like the fresh leather smell of a new pair of boots. I take the shoes out and admire them. The fabric feels thin, light, and breathable, and the bottoms are covered with ridges in strange patterns. I reach down to try one of them on when there is a small thump from the bathroom, and I hear the door open. I drop the shoe, sit up straight, and turn my head to see Adonis standing in the doorway of his bathroom wearing only a towel.

How in the hell is he so quiet that I didn't know he was in there? He must have just taken a shower and shaved, based on the look of him. His chest is glistening with moisture, and there is a little wad of toilet paper stuck to his cheek. My face is flush with embarrassment. "I thought you were out!" I blurt out.

"I got back about an hour ago," he replies. "Do you like them?"

"Huh?" I'm not able to pay attention to what he's saying; I'm too distracted by him.

"The shoes?" he prompts.

"Oh, yeah," I say, finally getting my focus back. "I love them. How are you so quiet? I didn't hear a shower or anything."

"I've been out for a while. I was shaving," he shrugs.

"Well …" I cough and clear my throat. "Do you need me to step out? So you can get dressed?"

If I don't get out of here in the next few minutes, I'm going to lose all self-control. I don't know if he knows it or not, but that towel is trying to become a tent.

"Why? Are you afraid of seeing me naked?" he teases.

"No, it's just …" I clear my throat and make a drastic downward movement of my eyes to call his attention to his situation.

He looks down and gets a wide grin on his face. "What can I say? Got a mind of its own," he chuckles as he walks over to the bed and sits down next to me. My face is getting so flush that I'm starting to sweat.

After our encounter last night, I feel so much closer to him. I'm still scared to move forward, though. He tells me that he loves me, and his touch is soothing, but I don't know how to respond to it. I'm afraid to let the words "I love you, too" leave my lips. Afraid that once I say it, he will no longer feel it.

Adonis puts his hand on top of mine in my lap, leans in, and kisses my forehead softly. "I'm glad you like them," he whispers.

He smells so damn good right now, even more so than he usually does. His hair is messy and shining with moisture, his skin is still a bit damp, and then there is the bulge in his lap ...

I can't take it anymore. I want him and need him, now! I squeeze his hand and lean my face near his. "Thank you," I whisper in his ear.

He turns his body toward mine so that we are facing each other completely. He reaches his hand behind my head and runs his fingers through my hair. "You're welcome," he whispers back, kissing me first on the neck, then my lips. Goosebumps erupt all over my arms at the touch of his lips on mine.

If he wants me, I'm all his. Right here, right now, no reservations. If we were to die right now, I would die a happy girl.

"I love you," he gasps after releasing from my lips. When I don't respond, he pulls back and looks at me expectantly. "Layla?"

"I know" is all I can think to say.

"I said I love you," he repeats. "All you have to say is ... you know?"

"I don't know what to say," I reply.

"How about 'I love you too'?" he suggests.

"It's not that I don't, I just—I'm afraid to say those words out loud. I haven't since ... well, I told you last night the last time that I said them, and it blew up in my face."

His face grows solemn, and he holds my hands in his. "You're not the only person to get burned like that. You have no idea how conflicted I felt inside when I fell for you, hook, line, and sinker. I knew I loved you the instant I saw you, but I was scared, too," he confesses.

"You didn't seem scared to me."

"I got over it pretty quickly when I saw that car. I also cover up my fear with being weird, if you haven't already noticed," he laughs.

"So, you're not weird when you're not scared?" I inquire.

"Nah, I'm always weird. Just different degrees of it, I guess," he answers. "I was scared, though. The last woman I said 'I love you' to cheated on me with my roommate."

"That's horrible!" I exclaim.

"Yeah, tell me about it. I came home from class, and I saw her car parked out front. I thought she was there to surprise me or something, but no—she was in bed with my roommate. We all get burned, Layla. It's whether or not we choose to heal that decides our future." He seems too young to have such words of wisdom. A young sage, wise beyond his years.

"I can't believe anyone would cheat on you," I say with disbelief, shaking my head. "I would think that girls would be throwing themselves at you and clinging on for dear life. I mean, come on. You were in the bathroom all that time. Did you look in the mirror?" I tease.

"Oh, they do, but I don't want those girls. The ones I want always make me have to chase them," he laughs.

"So I should keep running?" I joke.

"Take a break for now. I'll chase you some more later."

"Well, I'll be your bandage, then, if you'll be mine," I offer.

"Deal," he whispers in my right ear. His warm moist breath tickles.

I can't hold back any longer—I grab his face and kiss him. Adonis suddenly gets up and goes for the door. *Is he walking out on me?!* I sit there in stunned silence as he locks the door instead of walking out of it. He gives me a sly smile as he struts back to me.

"Now, where were we?" he asks playfully. Before I can say anything, he sits back on the bed and starts kissing my neck. I reflexively let out a sigh in response. He takes that as a cue to kick it up a notch. He lays me down and lies beside me, alternating now between kisses and gentle bites. That little bit of pain mixed in just gets me going. I never told him what I like, but damn has he figured it out quickly.

As we kiss and touch his towel becomes undone, and my hands find their way to his supple yet toned backside as I give his butt a good squeeze. He lifts himself up a bit and gives me a goofy look. "Why am I completely naked and yet you are still wearing everything?" he complains.

"You weren't wearing anything to begin with, remember?" I tease.

"Well, let's fix that then, shall we?"

"This dress isn't easy to get off, you know."

"Here." He pulls me upright. "I'll help you with that," he insists. He grabs my dress from the bottom and tries to pull it up over my head, but it gets stuck.

"There's a zipper in the back!" I say, my voice muffled through the fabric.

"Oops!" he chortles. He pulls the skirt back down so my face is uncovered and I shoot him a pretend-angry glare as he reaches around my neck to undo the zipper. I put my arms up to make it easier, and he pulls my dress over my head.

I now sit here in my underwear with him naked on his bed. I feel a tightness in my stomach as he looks at me. I don't just feel exposed physically but internally as well.

"Wow," he gasps.

"What?" I ask nervously.

"Just ... wow. You are gorgeous."

"Wasn't I with my dress on?" I ask incredulously, being the teasing brat that I am.

"Of course. But the more of you I see, the more gorgeous you become."

He slowly lays me back down and lightly caresses my chest and abdomen. I shiver at his soft touch as he continues his exploration of my body with butterfly kisses, starting at my bra line and descending down toward my navel. When his lips reach my panty line, he stops and comes up to kiss my lips. "Are you doing alright?" he pants, letting go of my lips only to catch his breath.

"Yeah. I'm fine. Why?" I ask.

"Just want to make sure that you really want this. I don't want to pressure you."

"That's very sweet of you, but I'm more sure about this than I have been about anything in a long time. I want you, and—" I pause for a moment as the words feel stuck in my throat.

"And what?" he asks.

I swallow hard. "And ... I think I love you too," I finally manage to get out.

He kisses me deeply, and my hands go up his back and grip his shoulders. He slides his hands under me and unclasps my bra. I help by pulling it off my arms, and he tosses it on the floor. Grabbing my breasts, he kisses them softly. A moan escapes me, and I pull at the hair on the back of his head. I've never felt so much pleasure in my entire life as I do right now. I've never wanted anyone so much. As we press against each other, he grabs my hand and moves it downward.

He places the tips of my fingers on his arousal. I retract my fingers reflexively but then relax and grab hold. He is very impressive there as he is in every other way—handsome, kind, sexy, and well-endowed. I grab his hand and lead it like he led mine. I guide his hand to my panties and slip his fingers under the band. He slowly removes them, leaving us both fully exposed. We are both breathing heavily and starting to perspire.

"Are you sure?" he whispers.

"Yes, but do you have a condom?"

"No. Do you think I just keep those lying around? I haven't been with anyone in years," he says. "Is that a problem?"

"Aren't you afraid of getting me pregnant?" I implore.

"Not really. If it happens, it happens," he says, sounding care-free.

"They'll kill me!" I exclaim, sitting up and pushing him off.

"If that happens, then we'll run far, far away. I promise. We'll take the family sailboat and sail off into the sunset together."

"You have a boat?" I ask.

"A nice one. So don't worry," he whispers centimeters from my face.

He pushes his body back against mine and runs his hands up the inside of my thighs, kissing me hard as he gently pushes my legs apart. We fit together like a lock and key. I'm not a noisy person in bed, but a loud moan from deep in my throat escapes and I don't want to stop it. Adonis puts his fingers to my lips, reminding me that we have to be as quiet as possible if we don't want to get caught together. He lowers his face to mine to give my mouth something else to do. "Now, shh," he whispers upon leaving my lips.

We have to keep it a secret, though I wish I could shout it from the rooftops and make all the noise I want. I don't want to lose him; I can't. *This is what love and making love is versus just sex!* I feel complete and at peace with him. *We should just take that boat right now and leave this place and find somewhere where we can be together without having to hide it.*

Adonis tenses up and digs his fingers into my back. "Layla! Oh, fuck!" he moans. He's so tense that he trembles before relaxing, laying all his weight on me. He rolls off to lie beside me, both of us panting heavily.

CHAPTER TWELVE

I'VE NEVER FELT HIGHER IN my life than I do right now, and I haven't even had any haze today! As I lie next to him, I feel truly happy. I wish that our time together didn't have to end. Why must the best thing that has ever happened to me have to be forbidden? *He mentioned sailing away together—to where? Where could we go in this messed-up world that would allow us to be together?*

"Where would we go?" I ask.

"What?" Adonis pants.

"That boat you said you have. Where could we possibly go that would not persecute us for being together?"

"Australia," he answers.

"Australia? Don't they have the same laws there too?"

"No. They didn't agree with the GI laws. Being isolated from other countries, they just do their own thing. It's not like their people are going to swim across an ocean to 'contaminate' "—he uses air quotes—"the gene pool."

"So no other countries have tried to force it on them?"

"Oh, they have, but those Aussies have a lot of fight in them. It wasn't considered worth it after a few failed invasion attempts. They take care of themselves, and no one bothers with them."

"Do you really think they would let us live there?"

"I would hope so. If they don't give us asylum, then we can just find an uninhabited island somewhere to call home," he proposes.

"Adonis," I say softly.

"Yeah?"

"I don't want to have to live a lie. I don't want to have to hide that we're together. Can't we just leave? Like right now?" I plead.

"No. This sort of thing takes planning. Give me a few months to get supplies stocked up and plan out a route; you can't just go off into the ocean unprepared. If you do, you're sure to die, and then what would be the point? We can die here," he explains.

"Okay," I say dejectedly. "Well, I better get cleaned up and get out of here before your family gets home." I go to sit up, but he prevents me from doing so. He looks intensely into my eyes.

"Don't be sad. Just give me some time to work things out and we'll be together forever. I promise," he assures me. He gives me a soft kiss and then lets me get out of bed.

I've never been with a man like this before; I've never felt this much love. I've also never had unprotected sex before, and I'm starting to regret it right now. The world we live in is dangerous for me in this situation. "Just so you know, I don't want kids, so you better do some shopping if you want to do that again," I call from the bathroom.

I clean myself up and fix my hair before returning to the bedroom for my clothes. His bathroom is way too clean for a guy. His mirror is almost spotless as I gaze at my naked self. My bruises have almost completely faded away. *I like how I look right now. I don't want to have kids and swell up like a beached whale.* I return for my clothes and see Adonis getting himself dressed.

"Why don't you want any children?" he inquires.

"We live in a fucked-up world. Why would I make someone else have to live in it?" I reason as I put my underwear back on.

"We're going to go to Australia, remember?" he reminds me.

"Still. I don't want to get all fat or pass on my bad genetics to some poor baby. I'd probably be a shitty mother anyway."

"There's nothing wrong with your genetics. That unknown variant shit could be anything. It could even be an advantageous mutation. They just use these labels to keep the rich, rich and the poor, poor. You know that," he objects.

"Even if that's true, I'm not mother material. How would you feel if your mom used to have sex for money?" I argue.

"The past is in the past. Parents never tell their kids everything."

"Why is this such a big deal to you, anyway?" I inquire as I have him zip my dress.

"I'd like to have kids one day. I always have. I'd want to raise them with the love I never got as a kid after my mom died. I know it's stupid and selfish to want to try to create the childhood I didn't have, but I do," he admits.

I sit on the edge of the bed to put on the shoes he bought me. They fit me perfectly, and the cushioning inside feels luxurious on my feet. I've never tied shoelaces before because I've never had shoes that had laces, but it can't be that hard, I figure. I tie a simple knot in the laces, but they are too long and hang over the sides and onto the floor. I go to tuck the laces into the shoe and Adonis crouches down in front of me.

"Let me show you," he chuckles. He unties the knots I made and demonstrates how to properly tie shoes. "You've got to make a loop and then take the other lace and go around, then under, and pull," he instructs while doing it for me.

"Thanks. I'll try to remember that," I say while rolling my eyes.

"You're most welcome."

"Okay, I seriously need to go now. After what we did, I need a shower and a nap," I chuckle.

Adonis pulls me in for one last long, sensual kiss, which makes my knees start to buckle. I steady myself and gently push him away.

"Seriously!" I laugh. "I'll see you later."

"I love you," he adds as I unlock the door.

"I love you too," I reply as I finally walk out. As I turn around in the hall to close the door, I blow him a kiss and head back to my room.

As the water falls over my body, I can't get the images of what happened out of my mind. *I wish he were here with me.* I don't like having to hide our relationship. I shouldn't need to scrub his scent off of my body when I wish I could be bathed in it instead. I take my time in the shower, grateful it gives me a place to be relaxed and alone with my thoughts. *If only we could be in Australia right now. Maybe get married and get an apartment ... I wouldn't want to take his last name, though.* It pains me to think that Donovan Caraway is his father. Being "Mrs. Caraway" would remind me of the phony bitch that is Adonis's stepmother. *Maybe he can just change his instead.*

As I open the bathroom door to go back to my room, I am immediately taken out of my fantasies and thoughts of Adonis. Lucinda is waiting for me, and she looks pale.

"Layla. I'm going to need you to"—she pauses to cough—"take care of a few more things today. I think I'm coming down with something nasty, and I need you to attend to the senator and his guest," she manages to get out before coughing again. I feel bad that she is feeling ill, but I don't want her getting me sick too.

"Sure, no problem. What do you need me to do?" I say quickly, wanting to get her away from me as soon as possible.

"Senator Caraway is meeting with a friend in the drawing room. Bring them coffee in half an hour and inquire if they have any requests from the kitchen," she instructs before turning away from me and being stricken with a coughing fit.

"I got it covered. Go and get some rest," I insist. I quickly return to my bedroom and close the door.

The last thing I need right now is to get sick! I get dressed and brush out my hair. *If I do, I wonder if Adonis will be able to treat me without anyone finding out.* I twist my damp hair, wind it into a bun, and pin it back so that it looks tidy.

I'm terrified of having to encounter Senator Caraway. I thought he was a horrible person before I came here, but after Adonis told me what happened to his mother, I find the man even more despicable. Unfortunately, I know that I'm going to have to run into him at some point; I'm living in his house, after all.

I head to the kitchen to pick up a tray sitting on the kitchen island that holds a container of hot coffee, sugar cubes, milk, and two fancy cups with saucers and spoons. Phillip is in front of one of the ovens stirring something around in a pan, preparing dinner.

"What happened to Lucinda? She seemed fine just a few hours ago," I call over to Phillip.

"She sometimes has breathing problems. Some kind of allergies or something," he speculates. "It makes her cough a lot and causes her to get winded and dizzy easily. She'll probably be fine by the morning."

"I'm glad it's not contagious!" I say with relief. "I hate getting sick." I carefully lift the tray off the island and balance it carefully in my hands. "See you at dinner," I add as I leave the kitchen with the coffee.

I carefully navigate the hallway to the drawing room. The door is closed, and I can barely make out a male voice coming from inside. I carefully balance the tray with one hand and lightly knock on the door.

"Come in!" a voice beckons.

I take a deep breath and open the door to the drawing room. Two men occupy plush chairs. One is facing with their back toward me, but the one opposite him I know instantly: Senator Caraway, a tall, lanky man with sharp facial features and close-cut hair that is so blond it's almost white. His blue eyes look so cold that they remind me of an ice storm. He shoots me a quick glance.

"Bring it over here," he commands.

I walk around the outer rim of a circle of chairs and slip in between two to advance to the table in front of him. There's a half-empty decanter on the table next to two short glasses filled with brown liquor. The room wreaks of alcohol and cigar smoke.

"You're too kind, Donovan! You ordered me a hooker with my coffee!" exclaims a vaguely familiar voice.

I look over to the man in the chair opposite the senator, a man I never thought I'd have the horror of seeing again. It's the third man from my last night at Andy's—the one whose name I wasn't able to discern in all the conversations in the room.

A mix of horror and anger consume me. I wish I could kill the bastard, pick up a shard of glass and slit his throat, but I wouldn't stand a chance. I couldn't stop him last time, and even if I could now, where would I run? I'd be hunted down like an animal. I can feel the bile in my gut rising as I become physically ill. My body feels weak, and the room starts spinning. My hands fail to maintain their strength and the tray falls to the floor with a crash.

"Clean it up, you fool!" the senator roars.

I fall to my knees in terror, fumbling to clean up the broken glasses and scattered sugar. *This can't be happening! Not him! Why me?* I try with futility to function, but I'm shaking so badly that I cut my right palm badly as I reach for pieces of broken glass. *Why am I not waking up? This can't be real! Why isn't the pain waking me up?*

"What on Earth are you talking about, Anthony?! This buffoon is our new housekeeper. Though not for long, at this rate!" the senator contends.

"She's a hooker," Anthony proclaims. The word feels like a knife jammed into my heart. I can't breathe; it hurts too much to breathe.

"A whore. Sex for hire. Some colleagues and I had our way with that one no more than a week ago! A good old-fashioned gangbang," continues the rapist scumbag.

"That's preposterous! Adonis wouldn't bring such filth into this house," Caraway insists.

"She probably blew him, and he gave her the job. Hell, I'd offer her a job at the desal plant for a good one," Anthony laughs. "Quite a nice pair of tits on her, too. You could make some good money with her."

I want to run, disappear, die—anything but to be faced with this situation. *I'm done for. I'm going to be fired, or worse.* I'm hyperventilating as I search my brain for what to do. I want to scream, but I know if I say anything it will just make things worse.

Anthony, the rapist piece of shit, crouches down in front of me. "Come on! Don't you remember, sweetheart? The best night of your life? How's that neck doing?" he taunts as he reaches up to touch my throat. I recoil at his approach.

I feel the tears welling up in my eyes. Tears of anger and shame. I clench my fists, moist and sticky with fresh blood, wanting to punch the son of a bitch.

"You, get out of my sight!" the senator hollers, pointing his finger at me as if it were a knife.

I stumble a bit as I get up, shaking all over with fury and fear. I grab the now empty tray and run for the door. My face is stained with streaming tears as I run down the hall to my room. I lock my door and sit up against it to keep anyone from getting in. I hug my knees to my chest and sob uncontrollably. *What are they going to do to me? What will they do to Adonis? We have to leave tonight, supplies or not. I'd rather take my chances out on the ocean than here! Why couldn't he have let that car kill me?*

How could such a wonderful day turn into this? Of all the scum that the senator is friends with, why that man? Then again, I shouldn't be surprised at such horrible people being chummy with each other. My insides feel like they are being shredded. I'm so distraught that each sob physically hurts every inch of my body. *I can't do this.* I've been trying to conserve my haze, to wean myself off of it, but I can't do it anymore. I don't want to feel anything. I want to black out and escape this; dying would be an easy way out of this hell.

I crawl over to the dresser and pull out my supplies. Only two bottles are left—that's it. Such a small amount used to be able to last me more than a week, but my tolerance has built up over the years. This supply could usually give me four fixes, but I need more than a little high. I want to be numb. Gone.

I draw the first dose from one of the bottles and my arms are shaking so much that I can't find a damn vein. I keep missing my mark, making small bleeding holes. I pull off my new shoes and socks and go for an easy one on top of my left foot. I press the plunger as fast as my veins can take it, draw another dose, and then administer it to the top of my other foot.

To my relief, my world goes hazy, and a reflexive smile and giggle escape me. I flop onto my back onto the soft carpeted floor and stare at the ceiling thoughtlessly. It looks like clouds when it's all out of focus; I see white, with patterns in the texture making pictures. One looks like a fat man's face smoking a pipe with birds flying out of it, and another looks like a bunny. The pictures start to move around and change shapes, swirling around like clouds in the sky. I giggle like a fool as the bunny turns into a possum and then a flower. *What was I worried about again? I can't remember.*

The ground feels cold and wet and my body, weightless. I move my arms, holding them out straight, and move them up and down across the water while I make a scissor-like motion with my legs. I bob up and down with the waves. As I stare at the sky above me, the clouds are growing dark, and the wind is making the water choppy. Water splashes up over my face and into my mouth. I spit it out and gasp for air as the water becomes turbulent. A bright streak of jagged white light cuts through the sky. The thunder cracks with a deafening intensity.

The warmth and safeness I feel as I curl up on the couch with my dad, clutching my patchwork quilt, is unparalleled. I lay my head in his lap, and he strokes my hair while he sings to me.

Blue like the sea, 'tis the topaz we have,
Blue are the hills like waves on the land.
Covered with flowers that sway in the breeze,
Blue is the color of my love for thee.

Blue like the eyes of my newborn babe,
Vibrant like cornflower petals in May,
Only your love makes me feel this way.

Blue is the sky,
Stretched out up above.
Blue is the color,
The color of love.

I love it when he sings that song to me. It's my favorite lullaby, the same song that his mom sang to him, that his grandmother sang to his mom, and so on for generations. It's a soothing song. The words feel like a warm blanket wrapped around my heart. His voice and caring touch make me feel safe and at ease.

"Nighty-night, Daddy," I whisper as I close my eyes.

CHAPTER THIRTEEN

(Adonis's POV)

YELLING AND A LOUD BANG violently awaken me. "Get your ass dressed and meet me in the drawing room in one minute!" my dad screams, ripping the sheets off of me. "I have something that you need to see." I can hear the slur in his voice and smell the whiskey on his breath.

"You're fucking sloshed again, aren't you?" I accuse. He always does this kind of shit. Being away at school was hard, but at least I never had to deal with him waking me up in a drunken rage when I was at Dartmouth. "I have a shift tonight, you know," I complain.

"One minute. Move it, if you know what's good for you," he threatens with a menacing hiss.

It's probably just a bunch of bullshit caused by Brenda again. Bitch is always making shit up and running to him about it. I think she actually enjoys it, and he believes anything she tells him. *He's such a moron.* I've told him about the times I've caught the boys that she sneaks into the house at night, but he doesn't believe any of it because she swears to him it isn't true. *If I just humor his stupidity, then maybe I can go back to bed.* I grab the clothes closest to me, my workout shorts and a T-shirt, and hustle for the drawing room.

I can smell the booze and cigar smoke from the staircase as well as hear more than one voice talking loudly, echoing through the foyer. The door is wide open, so I rush in to see what all his yelling is about. I see that he came home from golfing with his buddy Anthony Easton, who owns the desal plant. They both have rocks glasses in their hands more than half full of whiskey.

"Get over here," my dad beckons.

I go to meet him in the center of the circle of chairs when I see what he is talking about. On the floor is a huge mess of spilled coffee, broken dishes, and blood. I'm extremely anxious now. *Who was punished for this? Why is there so much blood? Did he beat them? Was it Layla or Lucinda?* I feel like I just swallowed a boulder. Fear and dread press down on me with the weight of the world as I imagine the possibilities.

"What happened in here?" I ask, trying to keep my voice calm.

"You knew, didn't you?" my dad says in an accusatory tone.

"Knew what?" I jeer.

"Come on, boy, don't play dumb," Anthony interjects.

I glare at him, stand up tall, and get in his face. "Who the fuck are you calling dumb?"

He gives me a sarcastic smile, tips his glass toward me like he's giving a toast, downs the rest of his drink, and then walks away from me.

"You knew! How could you bring such filth into my house? You've always been such an idealist fool, but this takes the cake! You're just like your mother. Stupid and foolish," my father rants.

"Don't you dare speak of her like that!" I yell. "I don't know what in the fuck you are trying to get at. Stop beating around the bush and out with it!"

"Did she give you a hummer in return for a job?" he accuses.

I'm dumbstruck. *How in the hell did he find out? What did he do to her? Is she even alive right now?* My mind races with panicked thoughts about Layla. She was supposed to be safe from that here.

"Where did you get such a stupid idea from?" I return, trying to feign ignorance.

"Don't lie, boy," Anthony interrupts. "I hope she at least gave you a good time," he chuckles.

"What would you know? No one in their right mind would screw you," I retort.

"Let's just say I know her intimately," he boasts.

If one's blood could really boil from anger, mine would be evaporating at this point. *He couldn't have—could he?* My stomach turns at the thought that he could have been with her and that I just had. "You must be mistaken," I say through clenched teeth, trying to hold in my rage.

"I don't believe so. How could you forget a pair of knockers like those?" he laughs.

I want to punch his teeth down his throat! But I also want to find Layla. *What if she's badly hurt? I need to get to her.*

"Some friends and I gave her quite the pounding no more than a week ago," he crows, giving me a perverted wink.

Less than a week ago was when I met her. *The bruises on her neck, face, and wrists were from that son of a bitch! Why couldn't I have found her before that happened to her?* I'm seething with anger. My fists are clenched so tightly that I'm likely to cut my palms with my fingernails, and I am shaking.

"Admit it!" my dad hisses. He stands so close to me that our noses almost touch. "Say it!" he bellows, spitting in my face. I take a stoic expression, not wanting to let him know that he can scare me, and look him straight in his dead, emotionless eyes.

"Yeah, I knew," I acknowledge. "I took her in order to save her from people like you and your golfing buddies."

"You're a disgrace to your DNA, wasting your time and emotions on caring for such low-life garbage. You really are your mother's son," he jeers.

How dare he talk about her like this! She was a sweet and kind person who deserved way better than the likes of him. *She died because of him!* I will never forgive him for that. I want to hurt him so badly, but I can't waste any more time on these pieces of shit; I need to find Layla. She could be losing a lot of blood based on what I can see.

"What did you do to her?" I demand.

"I didn't do anything to her. Slut dropped my coffee and bled all over my floor. I should do something about her, though. Probably could use a good belt lashing for ruining my evening and trashing the carpet," he says nonchalantly. "Probably cut herself pretty good as she tried—unsuccessfully, I might add—to clean up her mess." He shrugs.

"Allow me to treat her. Unless you want her bleeding all over the rest of your precious house," I suggest, trying to appeal to his love of material things. He ponders my suggestion for a few moments too long. "Do you want to have to replace all the carpets downstairs?"

"That would be rather bothersome. Clean her up, but that's it. No funny business. I don't need my only son screwing around with some GI whore."

I leave the room without further comment and run down the north wing. *She's got to be down here somewhere. Her room, the bathroom, possibly the garden.* I stop so fast that I almost fly forward from the momentum of my running. Her doorknob and door are smeared with blood. I try the door, but it's locked.

I knock loudly on her door. "Layla? Layla, open up. It's me," I call through the door. I wait a moment, hoping to hear a reply or for it to open, but it's silent. I pound on the door this time. "Come on, open up," I holler. I press my ear to the door and I hear something. A quiet giggling catches my notice and alarms start going off in my head. *Is she in shock? What's happening in there?*

I make a dash for the kitchen. I throw open the utensil drawer, rummaging through it loudly and knocking things all over the floor as I search for a butter knife or something that I can shove into that door to get it open. If I learned one useful thing in college, it's how to break into a locked room using things like butter knives and credit cards. How else can you put a tarantula in someone's bed?

"What in the world is going on?" Phillip asks in surprise.

I find a long, wide utensil. "No time to talk!" I holler back to him as I run back into the hall.

I can now hear her laughter from the hall. She is getting louder and sounds like she's gone completely mad. I jam the utensil in the crack between the door and the frame and push it down as hard as I can. The door latch slips back just enough for me to push the door open.

Terror and shock consume me as I survey the sight before me. She is on her back on the floor, drenched in sweat and smeared with blood. The shoes I just bought her are thrown about, and I see an empty bottle of haze and a needle sticking out of the top of her foot. She is moving her arms along the carpet in sweeping motions and laughing like a lunatic. Where her hands are moving along the floor is a streak of blood coming from her palms.

I drop to the floor beside her, pull out the needle, and grab one of her hands. She tries to wrestle it away from me, but I'm much stronger than she is. Her eyes are open, but she won't look at me. It's like she can't see that I'm here. I pry her hand open; it's gushing blood. I take off my shirt, rip it into strips, and wrap up her right hand tightly. Once I let her hand go she goes back to moving it along the floor, and I bandage her other hand.

I wave my hand in front of her eyes, hoping to see her track it or respond in some way, but she doesn't. *All the sweating and blood loss probably has her dehydrated and hallucinating. That, plus those fucking drugs could kill her.* I wish I could take her to the hospital and give her the treatment that she needs and deserves right now. If only I just had an IV line and a bag of saline, I would feel much more confident in her ability to get through this.

Brenda randomly comes into Layla's room, most likely just to get some sick amusement out of other people suffering, but I don't care why she's here right now if she can be useful. "Go get me a glass of water, fast!" I instruct her. She leaves without question, and I turn my full focus back to Layla.

I grab each of her hands in mine and squeeze them, trying to apply as much pressure as I can to help stop the bleeding without hurting her. She struggles to move her arms but I hold firm. "Shh, Layla. Don't fight me. I've got you," I say.

Brenda returns with the water and places it on the dresser. "Is she going to die? Can I watch?" she asks with morbid delight. I instantly let go of Layla and advance quickly on Brenda, shoving her back toward the door. "Get the fuck out!" I scream in her face. She goes white as a sheet and runs out. I slam the door and lock it. I place the glass of water on the table by the bed and push the dresser in front of the door. *I don't need her or anyone else coming in here and acting like this is some spectacle for their entertainment! They're such sick bastards!*

With the room secured, I get back on the floor and prop her head up on my lap and put the glass to her lips. I tilt it back a little to try to get her to drink, but she gags and spits it out. "Come on, Layla! Don't you dare leave me!" I plead.

I can't believe she would do this to herself and to me. I can see the streaks of blood on her feet where she injected herself. *A whole bottle? Was she trying to kill herself? I understand why she would be distraught from what happened, but was this the only option she could think of? Do I mean nothing to her if she can just try to leave me so easily?* I'm so angry with her, but I know I can't do anything about that right now. I have to save her, and then love and support her. I can't be openly critical of her at a time like this; that would only make things worse.

The only thing I can do for her now is to make sure she keeps on breathing and doesn't vomit and aspirate. I gently lift her from the floor to the bed. I lay her on her side and put her head on my lap. If she gets sick, at least she won't choke on it. I start stroking her hair and she settles down; her struggling and laughter cease. I shush her between my own sobs while slightly rocking us back and forth, caressing her beautiful curly hair.

The thought of losing her is like a hot knife in my gut. My grief from her being in this state is physically painful to me. *I can't lose her; not like this.* I wish we could just leave right now. I'd rather us die at sea together than have her leave me alone. I know I just met her, but I somehow know that she is it for me. She is the one person I'm meant to be with. *She has to get through this—she just has to!*

I wonder if she can even hear me. She's likely hallucinating from dehydration and drugs, but if coma patients can hear people, then maybe she can hear me. One thing that always made me feel better when I was sick or if I was afraid of a storm was singing. My nanny used to sing me this country lullaby that always calmed me.

Blue like the sea, 'tis the topaz we have,
Blue are the hills, like waves on the land.
Covered with flowers that sway in the breeze,
Blue is the color of my love for thee.

I stop for a moment as she starts moving around. She curls up her legs and starts nuzzling my leg with her head. *She must be somewhat conscious and hearing me to react like this.* Hope blossoms in my chest as I continue to sing, willing her to come around quickly.

Blue like the eyes of my newborn babe,
Vibrant like cornflower petals in May,
Only your love makes me feel this way.

Blue is the sky,
Stretched out up above.
Blue is the color,
The color of love.

"Nighty-night, Daddy," she mumbles.

"Layla, don't you close your eyes!" I plead, but she already has. I lightly slap her cheek, trying to get her to respond. "Come on, wake up! Show me those beautiful eyes." I put my fingers to her neck. She still has a pulse, but it's sluggish, and her breathing is shallow. I bend down, pressing my head against her back so I can hear her heartbeat and breathing.

I'm not going anywhere tonight. I don't care if my internship gets terminated. I can't leave her. She can't leave me. I hold on to her tightly, my body pressed against hers, and cry. I rock us, more so to try to soothe myself than her, for what seems an interminable amount of time, an infinity of fear and agony.

"Please! Just wake up! I love and need you. Don't you understand that? You can't just leave me without you." I sob.

If she dies on me, I'll lose my mind. I will deliver everyone who harmed her to the Grim Reaper myself before joining her. This world is so wrong—she's the only thing I've ever found in it that feels right. There's no point in suffering on in this hell if I don't have her with me.

She turns her head and makes a deep groan. I sit back up and stroke her cheeks. A warmth spreads all over me, a renewed hope from her stirring. I wipe my eyes with the back of my hand and perk up. "Open your eyes, Layla," I say over and over, now stroking her temple, hoping to feel her eyes open.

"Dad?" she mumbles.

I chuckle joyfully at hearing her speak. The tears I wiped away have returned, but not the sorrowful kind. "No, sweetie. It's me, Adonis." I feel her eyes open. My heart swells with so much relief and love that my chest can barely contain it. *She's going to be okay. We're going to be okay.*

"No!" she wails.

No what? Does she not want me to be here? Did she not want to wake up, to come back to me? That one word is like a punch in the gut. She sobs heavily, causing her breathing to become erratic and turbulent.

"I'm sorry. I'm so sorry!" she sobs.

I instinctively shush her and rub her back. "Don't be sorry. I'm here." I carefully lift her head and place a pillow under it. Now that she's awake, I need to get fluids in her. I crouch down beside the bed so that she can see my face. "I'm going to get you some water, okay?" I coo softly.

CHAPTER FOURTEEN

ADONIS MOVES TOWARD THE DOOR, but I don't hear it open. Instead, I see him leaning back awkwardly. He is struggling to move something large. As he moves, I see it's the dresser. *He must have put it there to barricade himself in here. I don't want to imagine the trouble he is going to be in for this. Why would he risk himself for me like this?* His chest is also bare and smeared with blood. I look down at my hands; they're wrapped in blood-soaked fabric. Unlike usual bandages, the strips aren't uniform in width. He must have literally given the shirt off his back for me. I can't process what all of this is making me feel. *How can someone loving you make you hurt so much?*

What have I done? His eyes were so red when he looked at me. *He's been crying. Crying because of me.* In my distress, I didn't even think once about how he would feel if I died; I only thought of myself during my inability to cope with my emotions. *If only he would just leave me, then I wouldn't have to feel so much guilt. I suck at having emotions. I can't deal with them; I don't know how. I just look for the easiest way out and take it.*

I'm angry, depressed, sad, embarrassed, and a slew of other negative feelings. I feel like there is a war raging in my mind. *I want to love. I want to be happy, but I'm not sure I know how. When something bad happens, I just want to run away from it, even if that means dying. When something good happens, like Adonis, I screw that up too. I suck at life. He deserves better than me. Why can't he see that?*

Adonis comes back in with a glass of water and sets it on my bedside table. "I called into work. I'm not going anywhere tonight." he states.

"I'm fine. Really. Don't get in trouble because of me. I can take care of myself," I argue.

"Nonsense. I'm staying—that's final. Now come on, drink."

He helps me into a sitting position and puts the glass to my lips. He tips it back, and I swallow the cool, life-giving liquid. It's so nice to have cold water to drink. It tastes better for some reason; it's not all warm and metallic tasting like back at home. I grab the glass from his reluctant hand so I can drink at my own pace. I don't like being treated like a baby with a bottle. I'm awake; I can do it myself.

I pass the empty glass to him and gaze at him. "You've been crying," I observe.

"Tears of joy," he answers steadily and kisses my forehead.

He's such a bad liar. Why won't he just say it—that I hurt him? That he's angry? That he wants to scream at me and ask me what the hell I was thinking?

"Liar."

"Let's get you out of that wet, bloody dress. Okay?"

He unzips the back of my dress, and I lift my arms the best that I can to help him get it off. He throws my dress to the floor, and his eyes are visibly full of pain as he scans me from head to toe. I feel so naked—not physically, but emotionally. *Now he can see who I truly am: a coward, and a scared little girl who can't handle life. I just wish I could bury myself under the covers and never come out.*

"We should probably clean you up before putting anything on. Wait here; I'll be back in a dash."

I can hear him rummaging around in the bathroom next door and turning the water on and off. He returns promptly with a small bucket of water and a washcloth. He places the bucket at his feet as he sits on the end of my bed. He dips the washcloth in the water, wrings it out, and starts wiping down my leg. I shiver at the sudden change in temperature. Time and time again, he submerges the cloth to rinse the blood and sweat off, sponge-bathing me like an invalid.

"We should change your underwear, too," he advises.

"Adonis! I'm not really in the mood for that right now!"

"Me either," he defends. "I'll get something for you to change into. I can be a professional, you know?"

He starts going through my drawers to find clothes. He pulls out some pajamas and then searches my underwear drawer. I see him place my last bottle of haze in his pocket. *He doesn't feel like he can trust me. I can't say that I blame him, but that's mine. He can't just take my things like that.*

He assists me in removing my underwear and changing into my pajamas. He is strictly platonic in his touching, nothing like the person who made love to me just earlier today. *He still cares for me, though. He has to or he wouldn't being helping me like this, right? But he seems so detached. Does he no longer love me? Did I hurt him so deeply that he feels nothing for me now but pity?*

"How about we get some fresh air?" he suggests, though I know that saying no is not an option.

I sit up and put my feet over the edge of the bed to get up, but my head starts spinning. I close my eyes tightly to no avail. With my eyes closed, I just feel like I'm spinning around in darkness instead of the bedroom. I lie back down, hoping not to get nauseous, and hear him exhale loudly as if he's annoyed by me.

"Here." He puts my legs over one arm at my knees and scoots me toward the edge of the bed. "Put your arm around my neck," he instructs. As he lifts my upper half with his other arm, I put my right arm around his neck and hold on tight.

Upon reaching the doors to the garden, I can see it's already dark out. *How long was I out?* He skillfully lifts one of his legs and opens the door with his foot while balancing me in his arms. "Neat trick," I remark.

"Do you know how dirty doorknobs are?" he asks. "I, unfortunately, know all too well. So, if it's a door that I can open with my foot, I prefer to do so. Same goes for flushing public toilets."

"I'll try to remember that."

He carries me through the winding garden in total darkness. I don't get how he does it; he must have it memorized or something. All I can see are somewhat darker shapes against the blackness of the night that are likely those giant bushes or whatever. It's actually quite pleasant out here. It's not too humid, and I can feel a refreshing sea breeze coming from the east. He walks in silence with me for a good distance before I can't take the awkwardness anymore.

"Where are we going?"

"Thought I'd take you down to the beach. It's a nice night, and after all that, I could use a quick swim to clear my head," he states matter-of-factly without a shred of emotion in his voice.

We arrive at the beach, and it is pristine. Even in the dark I can tell it's not all full of garbage like Gator Beach, and it doesn't stink of rotting seaweed. It's not totally dark out here either. It's a bit cloudy; the moon isn't out, but I see blue sparkling lights. It's like the ocean is full of glitter.

"Wow!" I marvel.

"Looks like we have a red tide. Pretty, isn't it?"

"But why is it blue at night? Why not call it blue tide?" I argue.

"Bioluminescent algae. Looks reddish by day, but at night it puts on quite a spectacle," he explains.

"I've never seen one this closely at night. Is it safe to swim in, or can you get sick from it?"

"For the most part. Just don't swallow any water and you should be okay. You're not going swimming anyway."

"Yeah, I know," I mutter.

He gingerly sets me down on a small boulder set back from the water. "I'll bring you some to check out." He runs toward the sea and comes back to me with sparkling wet sand in his hands. He brings his sand-filled hands in front of me, offering for me to touch it. I'm hesitant; red tide looks so gross in the daytime. "You can touch it, it won't hurt," he insists, moving his cupped hands closer to me.

I poke the pile of sand with the tip of my finger, and the sand lights up where I touched it before fading away. I giggle with wonder at this strange phenomenon. After a few more inquisitive probes of the microscopic creatures, he drops the pile of sand, rubs his hands off on his shorts, and sits next to me. I can feel the awkwardness between us as if it were a physical thing.

"You're mad at me, aren't you?" I murmur. I hope he will say no, but I know that he is. I need to hear him say it, even though I don't want to hear it.

"Would you be if you were me?" he inquires in a bitter tone.

"Yeah, I would," I admit. "But you have so much more to live for than I do."

"That's not true. I don't live for anything; I just live because I do. Or at least I didn't have anything until I met you. Even if I'd never met you, I still wouldn't have done what you tried to do. You hurt me, Layla! Did you even think about how I would feel if you died?"

I feel like such a jackass! Even knowing what I did to him, I would rather die than hear about how I made him feel. I don't handle guilt very well. "No, I didn't think."

"Yeah, I didn't think so."

"I couldn't think at all! I don't deal with stress and emotions that well. I would just rather not feel them than have to deal with them. So, I get high, or I drink, or if it's bad enough, I want to die. I'm sorry I'm such a sucky person, but I just am!"

"Well, next time you want to try and off yourself, you'll have to get more creative." He stands up and pulls the bottle of haze out of his pocket. "See this? No more! I won't allow it! I can get you all the kava leaves you need, but I can't trust you with this," he scolds. He runs toward the water, and I see him hurl the bottle into the ocean. He walks into the water after it and disappears beneath the waves.

I sit up tall in alarm. *Where did he go? Is he trying to scare me, to get back at me? He still has my blood on him! Sharks!*

"Adonis?!" I holler.

A few moments of panic later, I see him pop up a little ways out in the water. I breathe a sigh of relief. *He wanted to swim, duh. I wish I could join him, but that salt water would make my cuts burn like hell. I may as well let him take his time and cool off.*

I hate how hurting him makes me hurt. Why do emotions have to be so damn complicated? I want to kiss him and tell him I'm sorry, but then I don't want to completely invalidate my actions. I did what I know how to do. I know I was wrong, but I hate admitting it to other people. Knowing for myself that I was wrong is enough punishment. I've admitted enough as it is.

He eventually returns from the water and resumes his spot next to me. "Did you have a nice swim?" I ask.

"I needed it," he sighs. "I had to think."

"Think about what?" The panic in my voice is obvious to me but hopefully not to him. *Is he thinking about leaving me? I just had to fuck this all up!*

"Us," he answers directly.

"What about us?"

"Where we go from here."

"You're breaking up with me, aren't you?" I demand in a wounded tone. *I knew it! I knew he would leave me! Everyone always does! Why was I stupid enough to think he was different from any other bipedal primate with a dick?*

"Should I?"

"Well, if you're going to, may as well be sooner than later. No point in stringing me along just to …"—my voice cracks with a sob—"just to tell me in the end that it meant nothing!"

"I'm not leaving you. I love you, damn it! Why are you trying to push me away?" he exclaims.

"I don't know how to love you the way you need to be loved! You deserve better than me! I'm a mess! Do you like taking the sloppy seconds of assholes like your dad's buddies?" I know throwing that in his face will push him away, but I feel like I need to. I need to push him away and rebuild the walls around me to be safe again. Safe in feeling nothing.

"He's the one who hurt you, isn't he?" he asks, his voice laden with pain.

"Why does it matter? I'm damaged goods. If it weren't him, it would be someone else," I snap.

"I'm not going anywhere. You hearing me?" He grabs my shoulders and stares me in the face. "I love you, Layla! I don't care about that shit. I care about *you.* They'll never touch you again, I promise," he vows. "You don't have to talk about it if you don't want to. Just don't try to leave me again."

He kisses me firmly. "Where we go from here is Australia. Not tonight, not tomorrow, but soon. You just need to keep your head down and steer clear of my father until then."

"How am I supposed to do that when Lucinda is sick?"

"I'll go to the market tomorrow. Buy food for your family, get some medicine for Lucinda, and fresh bandages for you," he answers with confidence. He always seems to have an answer for everything. It is reassuring and annoying at the same time.

After everything that I've done, he still wants to leave with me to Australia. Leave his whole life behind him. I don't understand it. He also promised to take care of my family. If we leave, what will happen to them? Who will make sure they have food?

"What will happen to my family if we leave? Won't they starve? Or be punished for what we do?"

"I doubt my father will bother with them when we leave. They might be questioned, which is why you can't tell them anything. As for food, I have a plan for that; don't worry."

"You can't tell me not to worry. I'm going to worry about them! What are you planning?" I insist.

"When we leave, I'll have no use for the money I have here. I'm going to leave plenty for them to live off. They'll be fine."

"I'm just so torn about all of this," I confide. "If we stay here, we can't be together, but if we leave, then I leave my family behind forever. And what if we don't make it? What if we get shipwrecked, or they hunt us down?"

"We either take that chance or live a lie. You will be working here for a long time if we don't go. Eventually, I'll have to move out, get married, have a family. If I don't, then it would be suspicious. Would you rather me have to do that?" he surmises.

"Of course not!"

"Then we follow my plan. Keep a low profile and wait. Now how about we get you back in bed? You need to get your rest."

I start to stand up when he takes my legs out from under me and scoops me up. "I can walk back. I'm fine," I protest.

"You're not wearing shoes," he reminds me. "Besides, it's a good workout carrying you around."

"Are you calling me fat?" I infer with mock shock in my voice.

"You women take everything the wrong way," he replies, shaking his head and splashing water from his wet hair in my face.

"I was kidding!"

"I know," he says with a sly grin.

As he carries me back, I can hear his heart beating as my head rests on his bare chest. *I wonder if it's just the extra work of carrying me that makes it beat so fast, or if it is because of how he feels about me.* Either way, it is a soothing rhythm. I'll probably never understand why he's so good to me. *He's like one of those princes in a fairy tale. Love at first sight, at least for him, and wants to save me from my troubles.* I'd probably be less complicated if I were a distressed princess stuck in a tower than who I actually am. The fact that I have so many more problems than those girls makes his devotion to me even more absurd. It's hard to accept so much love when it's such a foreign feeling. Deep down, I'm afraid of getting used to feeling happy. Afraid of the pain being that much worse when it all gets ripped away from me. He says that he loves me and only me, but things change. People change, circumstances change, most of it beyond our control. If you never have the love at all, then you can't feel the pain of losing it.

He puts me down at the door, and we both brush as much sand off ourselves as we can before going inside via his foot trick with the door. He walks with me to my door as I try to bid him goodnight, but he opens my door and goes in before I can say anything. I nervously look down the hall to make sure no one saw that and quickly follow, closing and locking the door.

"I can put myself to bed, you know?"

"I know you can. I want to stay with you a little bit longer, if that's okay with you. Besides, I want to check your hands again, make sure that the bleeding has stopped," he replies.

He motions for me to sit on the bed, and I oblige. He unwraps my right hand and studies it. I have a few small punctures and long diagonal cut, but they don't seem to be too deep. He grabs the washcloth out of the bloody water that is still next to my bed and dabs the wounds in my hand to get a better look at them.

"I don't think you'll need any stitches on this one, but you're going to need to keep it clean," he advises. "I'll be right back, okay?"

Adonis returns in less than a minute with another T-shirt. "I never liked this one anyway," he says as he starts ripping it apart.

"Where did that come from?"

"The utility room. Don't worry; it's not dirty, just worn."

He uses the new shirt to rewrap both of my hands. It's already after ten o'clock at night according to my alarm clock. *It's insane how fast time goes by when you have to get up in the morning.*

"Thanks for the T-shirt, and for everything." I smile weakly. "We should get to bed, though. It's late."

"My thoughts exactly."

He puts his hand in the small of my back and kisses me. I tremble and feel like the wet sand he held in his hands on the beach—squishy, moldable, able to crumble at any given moment from his touch.

"That's not what I meant," I gasp. "Besides, you said you weren't in that kind of mood because of what I did."

"True; I wasn't, but I am now. I can't stay that mad at you. You're way too sexy," he confesses.

"Twice in one day? Seriously?" I chide. "You're an animal!"

"Hell, I would make love to you all day if I physically could."

He slides his hand up my shirt and scoots back to lay me down when the bed squeaks loudly.

"We can't do this here; we'll be caught," I argue.

"Grab a pillow and get on the floor," he says quickly.

"Are you serious?"

He gives me a sad puppy dog face, and I grin and shake my head at him. He is already on the floor looking at me expectantly. I throw a pillow at him and join him.

"Now, I know I rock your world, but we've got to be quiet," he teases.

"That goes for you, too, you moaner," I jest.

"Shut up and kiss me," he whispers.

How I wish our bodies could always be so close. I wish we could just become one person so that we would never have to be apart. As cheesy as it sounds, he's like the missing puzzle piece I've been searching for all my life. He makes me feel complete, whole.

After everything that I put him through, I'm not going to complain about the whole condom thing. *Fuck it. Who cares?* Making love isn't something that you plan; it just happens. *I was such a fool trying to kill myself. If I had succeeded, I'd never be able to be with him again. Of course, if I were dead, I wouldn't know any better, but still. If I have anything to live for, it's moments like this. The pure ecstasy of his body entwined with mine is worth living a hundred lives for.*

He stops suddenly and looks at me. "What's wrong?" I ask, concerned.

"Nothing. Just pacing myself," he pants.

"You have quite the endurance."

"I could be quicker if you don't want me to get you there." He gives me a suggestive smile.

"Aren't you thoughtful?" I giggle. I run my hand through his hair and then pinch his cheek. "That's not an easy task, you know?"

"I've never been one to turn down a challenge," he boasts.

Goodness gracious, can he defeat a challenge! The only other time I remember feeling this satisfied was from taking care of myself. I bite down on my lip and breathe loudly through my nose to keep myself from making a bunch of noises and giving us away. He's squeezing my shoulders a bit too tightly for my liking to stifle his own cries of pleasure. I don't want it to end, and I don't want to scream either. I can't fight the urge to hold on to him despite my almost unbearable pleasure. I wrap my legs behind his rear end and squeeze, pulling him in deeper.

"Mmmmmm!" he groans as he shakes violently. I release my leg lock on him and he rolls off to the side, breathing heavily. He grabs the pillow out from under my head and puts it over his face. He presses it hard into his face and makes a multitude of noises. I can't help but laugh at him. I also can't stop smiling. All of the happy chemicals in my brain are working overtime right now. *He is one hell of a lover!* A few months can't pass fast enough until we can do that all we want without having to worry about being caught.

"That's cruel!" he teases when he finally takes the pillow off his face. "We have to be quiet! How am I supposed to stay quiet when you do things like that?"

"It's a reflex," I lie.

"Yeah, right," he says, rolling his eyes.

He puts his shorts back on, picks me up, and drops me on my bed.

"Goodnight," he whispers. He kisses me once more and then throws the pillow at me.

"Goodnight stud," I tease, making kissing noises at him as he leaves.

I slip under my covers, not caring about pajamas or brushing my teeth, and fall into a deep, peaceful sleep.

CHAPTER FIFTEEN

5:30 IN THE MORNING COMES way too quickly. I'm groggy, sore, and smell bad. *I hate mornings!* If I were the ruler of the world, I would make having to get up before noon illegal. I need to shower, but I don't want to get my bandages all wet, so I remove them and am very careful as I wash up. I replace my bandages the best I can and get on with my daily routine, wanting to put the events of yesterday far behind me—with the exception of the amazing sex.

Doing laundry is enjoyable right now; it at least feels safe. *I wish I could just stay in here all day. I don't have to worry about messing up my bandages by getting them all wet in here. Maybe just a bit damp at times. How the hell am I supposed to do the dishes with my hands like this? Do the others know about what happened? About what I am and what I did?* I had the small hope of escaping my past by coming here, but it seems that I'll never be able to.

My growling stomach forces me to leave the sanctuary of the utility room in pursuit of breakfast. The kitchen is strangely still as I enter. I look off to my right to see both Lucinda and Phillip sitting there in silence as if they had suddenly stopped talking because of my presence. *They were probably talking about me. Why else would they be so quiet right now?*

SARA GROVER

I slowly walk over to the table, staring at the floor the whole time, and take my usual seat.

I don't look at or say a word to either of them. I just start eating, staring down at my plate to avoid eye contact. Still the silence continues; not even their utensils are moving. I can feel their eyes on me—staring, and judging. Even among the low class in this house, I'm on the bottom. *Lower than low in their eyes, I bet.*

Phillip clears his throat loudly and finally speaks. "What happened to your hands?"

"Like you haven't heard," I mutter, still looking at my plate.

"I know what I heard last night," Lucinda breaks in.

I slam my utensils onto my plate and glare at her. "Really? What did you hear? Huh?" I demand.

"Master Adonis in your room. Taking care of you. Saying he loves you."

"That's none of your business! My past, my relationships—none of it is your business! So you can take your judgments and shove 'em," I snap.

"You're a foolish little girl! If you want to die that badly, then you're heading in the right direction," she chastises.

"What are you going to do? Rat me out? You're just jealous!" I snarl.

"Layla, calm down! We're not judging you. We're worried," Phillip interrupts.

"Yes, so worried that you talk about me behind my back and get all quiet when I walk in the room, huh? Worried about the poor little whore? Worried about my love life? Yeah right!" I retort.

"We *are* worried. You're treading dangerous waters. If they find out about you and Adonis, you're as good as dead," he warns.

"Well, I tried doing the dead thing last night, but I failed. I guess they'll have to be better at killing me than I am."

"Stop your self-loathing and grow up. We want to help you!" Phillip pleads. "You're so damn stubborn. I'll take care of dishes

156

until your hands heal."

"And I'll take care of everything pertaining to Mr. Caraway," Lucinda interjects.

Yeah right! Like you fucking care about what happens to me, I spew in my head. They just want to keep the attention away from me in fear that they'll get caught in the crossfire.

"Given enough time, they'll forget all about the coffee incident. Just keep a low profile," Phillip advises.

"Yeah, I'm sure they will," I say sarcastically, rolling my eyes.

Lucinda adds, "You'd better clean up the drawing room today. The carpet shampooer is in the closet of the utility room; it has directions on it. Read them."

"If anyone needs to lecture me about anything else, I'll be doing laundry," I inform them as I get up and leave the kitchen.

She heard him taking care of me, but did she hear us having sex? What a nosy bitch! I bet she had her ear pressed to the door. I can see the judgment in her eyes and hear it in the way she talks down to me. *I need to face the facts. I can't trust anyone in this house but Adonis, not even the other GIs. Not today, not tomorrow, but soon,* I repeat over and over in my head. *Soon we will be out of here. I wish "soon" was a day on the calendar—that I could count down to it instead of it being some arbitrary time in the future.*

I emerge myself in my tedious work, trying not think about anything. Thinking just makes me anxious and feel helpless as I wait for "soon." I can't help but find comfort in his dirty laundry; it smells like him. As for the rest of his family, I wish I could burn theirs, especially his father's.

Desperate to see him again, I bring Adonis's laundry up first, no longer bothering to knock on his door. He is out, and hard. My moving about the room doesn't cause him to stir in the slightest. I can't help but feel a little disappointed by him staying asleep. I want to talk to him, want him to hold me, but he's exhausted. *I can't be so selfish as to disturb him when he spent the time he should have been resting taking care of my stupidity.* I kiss him on the cheek and leave him to rest.

My heart practically pounds out of my chest as I approach the room of the senator and his wife. I hesitantly knock. No answer. *Thank goodness!* I make their stupid bed as fast as I can and start piling the clean clothes on it. I'm setting down the last stack when I hear the door open behind me. I stiffen and almost stop breathing. *Please let it be the wife! If I don't move, maybe they'll just leave me be.*

"I believe you have a mess to take care of," Senator Caraway hisses.

If I could see myself right now, I'm sure I'd be whiter than the sheets I just straightened. I swallow hard, trying to collect my courage, which seems to have abandoned me. "I was just—" I begin. My words are cut off by a stinging pain on my back.

"Did I say you could talk to me?" he yells right next to my ear. I can feel his spit spray the side of my head.

I fall to the floor as another lash strikes my back and I cry out in pain. "I'm sorry!" I whimper. His belt cracks against my back again at my words. *Don't speak, damn it! Don't cry!*

"Shut your dirty mouth! Go clean it up, now!" he barks.

I trip over myself as I get up and run for the door. I hurtle down the stairs, skipping steps and almost falling twice. I slam the door to the utility room and scream into a pile of dirty towels. *I can't take this! Why me? Why? That fucking bastard!*

I scream so hard that my throat hurts, and I can't continue. *I need to fix this. I need to make it stop.* To avoid further wrath from the evil bastard, I retrieve what I need to clean the mess from last night and hurry to the drawing room. *If he's there waiting for me, I swear I'll kill him. Smash his skull in with a liquor bottle or something!* Luckily the room is deserted, and I can be alone.

I use a rag to pick of the shards of glass to avoid cutting my hands again and proceed to scrub the stains and shampoo the carpet, using my anger and frustration to scrub them with vigor. In truth, I wish I could just smash something instead. To be able to physically manifest my rage instead of trying to reason with it in my head would be relieving. I notice the decanter on the table still has some liquor in it, and without a second thought I drink what's left straight from the container. It burns my throat like fire, but if it helps to numb my back and my mind so I don't care … I wretch but manage to keep it down.

My day becomes a blur from there. I clean, eat lunch, and then seek refuge in my room. There's blood all over my floor too. *Damn it! I'll clean that up later. I doubt they care about what my room looks like as much as the rest of their precious house.* I flop down on my bed and hear a crinkling noise. What now? I roll over to find a bag of kava leaves, an ointment tube, a package of fresh bandages, and a piece of paper folded in half. *Great, another note!* I unfold it to find not another note from Adonis, but this time it's something that instantly makes me weep.

It's a drawing. It's from Daisy; I can tell. The kid is no great artist, but it's beautiful to me. Two little stick figure girls, one taller than the other, holding hands under a rainbow. Under the picture, in her rudimentary handwriting, she scrawled "I mis u sisy!"

I suddenly feel freshly angry with myself. I had never thought of Daisy or my mother, either, when I pulled that stupid shit last night. *How would they feel if I died?* It would probably kill my mother with grief, leave Daisy scarred for life, and then they would have no income. *I'm such a despicable person! I need to see them. I have to—at least once before I leave forever. How can I not tell them about leaving? Why can't we just take them with us?* I decide I have to talk to him, convince him to take my family with us. I can't leave them here, abandoning them more than I already have.

I need to get back to them. I promised I'd visit, and right now I could use the time away from here. The problem is getting someone to cover my work and getting Adonis to take me. I'd also have to pretend to be okay when I'm not. I had never let my mom know the truth about my last job, and I can't now either. I'd worry her to death with my problems. *Why couldn't my drug-induced dreams have been real?* I would give anything to be back home, to have my dad back and just be happy again. I'd even give up being with Adonis if I could have all that back in return, but I can't. Dad is dead, and I'm stuck here.

I put some kava in my mouth to help calm me down as I take off my bandages. It hurts pretty bad still, and the cuts look inflamed. I carefully wash my hands with soap and warm water before redressing my wounds. The ointment at least takes some of the pain away. Being that it's Sunday, and Phillip is doing dishes for me, I opt to skip lunch and take a nap. I lie down on my side, as my back hurts too much to put pressure on it, and awaken in time for dinner.

I have yet to see Adonis all day today, except when I saw him sleeping. His usual behavior is to leave me notes or to be there when I wake up, but not today. *Is he avoiding me? Does he know what his father did to me? If he is, I can't say that I blame him. What I did to him was unforgivable. If he had done the same thing, I'd probably just leave, too afraid to deal with it.* I want to tell him what happened to me today, but then I don't. I don't want him to feel like he has to protect me all the time. I can take care of myself, and I have for a long time. I'm not some damsel in distress; I just need to suck it up and deal with it. I've taken worse beatings than anything that asshole can do with a belt.

The rest of my day goes by without sight of him. I hug a pillow as I try to sleep when night comes, wishing it were him. How did I go from being resilient and hell-bent against being with someone not that long ago to suddenly feeling like I need him all the time? *What has he done to me? He's made me soft and weak somehow. Love does stupid things to me.* At least I think it's love. If what we have isn't love, then I can't imagine what is. I know my parents loved each other, but they didn't have to hide their small gestures of affection like holding hands or a kiss on the cheek like we do. Come to think of it, we haven't even held hands yet.

Three days pass, and there's still no sight of Adonis in a state of consciousness. I'm beginning to think that this is his way of breaking up with me. This place is big enough to avoid someone without a problem, especially with his schedule. *I'm a fool to think he really loved me. I knew it would end badly, but I went ahead and did it anyway. Stupid, stupid, stupid! He only feels bad for me. I'm like a charity project for him or something.*

I return to my room for a quick break after lunch to find him in my room. My heart stops at the sight of him sitting on my bed.

"Long time, no see. What do you want? Here to make it official?" I jeer.

"What? Make what official?"

"That you're breaking up with me. You've been avoiding me—don't lie. I knew I was a fool to believe this was real," I say flatly, not wanting to show any emotion, wanting to act strong.

"I haven't been avoiding you; I've been busy. I had to work a double after taking that night off to take care of you."

He puts his hand behind his back, and when he brings it back to the front, he presents me a pink rose. "I brought this for you, but if you don't want it, then fine by me."

I'm such a bitch! I only think of myself. I hate that about me so much. I never stop to think that maybe he was just doing something else. No, I have to think that he's avoiding me, wanting to break it off with me. Everything is either great or really shitty in my mind.

I'm either crazy in love, or he's breaking up with me.

"I'm sorry," I blurt out as he gets up to leave. "Please don't go!"

He turns away from the door to face me. "Why are you always pushing me away?"

"I don't know! I just have a hard time being happy, I guess. I'm not used to it. My mind always goes to weird places when left to think too long."

"Weird places?"

"Like thinking you don't really love me, feeling that I don't deserve someone like you. That I've abandoned my family and if I leave with you, it will destroy them," I blurt out rapidly. I'm talking so fast I fear I may bite my tongue, but I can't slow myself down. Thoughts cross my mind faster than I can get them out of my mouth.

"Stop," he cuts me off. He wraps me in his arms and hugs me firmly. I grit my teeth as he puts pressure on the welts and bruises on my back. I don't want him to know; I don't know what he would do if he found out. If he blows up about it, he will give us away, and I'm as good as dead.

"For the millionth time, I love you," he affirms. "Stop making yourself crazy with such negative thoughts."

"Lucinda knows," I interject.

"What?" he asks, releasing me and staring at me in surprise.

"She heard you. She heard you in here with me."

"She heard us having sex?" he whispers.

"I don't know! But she said she heard you say that you love me. What if she tells someone? How can my mind not wander such horrible places when such horrible things keep happening?" I implore.

"I don't think she'll tell, but to be sure, I'll have to talk to her. Just don't worry about that. There is no point in worrying about it. It only stresses you out."

"What about my family?"

"What about them?" he asks.

"Why can't they come with us? Leaving here without my mom

knowing anything—it'll destroy her! What if your dad has them killed even though they know nothing? What if they hate me for leaving?" I plead, growing more panicked.

He puts his hands on my shoulders. "Layla, you need to calm down, now," he states firmly.

My anxiety has been building for days, and I'm losing my head. All these worries I have are just spilling over, and I can't stop them. He guides me to the bed with strong hands and makes me sit down.

"Listen to me. Take a deep breath and calm down," he commands.

I take a deep breath in through my nose and out my mouth, trying to calm myself, but it doesn't help that much. What would help is answers.

"As much as I would like to take your whole family with us, we can't," he starts.

"Why not?" I demand.

"Because that boat can't store enough supplies for six people to sail for a month or longer. There wouldn't be enough to eat, or enough room for them to sleep. Do you want to risk them dying out there? They'll be safer here; I'll make sure of it. You need to trust me and stop freaking out."

"I thought you said it was a big boat."

"For trips that last a couple of days, or for a small number of people, but it's not a cruise liner," he elaborates.

"You saw my family. How are they?"

"They are fine. I swear. Yeah, they miss you, but they are well-fed and in good health," he affirms. "Stop worrying, stop trying to push me away, and just relax. Please."

"I wish I could! I don't know who I am anymore. I don't know how to feel or what to do. I'm losing my fucking mind here waiting for 'soon,' or to die, or for something to change the course of things. I feel like a rat in a cage!" I continue rambling on.

"How long were you on that crap?" he asks.

"What crap?"

"Haze."

"I don't know. Four, five years probably," I answer. "Why?"

"You're not crazy." He puts an arm over my shoulder and holds me gently.

Out of nowhere I feel a deep sadness swallow me whole, and I cry hysterically. "Well I feel crazy," I sob.

"You haven't actually dealt with having emotions for all that time. Anytime you felt pain you just shot up, didn't you?" he hypothesizes. I nod my head to confirm. "Your brain has forgotten how to cope, but it'll relearn soon enough."

"Why do you put up with me? I'm too much trouble. You could find a much prettier, smarter girl who isn't a basket case, you know," I point out, sniffling.

"Stop it, Layla. I mean it. You're not going to scare me off, so stop trying," he maintains. He puts his hand under my chin to make me look at him. "No more tears. Your family will be fine, they won't hate you, I'm not leaving you, and you're not crazy."

I throw my arms around him and grip him tightly. If I could just stay like this, I might feel okay, but I have to let him go eventually. I take a deep breath through my nose to take in his scent, to calm myself. I don't know what it is about him, but the way he smells just calms me.

"Are you smelling me?" he asks incredulously.

I nod into his shoulder. *He probably thinks I'm a freak. I can't help it.*

"Why?" he chuckles.

"I love the way you smell," I mumble into him.

"You're adorable," he coos. "If my stinky self makes you feel better, then whatever works."

I wipe my tears on his shoulder and sit up. "You don't stink," I protest.

"How about you wear one of my shirts at night instead of yours?

Then you can smell me all night if that will help you feel better."

"I'd like that. It's as close to you being with me at night that I can get."

"Then consider it done. I'll make sure you have something tonight. Anything else I can do for you?" he inquires.

"Yeah," I nod. "Just one more thing, at least that I can think of for now."

"Name it."

"Hold my hand?"

"That's it? Hold your hand?" he laughs.

My cheeks flush with embarrassment. I look down at my lap, feeling like a foolish child.

"I'm sorry. I was just expecting something more difficult." He grabs my right hand, but I have it closed in a tight fist. "I said I'm sorry! Now come on," he insists playfully. I allow my hand to relax as he laces his fingers between mine.

I look at our joined hands; mine is so small in comparison, like a child holding hands with their mom or dad. I give his hand a gentle squeeze. He returns the gesture, but it hurts. I wince a little. His hands are so strong yet somehow caring and gentle when he touches me.

He kisses my forehead. "Better?"

I smile. "Yeah, better."

"If it's okay with you, I'm going to take a nap before I have to get up for work. I'll bring you that shirt before I leave. Will that work?" he lovingly implores.

"Take your nap," I approve. "Dream of me, okay?"

"Always do. I love you."

"I love you too."

CHAPTER SIXTEEN

FIVE WEEKS AGO, I WAS scared out of my mind about being away from my family and in a strange new place. Now, I'm getting the hang of the routine around here and have, so far, been able to avoid any further contact with that evil bastard that somehow happened to help create the man that I love. I haven't had any time off, really, but Adonis has been sweet enough to deliver letters back and forth to my family for me.

I lie, of course, when I tell my mom how everything is going great over here. I'm highly skilled at lying about that stuff; practice makes perfect. If I can lie about being accosted by scumbags, I can lie about what goes on here. I want to tell her about Adonis and I being a thing. I wish I had someone to talk to about it, but I don't want to risk her knowing something that could bring her or the kids harm. I also don't want to involve my mom in my love life either. Not that we don't have a good relationship or anything like that, but some things are just meant to be private, only between him and me.

Now that I've been off haze for a while, I'm starting to get a new sense of "normal." I still have mood swings on occasion and think strange things, but then again, maybe I would have always felt these if I wasn't on drugs. Some days I just want to scream my love for

Adonis to the world, unafraid of the consequences—to marry him, have his children, grow old with him, the whole nine yards. Some days I want to successfully kill myself, setting him free to live the life he should have, which I seem to have ruined just by existing. Other days, I get random thoughts like: If I threw myself over this railing, would it be enough to kill me? What if I just "accidentally" fell down the stairs? Slipped and drowned in the shower? Days like today, I want to run away, burn the tattoo off my arm, take a new name, and start my life over.

I recount the days on the calendar. Forty-five. I don't know how in the hell I'm going to even bring it up. I know he told me it's something he wanted someday, but now? If I take a nasty fall or punch myself hard enough, maybe it will go away. It has to go away; I'm dead if it doesn't and someone finds out, which will happen sooner or later. Secrets like this can't be kept forever.

I should have known better. I do know better, but I did it anyway. Having passion, throwing caution to the wind—insanity at its purest. *Haven't I suffered enough?* Now I'm in a serious do-or-die situation. We either have to leave soon, or I have to find a way to get rid of it. I can't predict how he's going to react; I think that scares me more than what I ultimately end up doing. *Will he be happy? Angry? Scared away?* I like to imagine that he would be overjoyed. That he'll throw his arms around me and hold me tight, elated at the news, and set sail the same night to make a new life for ourselves, as a family. That's just a fantasy, though. He'll probably panic, be angry at me, at himself. *Maybe I should just try to take care of it myself, and if I succeed, never tell him.* What he doesn't know can't hurt him, right?

No, no, this is crazy. I have to tell him. I can't go around keeping secrets from him. You don't keep secrets from the person you love. At least, I don't think you do. I don't want a baby, though—not now. I can't even figure myself out, never mind some needy crying, pooping pain in the ass that will probably have all sorts of problems because I've been chewing semi-narcotic leaves, running myself ragged, and have defective DNA.

Why did I ever let him convince me to have sex with him without protection? Fucking idiot! Yeah, sure the odds of getting pregnant are low during certain times in a woman's cycle, but not impossible. I have always dreaded getting my period, as it meant I had to take time off work and be useless. Never before had I wished so badly that I was dealing with nasty cramps and blood. I'd welcome that monthly torrent of menstruation with open arms if it happened right now; hell, I might even jump up and down in excitement.

I told him I didn't want children, yet he does. *Did he have the intention of getting me pregnant on purpose?* I can't help but feel so damn conflicted. I almost kind of like the idea of having his child, but at the same time I hate it. Kids were never in my plan, but then again, neither was he, nor was working for the douchebag Senator Caraway.

The thought of it just going away, of just having a miscarriage, makes me feel hopeful and guilty at the same time. *I need to take care of myself first before I can take care of a baby, but then what gives me the right to kill something we created? Did my parents even want me? How would I feel if I knew they didn't want me, that I just happened by accident and they thought of getting rid of me? I don't know what nonexistence is like, nor will I when I'm dead, but who am I to decide to put something—someone—out of existence before they even know it?*

I hate my brain so much sometimes. What use is it to wonder what it would be like to not exist or be waiting to exist, not having any awareness of anything? Or wonder if it knows it exists and then what it would be like to just poof, be gone, not ever having a chance? *What choices do I have, though? Not many!* If anyone finds out I'm pregnant, I'm dead, the baby is dead, and Adonis is as well. If I can only sacrifice the currently microscopic thing growing inside of me without anyone knowing, that saves Adonis and myself. *We can al-*

ways have kids later, right? I just don't know what to do! He swears that he loves me. He will understand, I hope.

He's a doctor, for crying out loud! He should have known this would happen. Having spontaneous lovemaking sessions, sometimes two to three times a day, is bound to end in this kind of result. Even when he had the opportunity to get condoms, he argued that someone might find them in the trash and the gig would be up. I enjoy the sex. Hell, I can't get enough most of the time, but why do good things have to have such crappy consequences? It would be different if we didn't live in this time and place, but we do, and something has to be done. *I have to tell him.* I don't think I'll be able to bear looking him the eyes again if I lose it on purpose and have to hide it from him. I suck at lying to him anyway; he'll figure out that I'm hiding something, and then what?

I open his door to find him at his desk, shirtless, reading some massive textbook.

"Back for a fix of this?" he teases.

Damn it all to hell! It's as if he runs around half naked all the time on purpose to tempt me. I know it's summertime, but come on, the place is well air-conditioned. "No. We need to talk," I say cautiously. I shut and lock the door.

"Dirty talk?"

"No. Like serious talk."

"Did I do something wrong?" His eyebrows furrow and his nose scrunches up when he gets that weird worried look on his face.

"Not wrong, just something."

Did he do something wrong to me? Or was it something right at the wrong time? I don't know whether to call it wrong or right, but it's definitely something.

"Will the subject matter of this talk change at all in the next, say, fifteen to twenty minutes?" he asks.

"No. Why?"

He walks up to me, grabs my ass, and kisses me roughly.

Damn him! He's the addict now.

I break away. "Adonis! I need to talk to you about something." He always distracts me. *Why does he have to be so damn sexy?*

"Come on. Please! It's been while!" he wines, pulling me close to him and giving me another firm squeeze.

"It's been, like, two days!"

Horny bastard.

"Two long, agonizing days," he states, emphasizing each word dramatically.

I guess waiting another half hour or whatever can't hurt. He's already knocked me up—what's the harm in having sex before telling him? Maybe it will put him in a really good mood, and I can persuade him to have us leave immediately or help me terminate the pregnancy. "Fine," I concede. "We can wait until after you satisfy your insatiable sex drive." Maybe sex will help ease my mind too. *Can't hurt.*

Without a word he grabs me by the hand, leans back, and uses his weight to pull me toward the bed with him. Now, standing by the bed and facing him, he whirls me around so that my back is to him, unzips my dress, pulls it off, and throws it to the floor.

I want him now, too, but I have to tell him. *He is so damn frustrating!* Laying me on the bed, he caresses my chest as he kisses my neck. I can't help but let out a sigh of pleasure and longing. My mind is fighting a battle as part of me wants to stop him and tell him that I'm pregnant while the other wants him to ravage me—now.

"I've missed you so much," he whispers in my ear.

He is so dramatic. "I never leave this house."

"You know what I mean," he sighs as he unhooks my bra.

I run my fingers through his hair and gently tug at strands here and there. *Fucking A, I love his hair.* It's just the perfect length, not too short or too long. Long enough to get a decent grip to pull and tease him with, and it looks sexy as hell when it's messy after he wakes up or has just rolled around with me in bed. He kisses me deeply, our tongues doing a rough but graceful dance. I tug a little harder at the hair on the back of his head, and he gives my bottom lip a little nip.

"Not so rough, Layla. I don't want to go bald," he smirks as his mouth drifts to my neck, leaving a trail of sensual kisses and soft bites. He bites a little hard on the left side of my neck. I wince a little, to which he responds by sucking on the offending bite. *This is torture! Just take me already!* Our breathing is rapid as if we just ran for miles in the summer heat.

I reach my hand down to grasp the physical manifestation of his attraction, still veiled by his boxers, and run my fingers along it. He squirms and hurries to help me pull them off.

"You want on top?" he breathes.

I shake my head. "I'd rather you be in charge."

"If you say so."

As we connect, I can't help but make strange noises. Being with him is the most intense and intoxicating sensation I have ever experienced. It's like we're made for each other in every possible way. Though I am physically occupied, my stupid mind can't help but be a buzzkill and interrupt my fun. *You have to tell him!* Maybe if I can just say it while we're going at it. How could he possibly react badly if he's in such a state of arousal?

"Adonis," I utter between thrusts.

"What?"

"I … need … to … tell you … some … thing," I manage, panting hard.

"Hold on."

A loud bang sounds and he suddenly falls on top of me with all of his weight, squeezing me tightly.

"No! No!" he screams.

I can't breathe! I manage to turn my face to the side slightly to gasp for air. His hold is unrelenting as he continues to scream. *What the fuck is happening?* I hear a loud cracking sound, and he cries out in pain. I see his face pull up from mine and contort. With his face not pressed into me, I can see a menacing arm strike down on Adonis with a belt. *No! How can this be happening? No!*

We're caught red-handed—I'm dead! He has to know what they'll do to me and yet he is taking a beating, trying to protect me from the inevitable. *Protect me! Don't let them get me!*

"You can't! I love her! No!"

Strike after strike falls on Adonis's naked body, shielding me from the evil wrath of his father. I hear other voices in the room shouting inaudible things as my head spins with terror. My heart wrenches seeing him in pain, knowing that he is doing it for me. It all feels so surreal and like I'm not even here, my shock causing an out-of-body sensation, trying to detach me from the unfolding horrors.

My scalp burns with pain as someone pulls on my hair so hard that it very well could be ripped from its roots. I scream out in agony as I feel Adonis's protective body leaving mine, and I get pulled from the bed by my hair.

"No! Get off of me! Let him go!" I shriek.

I hear a blow come down and a thumping noise. I glance over to my side, and I see Adonis crumpled on the floor. The senator kicks him in the ribs, and he bellows in pain.

"I told you, Dad!" I hear Brenda blurt out in that I-told-you-so tone of voice.

The Ice Queen clutches on to my hair, using her grip to drag my naked body across the floor. I see Adonis in the corner by his desk, taking repeated blows from his father. He lands one good punch in the bastard's jaw, but the man is relentless in his fury.

"What did"—whack—"I fucking"—whack—"tell you!" I hear him yelling at Adonis as he punches and kicks him repeatedly.

"No! Adonis! No!" I cry out.

As I get dragged toward the door, I catch a small glimpse of him cowering, trying to protect his body from the assault to no avail. *I wish I could be the one protecting him. He doesn't deserve this.*

"Let me go, you bitch!" I scream.

A kick to the stomach takes the breath from my body, and I gasp for air as hot tears fall from my eyes.

"I'll get you out!"—whack—"I promise!"—whack—"I love you!" I hear Adonis cry out.

"The hell you will!" his father roars. I can hear the blows coming faster and harder as I am dragged out of the room, trying with all my might to get free, screaming in despair.

I'm being pulled along the carpeted floor, the rug burning my skin, as I kick and scream, trying to escape. I can't gain any leverage.

"Grab her feet!" Mrs. Caraway barks.

My feet are roughly snatched up and I'm airborne, carried at each end by the vile bitch and her cunt daughter.

"You piece of filth! Did you honestly think you were going to get away with it?" Brenda hisses. "I've known for a long time. Just had to catch you in the act."

"You cunt!" I scream.

"Oh, it's going to be such a joy knowing you're going to be locked up," Brenda beams. "Call me what you want, you dirty little whore. You'll be dead soon enough!"

We suddenly stop, and I drop. I hit the floor, hard, and gasp as I land flat on my back, the wind knocked out of me.

"Call the police. I've got it from here," Mrs. Caraway says to Brenda.

I'm picked up by my hair again and tossed into a room, and I hear the door slam behind me. A lock engages from the outside. "No, don't lock me in here!" I scramble on my hands and knees to the door, trying futilely to open it, but it doesn't budge. "Let me out!" I scream, pounding on the door with all the strength I have left, which isn't much.

"No, no, no!" I scream. "Adonis!"

"He can't hear you, bitch! You'll never see him again, so save your energy. The only place you are going from here is a cell," Mrs. Caraway taunts from behind the door.

"Fuck you! You bitch!"

I want to fucking kill her! If I could only get through this god-damned door, I'd choke the life out of her.

I curl up on the floor by the door and cry, my body being wracked with emotional and physical pain, constricting my lungs as I try to breathe. Every inhale feels like a knife in my heart as my chest tightens to resist my breathing.

This can't be happening. Stupid, stupid, stupid! I knew this would happen eventually. I just knew it! My life was never meant to have a happy ending. If he truly loved me, he would have left me alone, not made me fall in love with him. I'll never see him again, or my family for that matter. I'm going to die in prison. Why couldn't he just leave me alone?! My life sucked, but at least I was alive. Now I'm a dead girl walking—well, a dead girl curled up on the floor.

I didn't have much of a life ahead of me, but at least it would have been a free one, not locked in a cage like an animal, waiting to be put down. And the baby—I never got to tell him! He will never know that I could have had his child. It's going to be dead like me soon. Once they discover I'm pregnant, they'll kill me, killing it as well. Maybe it's better this way, him never knowing. I'm sure he will move on eventually, forgetting all about me. Not knowing about this baby will make it easier on him. I always knew my life would end in some horrible fashion, leaving him behind.

I love him, but I hate him at the same time. I would be home right now, living my normal life if he had just let me be.

Or would you? You would have been dead already from that car, the rational side of my mind interjects.

At least I wouldn't have seen it coming. Dying suddenly is so much better than anticipating a horrible death that you know is coming. If I had only died that day, he would be living his normal life, not being mercilessly beaten right now. What was the point in him saving my life that day just for me to die this way, because of him?

The door opens hard suddenly, pushing me across the floor and into the wall. Dazed, I try to make a run for it, but the door slams before I can reach it.

"Nice try! Put those on, tramp! Or they can haul you off naked. Your choice," Mrs. Caraway jeers from behind the door, now locked again.

On the floor are my clothes that I had been wearing earlier, left on the floor of Adonis's room. I gather them in my arms and huddle the garments to my chest, crying silently. I press my face into the dress. It still smells like him, like us. *This is the last time I'll ever inhale the aroma of that intoxicating man.* I get dressed and hug myself tightly, rocking back and forth on the floor, the waterfall of tears never ending. *My fate is sealed, but what about his? Is that asshole still beating him? Where is he? Why doesn't he come and save me?*

CHAPTER SEVENTEEN

I'M STARTLED AWAKE BY A cold drowning sensation. *What the fuck? Where am I?* I sputter and cough, expelling water from my mouth, flailing my arms and legs like I'm trying to swim. I'm dripping wet and chilled to the bone.

"Eat!" a male voice barks at me. A metallic bang follows. A small dish rolls around on its base after being dropped on the floor.

I can't see what the dish contains too clearly; it's too dark in here. I roll onto my side. My arm hurts so much that I hiss in pain. As I slowly prop myself up on my elbow, I notice a tightening around it. There's medical tape wrapped around my arm, just under my left elbow. I'm in too much pain to push up any further and resign myself to crawling across the cold floor on my stomach to the mystery food.

I prod it with my right index finger when I reach it, trying to figure it out. It feels stiff, yet slightly soft. *Stale bread probably.* I'm famished, so I shove the bread in my mouth. It's dry and hard to chew. I suck on the ends of my wet hair to create the moisture necessary to swallow.

I quickly finish my meager meal, hungry for more, as I try to recall what happened. *Where am I? How did I get here? What day is it? Where's Adonis?*

My heart drops at my last thought. *Adonis!* I don't remember getting here, but this must be the prison. I've only ever seen it once from the outside, and it's worse than I imagined. The outside has such a bleak appearance, sporting two gray chevrons that exude a sense of oppression, but it's far worse in here. It's dark and cold in here. *They must make it this cold in here on purpose, to torment people. It could never be this cold naturally in a place like South Texas.*

My memories come back to me like a flash flood, hitting hard and abruptly. The darkness around me deepens as my emotions plunge me into an empty dark abyss of despair. The air feels thin, almost nonexistent as I gasp for it between violent sobs. I'm cold, wet, and alone. *I'm going to die here. I'll never see Adonis or my family again! Why can't they just kill me now? Get it over with already.*

I hear a different male voice murmuring in the space around me.

"Who's there?" I call out.

I hear two men conversing quietly when one of them lets out a repulsive phlegmy chuckle that ends in a wet cough that echoes long after it ceases.

"Who's there? Let me out! I'll do whatever you want, just let me out!" I call out to them again.

I hear someone shuffle across the floor and then a click. I shut my eyes tight in response to a sudden blindingly bright light. The light is painful, and my head throbs. *How long have I been in the dark to have such an abhorrent reaction to light? This is worse than waking up with a bad hangover.*

I lean on my forearm on the floor and use my other hand to shield my eyes as I carefully open them just a bit, desperate to see what is going on around me.

"You'll do what we want whether you like it or not. You're not going anywhere," the first man mocks me.

Like hell, I'll do what you want. I blink rapidly, trying to acclimate myself to the light. I can hear the telltale hum of fluorescent lights. The hum is more eerie than usual as it reverberates through the cement and metal cell.

I see thick dull metal bars in front of me. *I'm caged, like an animal.* Beyond the bars, I see two burly men in black uniforms with heavy combat boots. I know I'll never make it out of here unless I can subdue them somehow. Then, if I manage to escape this cell, I can make a run for it. Where to run, I don't know, but anywhere but here.

I can see now that I am naked in here with the exception of my bra and panties. The floor has a drain in the middle of it. They probably just hose this place down instead of ever cleaning it. A rickety metal bed with a sagging cotton mattress is attached to one wall, and a filthy metal toilet stands in the corner. This place is disgusting. *I have to get out of here. I don't want to die like this. I can't just sit here, hoping for Adonis to rescue me. He probably can't or won't. I need to do something.*

Beyond the bars is a small room with a table. The guards are sitting there, cards splayed out on the table, an ashtray littered with cigarette butts lying on the edge. Behind them is a solid metal door, no bars. *Do they have me in solitary? Why are they isolating me? A personal favor for the senator?*

I've got to get out of here. If I can just get their keys, then maybe I can find my way out. Lock the bastards up in here and sneak my way to freedom. I can do this. I can do this. Put your game face on. Time to play.

"Hey! It's fucking cold and wet in here. Can one of you give me some clothes or a towel or something?"

"Shut up!" the second guard snaps.

"What do you think this is? A hotel?" the first guard laughs.

Pricks. Do they want to play it that way? Game on.

"Well, if you won't give me anything dry, then I'll have to dry what I have." As slowly and seductively as I can, I remove my bra. I twist it over the drain to wring some of the water out of it and then hang it over one of the horizontal cross bars of the cell.

My number one weapon is my body. If I can just get them to come in here, I may have a chance. They are hideous, but I have to do something, and this is all I've got to work with.

I look over at them and bat my eyelashes. They're taking the bait; I can see it in the way they're shifting around. They want to come in here. I slip off my panties and, without wringing them out, drape them over the bars so that they slowly drip water onto the floor. The dripping echoes loudly through the room. I can hear them breathing now, heavily.

I lay my back up against the bars as I plan out my next moves. I carefully examine the wrap around my arm. *Blood draw. Assholes tested me for their organ registry.* I wonder how long it will take before they come after me with a scalpel. I'd rather drown myself in that toilet than give life to some Normie cocksucker.

I take a deep, loud breath and use the bars to help me stand up. The cell swirls around me, and I almost lose my footing. *What the hell did they do to me? The last thing I remember is getting locked in that guest bedroom. Was I knocked out? Drugged?*

I brace myself against the bars until my head stops reeling. *Time to shake what my mama gave me.* I turn to face the guards, completely naked. Wrapping my hands around the bars, I press myself against the cold metal.

"It really is cold in here," I purr. "I'd use that blanket in the corner, but it's all wet."

They just stare at me. *Alright, Layla, reel them in.* "Could I maybe have one of your shirts? Or would you like to come in here and keep me warm?"

One of the guards—he has way too much facial hair—pushes his chair away from the table with such force that it scratches loudly across the floor. He starts to saunter over toward my cell. *Bingo!* He places one of his hands on the bar, going for my breasts. I back away, just out of his reach.

"You'll have to come in here," I tease.

"Hey! Who said you get dibs?" the other guard protests to his coworker.

"You're not coming too?" I say as seductively as I can.

The bearded guard pauses and looks back at his coworker, then back at me. "You're a dirty little bitch, aren't you?"

"May as well get my kicks while I'm still living," I reply with a sultry tone.

I fight my urge to shudder as he stares at my body, his eyes full of lust. As disgusting as they are, I've got to get them to open this door, no matter what. Their hesitancy is frustrating. Still out of the guard's reach, I start to slowly caress my breast.

"Won't you come and keep me warm? I might not be around for that long if I catch pneumonia from the cold."

The second guard whispers something in the bearded one's ear, and he nods and reaches for his pocket.

"I hope you like it rough," the second guard mutters as the first turns his key in the lock.

I nod and wink at him. *Perfect! Two swift kicks to the nuts and I'm out of here!*

"Get into the corner," the first guard commands before clicking the lock to open the cell door.

I slowly back into the corner, waiting for my opportunity. The two enter cautiously and, like fools, leave the door wide open. Putting on my best "oh I want you, baby" act, I pop my hip out to one side, rest my hands on my waist, and run my tongue across my lips. *Come on. Just a little closer.*

The guard with the beard suddenly advances on me before I can react and grabs my ass with one hand and pulls my hair with the other as he tries to kiss me. I reflexively knee him in the crotch and try to push him off of me. He crumples to the floor in front of me, and I go to make a break for the door when I fall hard on my face.

The second guard is on top of me, pinning me to the floor. *Fuck! Idiot! They were supposed to come on to me at the same time, not one at a time! Then I could have had them both on the floor and made my escape.* A warm pool of blood gathers under my face, the sweet metallic taste flooding my mouth. The first guard is groaning in pain and yelling profanities.

I've royally fucked up this time, but I had to try. I can't just go into oblivion without a fight like a coward. My head is jerked back by my hair.

"You stupid little cunt," the second guard hisses in my ear. He pulls me to my feet and slams me into the bars. The impact clatters with a bang that echoes like thunder through the concrete room as I fall to the floor. As I try to right myself, my wrist sears with pain. "I'll teach you to fuck with us."

The guard has both of my wrists squeezed in one of his massive hands. With his other hand, he pulls out handcuffs and swiftly attaches one to the bar and the other tightly to my left wrist. I pull at the cuff and it digs into my wrist, drawing blood. The guard is still holding my other wrist, looking at me with an evil grin.

"Let me go!" I scream and spit blood in his face.

His eyes are dead, his expression unchanging as he wipes the blood from his face with his free hand.

"Collect your balls and give me your cuffs, Pete," he calls to the other guard.

I can hear "Pete" still groaning as I see him crawling slowly across the floor to my captor.

"You bitch!" Pete gasps as he fishes his handcuffs from his back pocket and slides them over toward the other guard.

The second guard briefly releases my right arm to pick up the cuffs and I kick at him, hitting him in the stomach. He hunches forwards only slightly and glares at me, rage in his eyes. In an instant, he has my arm pinned again and is cuffing it to another bar. I kick, scream, and spit in resistance, but it's futile.

I'm so sorry, Mom! I tried! I had to try! I say in my head in what must be like a prayer.

Prison Guard Pete is back on his feet, approaching me menacingly. I shudder and try hopelessly at freeing my arms by pulling at my restraints, but I merely wince as the cuffs cut me more. I try curling my hands as narrowly as I can, thinking maybe I can slip through them, but all that manages to do is cramp my hands.

"You nasty little bitch! You think you can fuck with me?" Pete hollers in my face, spraying spit everywhere.

I close my eyes and take a deep breath. *I wish I had some haze. I need to detach myself from this.* I can't feel self-pity or sorrow; those emotions won't do me any good right now. I need to collect my anger, my rage, the emotions that numb me when they take over. I need that seeing-red, tunnel-vision, body-numbing rage right now. I slowly open my eyes, steeling my nerves, and stare the fucker straight in the face.

His hand strikes my face repeatedly. I can't see straight. My vision is clouded, and my eyes burn. "You tried to fuck us, and now we're going to fuck you," Guard Two jeers. I think it's him, or maybe the other, who punches me in the stomach. All the air leaves my body as I frantically try to recapture it.

I fall without warning as far as the cuffs will let me. My head is spinning so badly that I have to shut my eyes. My arms suddenly fall free, and I'm being dragged across the floor. With a jolt, I land facedown on a slightly less hard surface, and I hear the clicking of the handcuffs as they attach to another metallic surface.

I genuinely wish there were a God. Maybe, if he were real, he would help me, save me. What did I do to deserve this? All I did was fall in love, like a fool. Now I'm going to die in this putrid place—a nobody, abandoned and forgotten. Why did I ever let him into my heart? I knew he'd be the death of me.

I'm distracted from my self-pity by the forceful manipulation of my legs. *No! Not again!*

"Help! Somebody, please!" I scream.

"No one can hear your screams from here," one of them taunts.

"We'll show you what happens to little dickteases," the other adds.

I try to zone out the best I can, but the pain is unbearable. I scream until my throat is raw. The pressure and agony coming from my backside is more than I can take. Black spots and bright pulsating flashes invade the corners of my closed eyes.

How long have I been here? Days? Weeks? Months? My ability to track time has been lost for I don't how long. I know I get three meager meals a day, but nothing about them can help me distinguish breakfast from dinner. No windows; lights are on at what seems like random times. *I don't know how much longer I can take this.* I'm beaten and raped at what I think is a daily interval. I can't be too sure, though. Who knows how much time passes when I'm asleep? There are four different pairs of guards that tend to me—and by "tend," I mean hosing me randomly, throwing in plates of shitty food, and then fucking me. I guess seeing all four groups means that twenty-four hours has passed, but I can't be sure.

I wonder if my family knows what happened to me. *Did Adonis tell them? Would he lie about it? Is he even alive? I hope I'm not alive for much longer.* I'm always so cold and hungry here. My cough is getting worse, making sleep difficult. I have nothing but time to sleep when I'm not being bothered, yet coughing fits interrupt it so often that I spend most of my time awake, staring into the darkness, thinking about how insignificant my existence is.

Hundreds of billions of people had lived and died before I even came to be. Who remembers any of them? Unless they were famous for something, no one cares that they ever lived. My life is just a speck in the time of humanity. Compared to the time of the Earth, humans are just a speck, and compared to the universe, the Earth is just one of trillions of little planets. I am a speck, upon a speck, upon a speck. *My life is pointless. Humanity will not remember me, nor will the universe remember this pale blue dot in space. What's the fucking point of it all? In the grand scheme of things, I'm nothing. Why won't they just kill me already and let me meet my destiny? Oblivion, nothingness ... peace.*

Being alive is torture at its finest. Being a sentient being, even more so. Knowing that I am alive and that one day I will die is psychological torture. I'm cursed with knowing how insignificant I am, unlike an ant that doesn't know nor have the ability to care. They just go about their little jobs, completely oblivious to the fact that a foot could come and blink them out of existence. Ignorance truly is bliss. We are born alone, live alone, and die alone. Sure, people may be around us, but they are separate. All a person ever has is themselves. No one else can be inside our minds, to really know how we feel or what we want or need. We come from the void and return to it alone. The void, our one true home, and oh, how I long to go there. I close my eyes, willing myself to go.

"You're not good enough for him! You're garbage!" she hisses.

I try to pull away and run to him. "Adonis! Come back! Where are you going?" I yell. *He just keeps walking! Why won't he turn around?* "No! Wait! Let me go!" But she won't let me go. "You said you loved me."

He stops. *Thank fuck!* He's walking back toward me, slowly, but he's coming. "Please, Adonis. Tell her to let me go!" I beg. He stares at me, emotionless, his eyes dark and unreadable.

"I never loved you. It was just sex," he says flatly as he flashes me a wicked smile and saunters away.

"No! Please! Ahh!" I scream awake in emotional and physical pain. My insides are being squeezed and cramping in violent spasms. *It was a dream. A horrible dream. Am I still dreaming? This pain is much too real.* I scream and howl in pain. It's like period cramps plus getting stabbed with a hot knife. I double over on the floor, hugging my knees to my chest, trying to make it stop.

"Someone, please! Help me!" My screams and cries are either going unheard or ignored. They echo back to me as if the cell itself is mocking me. The pain churning in my belly is unlike anything I've ever felt. It's excruciating.

A warm sensation trickles down my thighs, and I have a sudden moment of clarity. *The baby! I've lost my baby!* I don't know how to feel. I'm confused—in pain! The infinitesimal speck that was growing inside of this speck in the universe is gone. The speck that I never got to tell Adonis about. Our speck. *I've lost it. I killed it. We were both doomed anyway.* My mind is trying to reason away these emotions, but I can't help but feeling an intense sorrow.

I crawl over to the disgusting toilet and sit down, clenching my stomach, trying not make any more of a mess in my already deplorable little hell. The pain comes in waves, my sobs only making it worse. I feel so empty, as if someone just hollowed me out like a pumpkin on Halloween. An emptiness that's as deep and dark as the infinite void that awaits us all grows inside me. I may as well already be dead. *I have nothing left to live for.*

Would they have had my hair? His eyes? His dashing smile? These useless thoughts keep emerging from the depths of my subconscious. I hate them. They do nothing but bring me more pain, yet I can't help but wonder these destructive thoughts. *If the world were different, could we have been happy? Could we have raised our little speck and maybe a few more in a loving home in that world?*

Before I can register the sensation and act on it, I throw up on the floor. With tears running down my face, blood between my legs, and snot and now vomit on my lips, I'm thankful for the darkness. I don't think I could bear to see myself unraveling. *Just take me now! God? Universe? Anyone! If only there were a place where I could hang myself in here. I'd do it without hesitation. The cruelty of these bastards is unprecedented. Even when I want to die, they make it impossible to do so. They enjoy watching me suffer.*

When the torrent of blood feels like it's finally ebbing, I stagger over to my pathetic filthy bed to rest. My hips ache from squatting on that unforgiving metal seat, and I feel dizzy. I tuck my blanket between my legs to soak up any more blood before letting my mind go blank and drift off to the world between here and nowhere.

CHAPTER EIGHTEEN

"WHAT THE FUCK DID YOU do in here?" a man yells, waking me from my sweet, dreamless sleep. The lights click on, making it impossible to ignore them and sleep longer.

"Looks like the bitch is ragging it to me," another man comments.

"Put a plug in it!" the first guard jeers, throwing a tampon at me.

Why did they wake me? Is it time for food? I'm not hungry. I sit up on the edge of the bed and look toward the bars, but I don't see any food. Scanning my cell, I see blood everywhere. *How can a person bleed so much and not die?* The smell of my vomit on the floor mixed with stale blood accosts my nose, causing me to gag. I turn my back toward the bars and use the bloody blanket to cover myself as I take care of the situation between my legs.

"Get up!" I comply and stand up next to the bed. "Stand in the center," the guard commands.

I know what they're going to do. One of the guards is fixing a hose to the wall. They never let me take a real shower; the best this cell and I get is a hosing down. The cold water hits hard, like always, with that pins-and-needles sensation. I briskly rub my hands over my body to wash away the dirt and dried blood.

"Can't have you looking and smelling like this," the guard with the hose remarks.

Since when the hell do they care how I look? The fact that they do should bother me, but right now I don't care. I want to feel clean, or at least not as filthy. I'm sticky, smelly, and covered in a reminder of my loss. I wish I could wash more than the blood away. If only pain and memories could wash away as easily, disappearing forever down a dirty drain.

To my surprise, a guard tosses a small raggedy towel at me. *Okay, this is weird. They've never given me a towel after a hose-down. Something isn't right.*

"Why the sudden hospitality?" I ask incredulously.

"Just dry off, shut up, and eat," a guard says, sliding a bowl between the bars.

Holy shit! Real food? The bowl is full of chili! They haven't given me anything with meat before. I love chili! Something is definitely up. A towel and decent food? Has the senator told them to lighten up on me or is this just some new form of torture? Bring up my spirits just to cut me down again? Fuck it. It smells too good to question further!

I wrap the small damp towel around my hair and sit down by the bars to eat my rare treat. *Oh yeah! Still warm!* Of course, I've had better chili, but compared to stale bread this is amazing. Just a little hint of garlic, some cayenne pepper ... delicious. The heat of the food warms me from the inside out. It's a comforting sensation, like being wrapped in a warm blanket not physically but emotionally. For the first time since I've arrived here, I don't feel cold.

I lean my head back against the bars. They don't feel cold either. A contented smile bows my lips as I breathe a sigh of relief. Clean, fed, and warm, I haven't a care in the world right now; all of my primary needs are satisfied. *This is as good as it gets.*

"How you feeling, sweetheart?" a man somewhere behind me says. I'm too drowsy to turn around. I nod my head ever so slightly. *Feeling pretty fucking good.*

"I hate to admit it, but I just might miss your ass. A good-looking one is a rarity around here. A pity your time came so soon," someone mumbles.

What! What are you talking about? I try to say these words, but my mouth won't make them. *What did you do to me?* I try my hardest to stand up, but my muscles won't cooperate. All I manage to do is tip over on my side.

"Stop fighting it. You're lucky we're making you comfortable. Makes it easier on the doctors too."

No! Just shoot me! I can't die like this, giving my organs to some rich bastards. Cocksuckers! I knew something was up. Why, you idiot? Why did you eat it? I should have known it was a trick. They laced it with something. *Sedatives? Muscle relaxers? This is it. Nothing I can do now.* My body has betrayed me by succumbing to drugs. May as well go to sleep now to avoid having any worse memories to take with me.

I close my eyes, the one thing I can still do. As I lie on the floor, which still feels warm, I hear the muffled banging of the metal door. I feel weightless for a few moments. Someone dresses me in a garment. I feel it fastened at the back and around my neck. Strange tickling sensations are playing at my nose, like a constant breeze. It's kind of refreshing. Without warning, my left eye is pried open and a bright light is shined into it.

I open my other eye in alarm and stare in disbelief. *Adonis!*

He's talking to one of the guards as he darts the light back and forth between my eyes. I hear my name and then something about my heart. *Are they taking my heart?* How appropriate to send him to do it! He already ripped it out once by abandoning me; why not again? The irony is almost too much to be real!

He reverts his gaze to me. I don't know if I'm crying. I can't feel anything anymore nor speak. *How could you?* How sick is it to have him physically rip my heart out? To be my Grim Reaper? *Why did our paths ever have to cross?* He lied; he's just like them.

I'm moving through the halls on what I assume is a gurney, florescent lights flashing above my face every few feet. There are beeping things and tubes attached to my arms and a mask on my face.

"BP is one ten over sixty-eight," someone says from behind my head.

He is walking beside me. His walk is casual, like what he's doing is no big deal. No big deal that he is here to end the life of someone who loved him. I hate him. I refuse to acknowledge his existence any further by looking at him. I close my eyes once more, hating that my last image of my life will be him.

The gurney bumps along the path. I hear buzzers and doors opening and closing. There is a change in the air and the sounds around me. *Are we outside?* I risk a quick peek, hoping for him not to see it. It's a dark, humid South Texas night. They're moving me across a parking lot. I hear an engine quietly start up.

"We'll be taking her around back," I hear Adonis say.

Around back to where? The hospital? Would make sense, I guess. Probably too dirty to cut my organs out in a prison. The gurney lurches and I hear clicks and bangs followed by the sound of the ambulance door closing. I can hear him talking with someone else close to me. I want to look, but I can't. I won't. *I won't let him see the pain in my eyes. I can at least die with my pride partially intact.*

"Should I administer the propofol now, doctor?"

"Not yet. I want to get a full examination in before doing that. I don't want to risk any damage," Adonis answers.

He sounds very professional and unemotional, his confidence and authority audible in his voice. *Why was I so stupid? I actually thought he loved me. I just lost our would-be baby, and now he's going to kill me. Had he been a day earlier, he could have killed us both.* If only my lips could move, I'd love to tell him how much I hate him. *I wish I had never laid eyes on you. I never will again!* Even with my eyes firmly shut, I can feel moisture pooling in the corners. I only wish those tears were from fear of dying, but they're not. I'm no longer afraid to die. Death will be so much better than the pain I feel from this ultimate betrayal. Death is numbness.

The ambulance comes to a stop, and the back door opens.

"You grab the back. You get the front," I hear Adonis ordering the paramedics.

My body tips forward as the paramedics take the gurney out of the vehicle. I'm on solid ground only a moment when I hear brief screams and two thuds. My eyes snap open. I'm dazed and stunned by the commotion. Adonis is leaning over me, breathing heavily. He pulls the mask off my face and is manipulating the tubes and wires. In a flash I'm off the gurney, bobbing up and down in his arms as he runs.

Even if I could physically react right now, which I can't, I don't know what I would do or say. I don't know what to think. I'm dumb-struck. *Is he saving me? What the hell is going on?* I hear him pant-ing loudly as he carries me. I close my eyes tightly. I can't bear the sensory input of the world shaking all around me.

He skids to a stop, and I hear a door open. I'm dropped uncer-emoniously into an upright position. Now stationary, I open my eyes. *His car?* I hear him get in, slam the door, and he floors it. I'm pressed back into my seat and manage to turn my head slightly to my left to look at him. His eyes flash back and forth between the rear-view mirror and the road, his hands gripped tightly on the steering wheel. Without even looking at me, he reaches over and pulls down my seat belt.

"I don't think anyone's following us. You looked upset to see me. Did you honestly think I would kill you?"

I try to nod, but I can't manage much. He's not even looking at me. *Yes! I thought you were going to rip my heart out for real!* If only he could read my mind to know just how pissed I am at him. Now, I'm happy to see him, to know that he is here to help me, but I'm also pissed that he left me there for all that time. Pissed at him for making me think that he was ready to off me like that. Why couldn't he have given me a wink or something to clue me in on things?

"Don't worry. We're getting out of here, baby."

My chest swells with joy at that simple statement. *How could I have doubted him? Leaving me to rot in prison is a good reason*, my anger and pride remind me. *Was this all part of some master plan?* I wish my body would cooperate and move. I have so many questions to ask. What happened to him? What took him so damn long? What day is it? What does my family know?

"Once we get to the docks, I'm putting you in the cabin, and you're to stay there. Get some rest. No arguments. Once we clear the bay, I'll check on you."

Not like I can move or talk right now, idiot. The docks—that means the boat. We're taking the boat! We're finally leaving this place forever. A new land, a new life. I should be thrilled, but I feel crushed too; *I'll never see my family again.* I'll never be with them for another birthday or holiday. Daisy's birthday should be soon, or maybe it passed when I was locked up. She'll feel hurt by my absence on her special day. I never even had the chance to get her a present like I promised.

The car lurches to a halt, and he's picking me up before my body can register the change in speed. *Whatever they gave me needs to wear off already.* It fogs not only my mind but my ability to sense my surroundings, which is getting annoying. So much is happening so quickly, and I can't sort it out in this state of mind and body.

His footsteps thump loudly on the wooden planks of the dock as we approach a large white sailboat with a blue hull. He makes a long step over the side of the dock, bridging the gap between it and the boat, and shakily brings me aboard. I breathe a sigh of relief. At least he didn't drop me. The sky above me is dark but dotted with a few stars that shine through the light pollution.

He pulls up on a handle with his foot and flings a door open; it makes a loud bang as it hits the deck of the boat. My body jerks as he drapes me over his shoulder and carefully takes us down a ladder, one hand on my back holding me firmly, the other quickly guiding us downward. The cabin is beautiful. It's not huge, but it's sufficient. It has a real cozy feel to it. There is a small couch, a table with bench seats, and a mini kitchen. We move further back through another door, and he deposits me onto a bed. I can hear his anxiety in his labored breaths as he bends down to plant a quick kiss on my forehead before leaving me.

Outside I hear the thumping of his footsteps and various things banging around. *This is all happening so fast. I don't even get the chance to say goodbye to anyone.* The day he slammed into my life in the street was a catalyst that changed my life forever. *There's no going back. No goodbyes. We either leave now or die.* I wish I could rewind time and never have gone to cross the street to the cemetery.

I think I still love him, but is it worth all that I've lost because of him? *At least I'm safe now—I hope.* The bed is so comfortable and warm compared to what I've become accustomed to in jail. The comfort of the bed, the drugs still in my system, and the rocking of the boat in the water gradually help me drift off into a deep sleep.

CHAPTER NINETEEN

THE SURFACE BENEATH ME SINKS and I snap awake, flinging my arms in self-defense.

"Whoa, there! It's okay. It's me," he soothes.

Adonis is sitting on the bed next to me. His presence still seems unreal. I stare at him in disbelief and reach out my hand to touch his leg. My breath catches as I feel his solid body beneath my fingers. *Feels real.* My nagging cough that I have been dealing with for what seems like eons now comes back with a vengeance. I take in short, sharp breaths in an attempt to get some oxygen before I involuntarily expel it in chest-hammering spasms.

I feel Adonis leave the bed momentarily and then return, running his hands along my bare back. I'm in one of those hideous medical gowns. Better than naked, I suppose, but not something I'd want him to see me in.

"Try to take a deep breath for me," he coaxes.

I try my best to bring air into my body before gagging on it. I feel him methodically probing my back with his stethoscope. We played around with it once before in his bedroom. He put the things in my ears and had me listen to his heart, to hear how fast it beats when I'm near him. The sound his heart made reminded me of a galloping horse.

"Sounds like you have some fluid in your lungs. You'll be okay," he informs me, rubbing my back soothingly.

Pneumonia! Just like Dad.

He must see the fear in my eyes. He pulls my head into his lap and starts stroking my hair. I don't see how I'm supposed to be okay—this is far from okay.

"I've got some penicillin with the other supplies in the other bedroom. We'll be alright. I promise."

The sedatives or whatever seem to have worn off. I can move normally but have yet to put my mouth to use. I have so many questions, but so little breath in which to ask them.

"Where are we?" is the first thing I can think to ask that isn't too many words.

"Middle of nowhere, baby. Don't worry. Now, if you can handle it, I can give you a shot of penicillin now. It'll be sore for a while, and I have to administer into good muscle—so, most likely, your ass."

I nod, and he gently moves me to get up. He walks into the main cabin and then to the far end and opens another door. Of all the pain I've put up with in my life and recently, a needle in my ass doesn't seem like a big deal. *I'd gladly take many needles instead of being used as a sex slave and a punching bag. He left me there way too long. Those things should never have happened. When I have the energy to launch my inquisition, he better give me some really good answers as to why he took so damn long, or I may just have to throw him overboard.*

"Okay. Let's roll you onto your stomach."

I wince as I slowly turn over, my bruises from prison still fresh and smarting. I feel a chill as he wipes a wet cotton ball in a large circle on my behind and the pressure of his thumb and forefinger on my skin. "Count of three. One. Two." The needle plunges deep into my backside and he holds it there. I clench my teeth and draw air in sharply, making a hissing noise.

"You didn't say three!" I groan.

He finally withdraws the needle and wipes the spot with a cotton ball again. "Element of surprise works better, I think." He secures a small bandage to the injection site and rubs it. "You okay?"

"Mm-hmm."

I've had worse. I hate to admit it, but I don't mind the shot that much if that means he is going to rub it after. I've missed his gentle touch.

"Are you hungry?"

"I guess."

"We have a good stock of food, mostly nonperishable. How about I make you one of my favorite comfort foods?"

"You can cook?" I manage through a cough.

"Don't sound so surprised. I'm a man of many talents," he chuckles.

"What are you making?"

"You'll just have to wait and find out. After we eat, we can sleep."

"Who's steering the boat?" I ask. "Are we anchored somewhere? What if someone finds us?"

"I dropped the sea anchor. We shouldn't drift too much. I need to sleep, too, you know. Breaking you out of prison and then being up all night was an exhausting ordeal."

I give him a small smile and leave it at that. I have so much more to say, but I'll save it for when I feel better and have more energy. My whole body is sore. I have a pinch in my left shoulder and neck, and now my right butt cheek hurts. Even though I don't necessarily feel hungry, I know I probably should eat. Unlike my last meal, I doubt Adonis is going to drug my food.

I watch him at the stove in the cabin through the open bedroom door. It's obvious that he doesn't cook often; he's never had to. He's spent most of his life with a private chef. He probably lived off of ramen noodles and macaroni and cheese in college and considered that cooking. From what I can gather from my observations, he's mak-

196

ing some sort of hot sandwich and maybe soup. I smell my favorite spice: garlic! Tasty and useful, as it clears the sinuses well when you eat a large amount of it. I used to chew on garlic cloves whenever I got a cold. My dad would joke that my breath could kill vampires. I giggle quietly at my dad's overused joke. It's crazy how smells can trigger your memory.

He's using a knife to flip a sandwich. If I weren't incapacitated, I'd go in there and show him the proper utensil to use. *Get a spatula, dummy!* I shake my head. The stove is going to be filthy after this. Adonis reaches his hand into the pan to center the top slice of bread that came off during his attempted flip of what smells like a grilled cheese sandwich. *I hope he's better at using the right medical equipment than he is at using the correct cooking utensil.* I thought such things were common sense.

As horrible as he is in the kitchen, he's still pleasant to watch. His hair is messy in that sexy way, probably from being out on the deck with the wind off the open ocean. He's changed his clothes since I last saw him. He's no longer wearing his green scrubs but a black T-shirt and faded blue jeans. I like this look. He looks much more down-to-earth like this. In this time and place, he isn't Adonis Caraway, son of the evil senator, Normie, doctor, rich brat; he's Adonis the twenty-two-year-old sexy but clueless guy who couldn't cook his way out of a paper bag.

He pours some soup straight from the pot into a plastic bowl and curses from burning his hand while holding the hot pot handle. *Use a ladle or a potholder!* It's a good thing he can treat his own injuries. If I allow him to cook much longer, he'll have to be the one resting in this bed instead of me. He sets the table, and I creep to the edge of the bed to get up. The smell of garlic makes me hungry. I go to push off the bed and my shoulder pinches and tightens with a burning pain. *Fucking shit! Work, useless body!*

"Let me help you." Adonis is suddenly at my side and puts his arms underneath mine, pulling me up against his chest.

"Ahh, fucking hell!" I groan. I'm so stiff and sore. My body feels like it's broken—out of order and in need of major repairs. Adonis walks slowly backward, holding his chest against mine as we make our way to the little table. I look down at the table, and I'm slightly impressed. Grilled cheese sandwich and tomato soup. It looks edible enough. The sandwich is a bit burnt around the edges, and the slices of bread don't line up, but it smells good. I look across the table and smile at him, more so with my eyes than my mouth, as my facial muscles still refuse to cooperate fully.

"Smells good. Thank you." I shakily pick up half of my sandwich, which he so kindly cut in half, making two triangles, and dip the end into the soup before taking a bite. The taste and sensation of the warm food traveling through me awakens every inch of my body. "Mmmm." I take a spoonful of the soup. *Wow!* The tangy and slightly spicy soup makes my taste buds dance as the thick, hot liquid cascades over my tongue.

I shift in my seat to put more of my weight on my left side. My backside is killing me from where he gave me that shot. An unwelcome cough makes me sputter some of my food on the table as I angle my head downward, trying not to cough on him.

"Sorry," I mutter as I wipe my mouth with my hand.

"Don't be." Adonis gives me a sympathetic smile.

"Don't look at me like that."

"Like what?"

"Like I'm some …" I say before a coughing fit interrupts me. "Like I'm some poor wounded creature in need of your sympathy."

His expression is a mixture of anger and grief as he stares at me. His mouth opens like he's about to say something and then closes again without a word. My emotions are a mess; I'm happy to be with him and don't want to be with him at the same time. *He left me there for all that time. I ended up pregnant and in a prison cell because of his carelessness.*

We both return to our food without further conversation. I finish as quickly as I can. I feel awkward sitting here across from him, knowing he is looking at me as I try to ignore him by concentrating on my food. With food in me, I feel some of my strength returning, and I move to get up on my own before he can offer to help.

"Where's the bathroom?"

"Through that door by the couch." He points to my right.

I scoot off of the bench and start for the bathroom.

"Are you sure you don't need help?" he asks. I can hear the concern in his voice, but I'm a big girl. I can take a piss on my own.

"I'm fine."

I hear him following behind me. I close the door before he dares try to come with me. The bathroom on a boat is small, but at least it's clean. There's a small standing shower against the wall, and a toilet and a sink pushed up right next to it in a little row. I sit and relieve myself. *Toilet paper!* I never thought I'd be so happy to see toilet paper. The small shower looks inviting. I pull back the curtain to see a washcloth and a bar of soap. I try to reach the ties on my gown to take it off, but soreness causes me to wince and retreat my hands.

Great! I'll have to ask for help. He already "rescued" me, and now I need him to help me shower? I'm pathetic. I open the door, and Adonis is waiting there.

"Everything okay?"

"I'm fine. Need tampons and a shower, but I can't get this stupid thing off." I tug at my gown.

"You really should rest," he admonishes.

"I'm dirty. I'm sore. I just want a shower."

"Fine. Let me get you some painkillers first and I'll get you what you need."

He pulls some towels and a bottle of pills out of a cupboard.

"Feminine supplies are in the cupboard under the sink. Take this." He hands me two white pills and a cup of water. I pop the pills in my mouth and gulp down the water. It's not super cold, but better than the metallic-tasting shit they let me have in my cell. I turn my back to him.

"Untie it, please."

His deft doctor fingers swiftly undo the three ties down my back. I let the gown slide down my arms and fall to the floor in front of me. I've had so many sick perverts see me exposed lately, yet I feel more naked now in front of Adonis. I feel ashamed, embarrassed, and exposed all the way to my soul. All the things that were done to me while we were apart, what we had and lost that he doesn't know about—I feel like they are written on my skin and that he only has to look and read them. If only there were someplace that I could hide from him, but there isn't. We're on a boat together in the middle of the ocean. There's nowhere to run or hide.

"Thanks," I murmur, and without looking back at him I step back into the tiny bathroom. I go to close the door, but he blocks it.

"Keep the door open. Just in case. Okay?"

"Fine," I sigh. *He is way too concerned. I can take a shower. There isn't any room to fall over in this tiny space anyway.* I slowly bend down to open the cupboard under the sink and retrieve a tampon before turning on the shower.

"Oh! Yes!" I moan as the water envelops my body. It feels heavenly. I lather up the washcloth, rubbing the places I can reach and squeezing soapy water over the areas I can't. I don't see any shampoo, but clean water and a bar of soap are good enough for now.

How am I going to tell him? Should I? I'm stuck here with him. We're going to end up talking in depth sooner or later. I shake my head under the water, wishing my thoughts would shut up. *Not now.*

I grab a towel off the sink and drape it over my shoulders. My arms are too sore to wrap my hair properly. I wrap a second over my chest and go back to the bedroom. Adonis is sitting on the end of the bed, waiting for me.

"Hey," he mutters

"Hi."

I sit down on the bed next to him, trying to cover myself even more by crossing my arms over my chest. "Did you bring any of my clothes?"

"Yes. I also bought you some more. I stocked up on everything."
He opens a drawer under the bed and hands me panties and an over-sized shirt.

"Thanks." I smile weakly at him and look down at the clothes in my lap. *Sleeping clothes. I hope he brought more than stuff like this for me to wear.*

I clear my throat. "Would you mind ... you know?" I motion my chin toward the door. "So I can get dressed."

"Why? I've seen you naked before." He sounds alarmed and confused.

"I don't know. I just ..."

"I'll turn away. Okay?"

"Okay. No looking." I watch as he turns his back to me and pull the shirt over my wet head. It reaches almost to my knees. With all the important stuff covered up, I slip on my panties. I haven't been this clothed in ages. I feel safe like this, like I'm protected from the world somehow.

"I'm done."

He turns around and faces me. A look of longing and deep sadness shows through his eyes. How can he make me feel so guilty with one look? *I'm the one who should be sad. I was the one left for dead!*

"Why are you looking at me like that? Stop it."

"You're acting like this is all my fault."

"It is!" I snap. "I told you this would happen. You wouldn't listen to me."

"When they took you it damn near killed me, Layla! I've spent every single day since preparing for this. For *us*. To get the fuck out of there and be free."

"We could have left when I asked and avoided all of that," I return with venom.

"Damn it. I don't want to fight with you! I'm sorry. I can't change what happened, but I'm here now. You're here. I'm going to take care of things. Just trust me," he pleads.

"I'm tired. Let's just go to sleep." I don't want to discuss any of this right now. I'm fatigued and drowsy. I don't have the energy to argue with him.

"Okay," he says dejectedly.

He pushes a switch on the wall, and the lights go out. I crawl into a comfortable position, laying my head on a pillow. *Oh, yeah. That feels nice.* I pull the sheet up and roll to my side. My ass hurts too much to lie on my back.

"Goodnight," I whisper.

"Goodnight."

CHAPTER TWENTY

IT'S TOO WARM IN HERE. My pain is not as bad, but the heat and my nagging cough make it hard to sleep. I try to roll over, but my path is blocked. Adonis is snuggled up against my back—that explains the heat. I wish things could go back to the way they were. I love him, but I can't help but feel so much resentment toward him. Part of me wants nothing more than to cuddle in bed with him for the rest of my life. I miss his gentle embrace.

I hate feeling so conflicted, like letting him back in would some-how invalidate my pain and suffering. *Why should I be the one to bear all the pain? He should have to suffer too. I know that hurting him for what happened to me doesn't fix anything. I get that how I feel toward him isn't fair, but what he did to me wasn't fair either.* It sickens me that the thought of breaking him down gives me a feel-ing of justice. I hate feeling like he deserves to feel pain like I do to make me feel better. I'm a horrible bitch and feel guilty for being so, but I just can't help feeling what I do.

I get up, grab a glass of water from the sink, and head for the bathroom. The face in the mirror hardly looks like my own. I'm paler than usual, have dark circles under my eyes, and bruises dot my body. I've lost a lot of weight. I look like a ghost of myself.

I find a toothbrush in the cabinet behind the mirror and relish in the sensation of having the grime cleaned away. The taste of mint helps to wake me up. I splash water on my face, towel off, and head for the little kitchen.

My appetite has returned with a vengeance. I look through the cupboards to find mostly rice, beans, and a bunch of dehydrated food in pouches. The mini refrigerator wields much more desirable results. *A half gallon of orange juice. Nice!* I unscrew the top and drink from the carton. I haven't had orange juice in so long that I don't care to waste time pouring it in a glass.

"Glad to see you're moving around okay," Adonis says behind me, startling the hell out of me.

How the hell is he always so damn quiet? I lower the carton and place it on the counter.

"The painkillers seem to be doing their job," I state casually.

"I enjoyed you being next to me," he admits quietly.

Seriously? He's awfully direct. What ever happened to "Good morning"?

"Listen, Adonis. I can't …" I begin as I turn around to face him. My brain stops working, and I can't form the words. He's in his boxers. He's such a magnificent sight to behold. *Pull yourself together!*

"I can't do this"—I gesture to him—"right now. Too much has happened—I just can't."

I can't bear for him to touch me sensually. My body is tainted. Even the thought of him touching me scares the hell out of me. Those parts of my body are reminders of what happened in there. Reminders that I can never get rid of.

His eyes are like a sad puppy's, big and shining with budding tears. "Please. At least talk to me. What do you want me to do?"

"I want answers," I mutter.

"Ask me anything! I'll tell you anything you want to know."

"What day is it?"

"The twenty-eighth."

"Of July?"

"No, August."

"August! You left me there all that time!"

He grabs my shoulders. "I had no choice. I got to you as soon as I could. I swear!"

I push his hands off and stalk off to the bedroom, slamming the door behind me. *Almost two months! He let me suffer all that time.* My hunger has vanished, replaced by anger building in my belly. The door swiftly opens; the stupid thing doesn't have a lock on it. I crawl to the back of the bed to get some distance from him. His face is anguished.

"Please. Just listen to me. Goddamn it, Layla. I fucking love you! I took the beating of a lifetime trying to protect you. I worked nonstop, planning and preparing to get you out of there and to leave with me. I drugged two paramedics, for fuck's sake! I've done all that I know how to do to be back with you, and now you want ..." His voice cracks before he continues, "Nothing to do with me?"

"Do you know what I went through? Huh?" I seethe. "I was kept in a cold, dark cell, no clothes, eating stale bread while getting beaten and raped every fucking shift change of the guards! And you want me to feel sorry for you?"

His expression is complex and pained. His mouth is agape as he stares at me, looking wounded and lost.

"I ... I don't," he starts, his voice faltering. He swiftly embraces me, taking me by surprise. His grip is almost too tight to bear. He's clinging to me like I'm a lone life raft in this ocean we find ourselves in. I let myself relish at the warmth and safety of his embrace for a moment before gently pushing him away. He seems so fragile, yet I'm the one who went through hell and back.

My rejection of his embrace makes him more upset, but I can't handle to be touched right now. I want him to hold me, but I'm afraid he'll want more, and I can't give that right now. The thought of being touched in my most private areas is a sickening thought.

He has his hands covering his face. *Is he crying?*

"Adonis, please. Don't do that. I just don't want to be touched by anyone."

I don't know what else I can say to help him understand, to make him feel better. *Why do I suddenly feel like I'm the one who needs to be apologizing? Am I too hard on him?*

Yes! Stop being a bitch. He loves you! my subconscious chimes in.

I grab his hands and pull them away from his face, which he has pressed into the bed. "I'm sorry," I whisper.

"No," he croaks, shaking his head. "I'm sorry. I should have gone for you sooner. Should have listened to you. Should have left you alone. Should have—"

"Stop it!" I cut him off. Tears are building in my eyes now, and I can't hear any more of this or I'm going to lose it. "I can't imagine a world in which I never met you. I'm sorry. We've both suffered from this. I'm sorry for lashing out at you. I just have so much anger inside that I don't know what to do with. I'm angry at the world. Angry what it did to us. Angry that I had to leave my family. Angry about …" I stop my rant. I can't say it. *Angry about losing our baby.*

I try my best to fight back my tears by taking deep breaths, but they fall unbidden down my cheeks anyway.

"If I promise not to touch you sensually, will you let me hold you?" he begs. I nod.

Fuck it. I can't control my feelings anymore. Violent sobs wrack my body. He rubs my back, trying to calm me, but I can feel his ragged breathing from his silent but noticeable sobs.

"Shhhh. You're safe now."

I may be "safe" now, but I need more than that. I feel broken and lost, like someone took my life, blew it up, and ejected the remains into deep space, each fragment drifting light-years away from the others, making it impossible to be whole again.

"Layla?" he whispers.

"What?" I murmur into his shoulder where my head rests, drenching his soft skin in my tears.

"I need to know something."

What else could he possibly want to know? I should be the one asking him. I still have so much I need to know, but I can't handle my current situation and don't want to add anything else to my already overloaded brain.

"What?"

"That night—when …" He pauses momentarily, taking a deep breath. "When they took you."

Oh no. Where is he going with this? I don't want to relive that night!

"You said you needed to tell me something. What was it?"

My heart drops like a stone. *Why, Adonis? After everything that has happened, how does he still remember that? Why couldn't he have forgotten?* I would never have to tell him if he would just forget. I swallow hard. *How do I tell him?* The memory of the miscarriage. The pain, physical and emotional, rises from the depths of my gut like rising vomit, burning and wanting to escape from my mouth in a heaving torrent.

He puts his hands on my shoulders and pushes me back a little, looking into my tear-swollen eyes, searching them for answers. "Layla, please. Tell me. It sounded important to you then, and I selfishly ignored your need to talk to me because I was thinking with my dick."

"It doesn't matter. Just forget it." My voice is a halting, broken strain of syllables.

"If it didn't matter then you wouldn't be crying. Tell me," he coaxes.

I stare down at my hands, my fingers knotted around each other in an intense grip. *Maybe if I squeeze hard enough, I'll awake from this nightmare. How do you tell the man you love, yet who also abandoned you for almost two months, that he knocked you up and then you lost the baby from the abuse you suffered because of him?* He always wanted children; my revelation might destroy him or, at the least, wound him deeply.

"Please," he begs again, the need and sadness evident in his voice.

"I was going to tell you ..." I take as deep of a breath as I can to ward off the tears and building nausea. "I was ... I was ... pregnant." My last word is just a breathy whisper as I tightly shut my eyes.

A deathly silence falls over us. The only sounds I can hear are my shallow breathing and my heart pounding in my ears.

"Was?" he finally chokes out. The agony in his voice is almost tangible. "When?"

"When what?"

"When did you ..." His voice fades out. I don't think he can bring himself to ask.

"Before the last time I slept. Before you came to get me," I mutter.

I hesitantly look up at him. His face contorts in pain. His eyes are squeezed shut, but tears still manage their way out. He gets up suddenly from the bed and almost sprints for the ladder to the deck of the boat.

I curl up on the bed, hugging my knees to my chest, and let the tears flow in a cathartic release of emotion. I hear Adonis up above stomping around, various loud bangs, and screams of rage. "Fucking shit! Goddamn it!" *Bang.* "Motherfucker! *Ahh!*"

His emotional release only deepens my despair. We're both lost and suffering and can't separate enough from our own pain to comfort each other. *Why does this affect him so much? He's the man. He's supposed to be stoic, a stable place for me to cling to. Yes, he wants children, but this could have happened even if I wasn't locked up. Would it have been as bad if I just miscarried without being beaten and sexually abused? Does he blame himself? Blame me?*

It's his fault I got pregnant. My negative thoughts creep to the surface, wanting to blame someone, and Adonis is an easy target. I have every right to be mad at him, to blame him, but seeing him suffering makes me hurt more than I already do. I can't stand to see him in pain. I feel a primal need to protect him, like a mother bear or a lioness. I can take pain; I've had my whole life to learn to live with it, to become emotionally sturdy or numb. *But can he take it?*

Why does everything have to be so fucked-up and complicated? What I wouldn't give to have that perfect happily-ever-after life with him. A life without GIs and Normies—just people. A life in which I don't have to choose between the man I love and my family. I had never envisioned having children before Adonis, but now the vision I wish could exist would be to have my mother by my side to help me. To have her teach me what to do and be a part of my kids' lives. For them to grow up having a loving grandmother and an aunt and uncles to play with them.

The boat jerks, and I can feel that we are on the move now. *Should I go topside to talk to him?* I want to see where we are, but I wonder if maybe I should give him space to sort his feelings out. *Does he want space or want me? Maybe he wants me to go to him but is too proud to ask. If I go to him, and he doesn't want to see me, how will he react?* I don't know what I should do. What's the right course of action?

As much as I want to lie here all day and wallow in my self-pity, I can't any longer. *I have to try to fix this—fix him.* The sight of Adonis in so much emotional pain crushes me. I need him back. I need the strong, caring, optimistic Adonis back, the man who always tells me not to worry when that is all I know how to do. I need the man I fell in love with back to bring me out of the darkness, not wallow in his own.

For once, I need to do more than put on a facade of strength. Screaming and punching won't fix anything. I no longer have drugs to help me escape. I need to be strong for real—for both of us. I've had far more practice in dealing with pain in my life than he has.

Yes, he lost his mother, but that was so long ago. Most of his life has been easy and full of privilege. *I need to help him through this.*

I listen intently. He's no longer screaming and cursing; all I hear is the water moving against the boat. I splash my face with water to wash away the tearstained look and head up the ladder to the deck.

CHAPTER TWENTY-ONE

HE'S STARING INTENTLY AHEAD WITH indifference when I reach the deck. Though I make enough noise, he doesn't move a muscle. The wind is constant, whipping his unruly chestnut hair in waves. I look off in all directions and see nothing but the sea. Not a speck of land anywhere. The water is calm; most of the turbulence being caused by our wake. White popcorn-like clouds dot the sky. The weather is perfect, which is a big relief, as it is currently hurricane season. I don't know what we would do if we were caught in a storm with nowhere to seek refuge.

He looks pensive and sullen. I wish I knew what was going through his mind. Seeing and hearing him so upset is by far more painful to me than what I just went through, though I don't know why. My emotions are at war with each other. Half of me wants to be angry as hell at him, and the other just wants to hold him.

I approach him slowly from behind as if he were a wounded animal that may or may not lash out in pain and maul me to bits.

"Adonis?"

He ignores me. I step just close enough to touch his shoulder.

"Adonis? Talk to me," I coax.

"I just want to be alone," he mutters, never breaking his thousand-yard gaze.

Alone. The word echoes through my mind. That's how I feel right now. *I don't want to be alone.* I want to be angry, and apparently he does too. All anger will do is make us both alone on this boat in the middle of nowhere.

"I don't want to be alone," I murmur.

He sighs loudly and relaxes his shoulders. He applies two clamps to the helm and turns to me. "You're not alone, Layla."

His eyes are red and his cheeks tearstained. I've never seen a man so upset in my life. Having to be the one comforting him feels alien. I want to take away his pain. Before I can overthink the situation anymore, I wrap my arms around him, squeezing his chest into mine.

Unbidden tears crest over the bottom of my eyes and stream down my face. All of our pain is unleashed together as he reciprocates my embrace. I can feel his heaving breaths giving away his crying, though he makes no other sounds.

"I'm so sorry," he whispers.

"Stop. No more apologies. Just hold me."

Without letting me go, we shuffle to sit on one of the two benches that enclose the helm and let a peaceful silence fall between us. The billowing sails and the sound of the hull skipping over the water have a tranquilizing effect, helping me relax and just enjoy our proximity. With my nose pressed into his chest, I inhale deeply, taking in his intoxicating scent. *I've missed his smell.*

"Mmmmm," I groan quietly. I wish I could bottle the way he smells and keep it with me always.

"What?"

"Nothing. Just enjoying you," I mutter.

He kisses the top of my head. "I missed you so much."

"Ditto."

"I bet I missed you more," he says, his voice sounding a little less solemn.

There he is! He's coming back to me! My sweet, confident, happy Adonis is coming back. Just that little lift in his voice is enough to give me hope. My heart swells and I squeeze him tighter.

I smile against his firm, heavenly smelling body. "No. I missed you more."

"I thought you were mad at me."

"I am—I mean, I was." I relinquish my hold on him and sit up straight. I gingerly hold his face in my hands. His face is stubbly, yet still so soft. Gazing into his eyes, he looks years older. Lack of sleep and sadness has taken away some of their vibrancy and has left behind dark circles and little lines in the corners. "I can't stay mad at you," I admit, and I plant a chaste kiss on his gorgeous lips.

He gasps in surprise and pulls me back into him.

We stay wrapped in each other's arms for only a few minutes, but it feels like forever. A wonderful forever in our little bubble of a world that exists when we're together and no one or anything else matters.

Our blissful paradise is broken by my stomach loudly growling at me. I realize then I never ate after getting up; I only had that swig of orange juice.

After five days I am seriously starting to get sick of freeze-dried beef stew, rice, and beans. There are only so many ways to make rice and beans, and with limited spices and no fresh meat, it's getting old—fast. The seas have been fair so far. Adonis says we are getting closer to the Strait of Panama, but I have yet to see any sign of land. It will probably take us months before we get to Australia. That is, if I can stay sane aboard this damn boat for that long.

My cough is almost entirely gone now, and the salty sea air is very therapeutic. If only it could cure the tension between us. We have reconnected some, but it feels more familial than romantic. We've discussed so much, but I still feel the gaping maw between us. I long to be with him, but I can't seem to bridge that distance.

He emptied his bank accounts before coming to break me out of prison. Over four hundred thousand Ameros were given to my family and stashed in different places all over the house—under floorboards, in the walls, in the attic—so that if anyone came looking, they could never find it all. Adonis also bought Daisy a pretty porcelain doll with curly red hair and a sun hat for her birthday and told her it was from me. That was sweet of him.

My family is financially secure, and they know what we're doing. He only told my mom, but still, it gives me a little peace of mind. I'm sure Mom has been crying her eyes out every night since I've left, and Daisy along with her. I miss them. I even miss my annoying brothers. Who would have thought? I miss feeling loved by my family.

I'm no longer bleeding and I'm less sore than I was a few days ago, but I am still afraid to have him touch me intimately. I want him, but then I don't. I wonder if we'll ever be as close as we once were. *He's all I've got now. What choice do I have?* We've sailed off into the sunset together to seek a new life in a new land. I'm going to have to learn to love him again. I have no one else. I need to put aside my pride and self-righteous indignation and try. *It would be easier if he came to bed. The sunset was hours ago, and yet he is still up there at the helm.*

I climb the ladder to the deck. The sky is stunning. There isn't a single cloud, and the stars are brighter than I have ever seen. *Wow! Were they always this bright?* The galactic center is like a sparkling necklace in the night. Even though it is a new moon, the sky isn't dark and brooding but rather breathtaking and full of light.

The waters are calm as the stars reflect off them, making terrestrial blinking twins below who dance on the gentle waves. A shiver runs through me, and I wiggle to shake it off. It can get pretty cool out here on the open water at night.

The sails are already down for the night yet Adonis still stands on deck, leaning against the top of the cabin, looking out into the vastness of ocean and sky. *Is he up here to stay away from me?* I can't think of anything I said earlier today that could have this effect on him. Maybe it's because I won't let things be the way they were. I want to want that closeness with him again, but it just feels weird. *I have to try,* I remind myself.

"Hey. What are you looking at?" I say softly, trying to coax him out of his trance.

"The world. Just thinking," he answers, not shifting his gaze from the horizon.

"It's beautiful out here. I never thought the stars could be so bright!"

He turns to me, the left side of his face slightly illuminated by the small amount of light leaking from the cabin. In the eerie glow of the half-light and the stars he looks heavenly, as if from another world, mysterious and perfect.

He takes three paces and stands almost too close to me. "Would you like to watch the stars with me?"

"Sure," I answer, my voice so weak from sudden indescribable feelings that it's barely audible.

I shakily lie down on one of the benches by the helm and turn my eyes skyward. A shiver runs up my spine again, and I can't tell if I'm really cold or if it is just nerves. I do want to be with him as we were; it's just hard for some stupid reason. I want to snap him out of his introspection and melancholy. *I need to bring him back.* His habit of staring off aimlessly all the time is starting to worry me. I wonder what it is that he thinks about when he does that. Does he even think at all when he does that or just space out to stop feeling things? I wish I could stop feeling, but I can't.

"I can't wait to see the stars in the Southern Hemisphere," Adonis declares, interrupting my thoughts.

"The stars are different there?" I thought they were the same everywhere. *Space doesn't change, does it?*

"You can see different stars there that you can't back home. Just a different view, like looking out the back window instead of the front. Same space, different view," he says simply, as if this should be obvious to me.

"That makes sense, I guess."

Not really, but whatever.

"You'll see it soon. A few weeks more, maybe, before we get south of the equator."

"And how soon until we reach Australia?"

"Three or four months."

I sit up quickly and gape at him. "Four months? Do you think I can eat nothing but freeze-dried food and beans for four months?! Please tell me you brought fishing gear."

He props himself up on his elbow as he lies on the bench across from me and chuckles at my exasperated response. "Yes, I have fishing gear. I'll leave all that gross fish butchering to your expertise."

"Squeamish?" I tease.

"No. I deal with human bodies for a living, and you used to deal with dead fish for a living. Besides, I have to steer the boat. You need to make yourself useful somehow," he jokes.

I lie down hard in exasperated annoyance, my head causing the vinyl upholstered cushioning of the bench to whistle. *Smart-ass.* At least he is engaging me and in a good mood.

The rocking of the boat combined with my view of the serene sky makes my eyelids heavy. I feel relaxed and content, maybe even happy at this moment. My eyes start to droop, but I snap them back open in surprise.

"Did you see that?" I almost shout at him as I point to the sky. *A shooting star!*

"Yeah. Make a wish."

"A wish?"

"Yes. You're supposed to make a wish when you see a meteor."

"That seems rather silly. Wishes, prayers, magic, and such things are just myths," I admonish him, shaking my head. *Ridiculous!*

"Don't knock it till you've tried it," he replies in a singsong tone. "I already made mine."

"Did you, now?"

"Yup."

"Ok fine. I wish for—"

"No! In your head. You can't say it out loud, or it won't come true," he scolds me.

"You are ridiculous!"

I shut my eyes tight and think of the one thing I would want more than anything right now. *I wish my dad were here.* A stupid wish, one that could never come true.

I breathe a loud sigh as I think fondly of my dad. He was always so happy, even though he had a crappy job and we lived in a fucked-up society. At least he made me think he was happy. If he wasn't, he never showed it.

"What did you wish for?" Adonis interrupts my reverie.

"You said I couldn't say it out loud."

"I know, but I'm curious. Tell me." His voice sounds so young, like a little kid asking what they're getting for their birthday. It's cute.

I stare up at the sky, longing for another shooting star, as a grin spreads across my face for a moment before fading. I can't tell him what I actually wished for; that would take away the good mood he's in right now.

"A blanket," I lie. "It's cold out here."

In a flash, he's off his bench and vanishes through the hatch. I sit up, resting my elbows on my knees, my head in my hands, bemused. *Is he just going to leave me up here all alone?* The lights inside the cabin go out. *Did he just go to sleep without saying anything? Ass.*

I sigh and flop down on my back on the bench again, closing my eyes. If he is going to keep acting like this, I don't know what I'm going to do. Happy one minute and standoffish the next. *I'll just sleep out here. I don't have the energy to go down there and discuss this crap.*

The hatch flies open loudly, the door banging against the deck. I stand up instinctively, startled and ready to act. Out of the hatch comes a dark bundle followed by Adonis. I take a deep breath to calm my adrenaline rushed mind and shake my head. *A blanket.*

He takes the blanket and lies back down on his bench across from me. I thought he had brought it up for me, but he's wrapped himself in it. *What am I going to do with this man?*

"You cold?" I ask, making the sarcasm in my voice obvious.

"No. You said you wished for a blanket. Well, here it is. See? Wishes can come true," he muses.

"I meant for me, not for you."

"You didn't specify."

"I would think that's obvious."

What a brat! I can tell he's enjoying this. *What does he think I'm going to do? Beg for him to give it to me?*

"What about my wish?" he chimes in.

"What about it?"

"I'll grant yours if you grant mine," he teases. I can almost hear the smirk on his face.

Oh boy, here we go. I roll my eyes though it's too dark for him to see me do so. *What did he wish for? For me to throw myself at him?* I do prefer his playful mood now as opposed to his melancholy. I guess it can't hurt to play along a little bit.

"What was your wish?" I ask, exasperation evident in my tone.

"For you to join me."

"I've been here the whole time."

He scoots over to the far end of his bench and pats the side closest to me loudly with his hand. He props himself up on his elbow and flashes me his dazzling smile, so dazzling that I can see it clearly in the dim light of the stars. "I mean over here. We can share the blanket," he cloys.

Is he ever laying it on thick! His emotions have gone back and forth so much tonight that I'm bound to get whiplash. *I have to try, I have to try,* I go on repeating the mantra in my head.

"Okay," I say with extra enthusiasm. "Scoot over."

I slide onto the bench, pressed up against him yet still dangling a little bit off the edge. He tries to scoot over more, but it just makes it worse.

"On the deck?" he suggests.

"Why not just go inside? I don't want to lie on the floor."

"The deck," he corrects me. "And I want to watch the stars while we cuddle."

"Fine," I concede.

I sit on the deck—basically the floor—and he joins me, spreading the blanket and then sitting on it.

"Get up for a second."

I comply as he spreads it out flat, covering the deck (floor) between the two benches in front of the helm.

"This doesn't look very comfortable," I complain.

"I'll get some pillows."

And with that statement, he is back down the hatch, returning promptly with two pillows. He lays them next to each other and I rest my head on one, trying to get comfortable, but a wooden deck is not a very forgiving surface for your back.

"Better?"

"I'm still cold. I wanted to cover myself with the blanket, not lie down on it."

"What if I keep you warm?" he whispers into my ear. His head is turned to the side on his pillow so that he is almost touching my ear with his lips.

I shiver with feelings of arousal at his proximity and his hot breath in my ear. Staring at the stars above and with him next to me like this, it would almost be perfect if we weren't in this place because we were running away. If only this were a normal pleasure cruise, just a young couple enjoying their time together without a worry in the world. A beautiful and romantic scenario in the wrong setting.

I nod almost imperceptibly and he scoots closer, draping his arm across my abdomen. He makes a deep inhale and exhale and feigns a casual stretch, one of his legs just happening to end up over mine.

"I've missed you," he whispers.

Oh, Adonis! I've missed you too!

"I know," I whisper back. It's all I can manage to admit.

"Do you know? Without you in my life, it was like the Earth stopped turning. Time just went on and on, interminably, slow and agonizing," he murmurs, his head now on my chest.

He gives me a slight squeeze and my heart swells with joy. *I want what we had back. I want him. I want us. I want a lot of things.*

"I missed you too." I stroke my fingers through his messy hair, long overdue for a haircut.

He quickly rolls on top of me, set off by my touch, and gazes at me intently with desire and need. My senses heighten; I want and need him so much. Desire flows through my veins as the hairs on my arms stand on end.

"Let me make love to you under the stars," he whispers in a husky voice.

Those words light a fire in me, and I pull his face into mine and kiss him deeply. He returns my kiss with fervor. I feel his need, his love for me, and I become lost in him, my previous shivers and cold sensations now far away.

I flinch slightly as he moves his hands up under my shirt near my navel and he pulls back. He looks searchingly into my eyes, his eyes touched by pain and rejection.

"I'm fine," I insist. "Please."

I grab his hand and place it back on my stomach, resisting my reflex to pull away from him. *Try harder, damn it!* I scold myself.

Reassured, he kisses me again as he runs his hands along my

stomach and up to my breasts. I squirm and try to stifle a moan, but a small one escapes.

"Mmmm."

"Don't hold back, Layla. We can be as loud as we want now. Only the sea can hear us as the stars watch in wonder," he whispers into my neck.

I've never heard anything so beautiful and sexy in my entire life, and the floodgates that were holding back my last bit of self-control burst. I grab at the back of his shirt and pull it up and over his head, revealing his stunning chest with just that little bit of chest hair. I rake my fingers down his back, causing him to let out a primal groan.

As I've been only wearing his T-shirts and panties since I've been on the boat, there isn't much to remove. There's no point in getting dressed every day; it's not like anyone else is going to see me, and this is just so comfortable.

He runs his hands up my bare legs, stopping at my panties briefly before tugging them off. He rolls off me only for a moment and swiftly discards his denim shorts.

"I love you so much, Layla Mason. You have no idea," he gasps as he rubs his hands over the area that my panties were covering.

"I think I might have a clue," I giggle as I trail my fingers along his boxers, tracing the obvious physical manifestation of his feelings.

He grips my hand and squeezes it, making me grip him *there.*

"Oh, fuck!" he gasps.

I pull his mouth back to mine, and my lips and tongue greedily consume his. With one hand I pull down his boxers, releasing him. He moves his legs between mine and in one slow, gentle motion, lock and key reunite. My heart soars as we unleash our tension and love under the twinkling night sky.

CHAPTER TWENTY-TWO

IT'S TOO BRIGHT. THE SUNLIGHT casts an orange glow in my vision through my closed eyelids, and a light wind tickles my face as I will my heavy eyelids to open. It must be midmorning, like eight or something based on the angle of the sunlight. The ends of the blanket under us are pulled around us like we're a burrito, and Adonis is snuggled up behind me, one of his legs wrapped over both of mine. My shoulder aches from sleeping on the hard deck. I groan slightly as I wriggle myself free of his cocooning embrace and sit up to stretch out my limbs and yawn.

Last night was magical, but my shoulder and back are paying the price for it now. We should have just gone back inside afterward, but I was so tired and he wanted to sleep under the stars, so I just went along with the idea. Even with my body aching from the uncomfortable sleeping arrangement, I can't stop smiling. What he did—no, what we have … it's beautiful. Of all the times we have made love before, that was by far the best. It just felt so right. I felt free. Free to express my love and receive it without having to worry about being caught.

My moving around rouses my sweet, sweet man from his sleep. As I sit up, stretching my arms behind my back, trying to pop my shoulder, he nuzzles his head against my hip. I run my fingers through his messy bedhead/sex hair and his eyes open lazily. They are luminous and look happy, a welcome change to the sadness that had been emanating from them lately.

"Good morning," he mumbles, a wide smile spreading across his face.

It is a good morning. Usually when people say "Good morning," it's just because that is what you are supposed to say; it could be a totally shitty morning, and you still greet someone by saying "Good morning." I hate such mindless chitchat. It's just a bunch of lies anyway, except for this morning.

"Good morning. Do you want breakfast?"

"Sure. Gotta love those dehydrated eggs," he laughs.

I bend down and give him a quick kiss on his forehead before I get up, taking my pillow with me into the cabin. I toss the pillow onto our bed, half tempted to join it and sleep a little longer on a soft surface, but I can take a nap after we eat. I need to get Adonis fed so he can get us on the move again.

I pull one of the numerous pouches of dehydrated scrambled eggs from the cupboard and dump its contents into a bowl, add hot water, and stir. I miss being able to truly cook. Maybe when we stop for lunch time, I can try doing some fishing, though I don't know how much luck I'll have with the lure Adonis brought. I'm used to fishing with real bait, not that fake crap. Fish are stupid, but not that stupid. Why go after fake food?

Adonis scoots by me with the blanket and his pillow and then joins me in the "galley," as he calls it. It's a damn kitchen. Small, but still a kitchen. I don't see why things being on a boat need a different name. The floor is now the "deck," the bathroom, the "head," and the bedroom is called a "berthing area." I laughed like crazy when he called it that.

"Why the fuck would they call it that? Men don't give birth!" I laughed.

"It's spelled with an *E*. B-e-r-t-h, not b-i-r-t-h."

"Even so, it still sounds stupid. I'm not calling it that. It's a bed-room."

He is really into his technical terms with this whole sailing thing. I don't get all these maritime names for crap, but I play along with him for all of them except for the bedroom.

I place two small plates of eggs on the table and take a spot on the bench. At least he had the sense to stock some spices and con-diments. I don't think I could eat these eggs without pepper and Tabasco sauce.

He takes the spot next to me and drenches his food in Tabasco.

"You shouldn't use so much," I scold him. "We need that bottle to last."

"When we get to South America, we'll dock for a day or two so we can refuel the generators and buy a few things. Don't worry. I'm betting that they have much spicier stuff there than Tabasco."

"Great! I can't wait to walk on dry land again!"

"You can't leave the boat, Layla. They have the same laws there as they do back home. If someone saw us together and got a glimpse of your tattoo, they would haul you off. We can't take that kind of risk."

"I can cover it up," I counter.

"No. You're to stay inside the cabin unless I say otherwise."

"You expect me to stay trapped in here like a prisoner? I've al-ready been there, done that, thank you very much," I snap.

He grabs my face and turns it toward his. He looks forlorn and angry at the same time. "I mean it. I'm not losing you again."

I want to argue the subject and get him to see things my way, but the look in his eyes extinguishes my rebellious behaviors. I hate seeing him like this. I want him to be happy, and making him have to think about the possibility of something happening to me again clearly torments him.

"Fine," I concede. "I'll stay hidden away while you do whatever."

"Thank you." He smiles ever so slightly and plants a light kiss on my cheek.

He places his empty plate in the sink, grabs a glass of water, and returns to the bench to sit next to me.

"Aren't you going to hoist the sails there, captain?" I tease.

"I thought maybe you would like to help me. It would be good for you to learn too. Or at least be able to assist me or take over if I need a break or something."

I put another forkful of food in my mouth and chew slowly, delaying my ability to respond. I don't know the first thing about sailing; I'd probably sink us. He puts way too much faith in me. Sailing is his thing, not mine. His boat, too.

He looks at me expectantly as I chew. It's annoying.

"Well?" he asks when I swallow.

"I don't think that's such a good idea. I don't know anything about sailing. I don't want to break anything."

"You won't break anything. Come on! It'll be fun," he coaxes. "Just don't knock yourself or me overboard with the boom and we'll be fine."

"Knock you overboard!" I squeak. "That can happen? No, I can't do this!"

"If it scares you that much, you can just stay down here. Maybe another day."

He lets out a long sigh. I can tell he's disappointed, but I'm sure he would be more disappointed if he got stranded in the ocean because of my stupidity. I don't even have the first clue of how to turn the damn boat around. He'd be shark bait.

I go to the "the head" and freshen up a bit. As I brush my teeth, I can't help but notice how different I look. Maybe it's because I am finally feeling happy for the first time in what seems like forever. My cheeks have color, my eyes are a little brighter. Last night was just what I needed—what *we* needed. My pre-Adonis self would spit at the idea of me needing someone, but I know better now. I *do* need someone. I can't do it all on my own. I need him.

Still tired from our lack of sleeping last night and fighting a stiff back, I crawl into bed for a much needed few extra hours of sleep.

The silence is eerie. Even the waves have stopped lapping at the side of the boat.

"Adonis?" I call out into the cabin. No reply. I call out again with the same results.

I quickly get to my feet and ascend the ladder to the deck. It's deserted. *Oh no!* The winds pick up suddenly, howling in my ears.

"Adonis? Where are you?" I try to scream above the wind.

In a panic, I carefully inch along the deck under the sails while I call for him, but he isn't anywhere. Tears prick the corners of my eyes as I scream for him. I lean over the starboard side to look into the water when I slip and plunge headfirst into the ocean.

I wake to the sound of thunder and myself screaming. I'm dripping in sweat. *Oh, thank goodness!* It was just a dream—a nightmare, to be precise. Adonis bursts through the bedroom door and quickly embraces me.

"Shhh. You're okay. It's just a little thunder," he says soothingly.

I pull out of his hug and grab his face, kissing him aggressively, making sure he's real. His mouth is slack with surprise momentarily before reciprocating my fervor. Needing desperately to breathe, I relinquish my possession of him, resting my forehead against his as I try to calm my breathing.

"I wouldn't have taken you for someone so frightened by a little storm," he breathes.

I shake my head. "It wasn't that. I had the most horrible dream, but I'm fine now. You're here."

He gently kisses my cheek. "Of course I'm here."

A loud crack of thunder snaps me out of my nonsense over a stupid dream. *A storm at sea! Could it be a hurricane? It's the right time of year for that.*

"How bad is it out there?"

"Nothing we can't handle. Just a bit of wind and lightning." The confidence in his voice is reassuring. He at least sounds like he's dealt with a storm on the water before; whether or not he has, I don't want to ask.

"Not a hurricane, then? How can you be sure?"

"It just kind of popped up. It formed quickly. Just a passing summer storm."

"What about the sails? We're the tallest thing out on the water. What if we get hit by lightning? We're sitting ducks out here!"

"This baby has a lightning protection system. We're fine," he insists. "If we get hit, it will just hit the mast and travel down the lines to ground with the water. Stop worrying."

"What if we get blown off course?" I can't stop coming up with new concerns. *We could capsize! I don't want to die out here and be fish food.* My panic about the storm is perpetuating my already existing anxiety from my nightmare. I hate when I can't shake my unconscious emotions after I'm awake. Why can't the weather just give us a break? Like we haven't had enough difficulties in our lives. Would a few months of perfect sailing weather be too much to ask?

"We're heaving to. We shouldn't get too far off course."

I shake my head and stare at him with bemusement. *What the hell is that? This turbulent water might just make me heave!*

"It's a sailing maneuver to keep us from going too far or capsizing," he explains, answering my unspoken question.

"So, we'll be okay?"

"Yes," he says, his voice steady and calm.

I'm a cocktail of emotions. I usually love thunderstorms, but the thought of being so vulnerable on the open ocean frightens me. Inside a building I feel protected, but out here it feels dangerous. At the same time, I'm also relieved—relieved that he didn't fall overboard and is alive, here, and mine. I'm also strangely turned on. In short, I'm a tangled ball of crazy right now. The thunder and lightning light up my desire like they do the sky.

"Are you positive we'll be okay?" I ask again, just to be super sure.

"Yes," he says, exasperated, rolling his eyes. "We'll be fine. I've weathered worse than this on weekend trips."

With that extra bit of reassurance, I pounce. I shove his shoulders, causing him to fall onto the bed, and straddle him. He is gaping at me, confused and stunned, I think. I lean down, grab his face with both hands, and kiss him savagely. When I release him, he is slack-jawed and panting. Another crack of thunder roars close by and it's like a signal for me. I scoot down onto his legs and unbutton his cut-off jean shorts.

He sits up and grabs my shoulders. "Are you okay?" His voice is full of concern. He probably thinks I've totally lost my mind.

"I'm fantastic," I pant. "I just want you." I tug at his zipper and his eyes widen.

"You woke up screaming. Are you sure?"

"Oh, for fuck's sake, Adonis! Yes, I'm sure. I want you. I need you. Now!" I need this to feel better, to feel grounded back in reality. Physical intimacy with him soothes me, and I need some soothing right now.

I scoot off him to stand at the foot of the bed and remove his shorts and boxers in one pull, exposing the truth.

"You want it, too," I whisper.

A bright flash lights up the cabin and the thunder quickly follows, shaking the walls a little. *Damn, Mother Nature is hot when she's bitchy!* I flick the lights off, and only the faint light from the gray sky penetrates the room. I want only the lightning to illuminate us. Another bolt flashes and I briefly see his stunned face and glorious nudity.

I crawl back into bed, lying on top of him. I kiss his chest as I run my hands teasingly across his hips.

"What has gotten into you?" he pants.

"Can't I just want you?" I lightly bite one of his nipples, and he practically levitates off the bed.

"Ahh! What the hell?" he hollers.

Astonished, and a bit offended, I sit up abruptly, straddling his hips. "You don't like it?"

Is he rejecting me?

"No. I don't not like it. It's just … different. You're never like this."

"We've never experienced a thunderstorm together," I whisper as I return to soft kisses. *What a baby!*

He laughs and another bolt flashes, letting me glimpse his face. He looks relieved. *Oh, thank goodness!*

"That's what this is, huh? You have some fetish or whatever for storms?"

"Mm-hmm," I mumble into his toned abs as I slowly make my way downward. "I've always wanted to do it in a thunderstorm. A fantasy of mine," I reveal.

"Well, who am I to deny you your fantasies and dreams?" He grabs my arms and pulls, flattening me along him so that my face is up against his. "I'm all about making your wishes and dreams come true from now on," he whispers, then slowly kisses me.

I nip at his bottom lip.

"Ow! Play nice," he admonishes.

"We did slow and lovey last night. In my fantasy, it's rough."

"Rough, huh?"

He swiftly flips me over and is on top of me. I squeal with delight. *Yes!* Intense light flashes through the room, and the roaring of thunder is quick to follow with an almost deafening crack. In the light, I glimpse his eyes. They are alight with amusement as he gives me a quick grin before everything goes dark again.

Without warning, he collides into me and I cry out in surprise, pleasure, a little bit of pain, but I can handle it.

The rocking of the boat plus our movements makes it feel like we are physically shaking the earth beneath us, only it's water, but it's a nice illusion.

All too soon he cries out and goes rigid, momentarily crushing me as he collapses onto me. *Damn it!* It was still good, but oh well. That's how it goes sometimes.

He rolls off of me and drapes an arm across me, his breathing still heavy.

"I'm sorry," he pants.

"What? Why?" I ask, bewildered.

"Too quick," he sighs.

"Don't worry about it. There will always be another storm," I reassure him.

I turn my head to the side and kiss his nose. Whether or not he gets me there doesn't matter in comparison to how happy I feel just to have him. I love him.

"Thank you for indulging me."

"It was my pleasure," he murmurs into my neck. It tickles. I giggle and try to scoot away from his face. "Are you ticklish on your neck, too?" he teases.

Oh no! The feet were bad enough!

A low, rolling thunder creeps through the cabin. The storm is moving away, I think. It's not as loud, and I didn't see any lightning.

"No," I lie.

"Are you sure?" he murmurs into my neck again, causing me to squirm though I try hard to stifle my reaction. "I think you're lying to me," he teases.

I feel his lips spread into a mischievous grin right before he rolls on top of me and unleashes a tickle assault on my neck and collarbone.

I haven't had any luck with fishing out in the deep waters of the middle of nowhere. However, we can finally see land. We're almost at the southern tip of North America. The last twenty days have been very routine: eating more freeze-dried food, trying to fish to no avail, and making love.

I would be completely content with everything if it weren't for the food situation. I can't wait until we dock and Adonis procures us some real food. The mini refrigerator is empty now, not that it had much to start with. He couldn't let the generator run to keep things cold while he was preparing for us to leave, so all that we had was what he could bring a few hours before he broke me out of prison. Hopefully, we get enough perishable food to fill it to capacity. I could kill for some milk or cheese.

My fishing pole dangles lazily in my hands. The most action I've gotten on this thing has been from seaweed.

"Nothing, huh?"

"Nope. Stupid fish."

"You would think they'd be more polite. You're the birthday girl, after all," Adonis chuckles as he sits down next to me, dangling his legs over the bow.

Oh yeah—I'm old today. It keeps slipping my mind. *Twenty.* I'm no longer a teenager. Time has been such a blur since that night I was hauled off. At times it has gone infinitely slow, and others it's just been a whirlwind, causing everything to blur together, but time is supposedly relative. That's an understatement if I ever heard one. *Relative—ha! I feel like I've aged years in the last few months.*

"I don't think fish care about birthdays."

He wraps his right arm around me, pulling me close to him.

"You don't seem to care either. Why not?"

I shrug. "I haven't cared since my dad died. Time may as well have just stopped then for me anyway. Every year I age is a reminder of how long he's been gone—almost six years now." I let out a long sigh and rest my head on his shoulder.

"Don't you think he'd want you to be happy?"

I've never thought of that. "I guess. I don't know."

"I think you've been sad long enough, my beautiful girl. It's going to give you wrinkles," he teases.

"Well, I am officially an old lady now, you know."

"My old lady. Happy birthday." He kisses my temple and helps me to my feet.

I reel in my empty line and carefully make my way to the stern, depositing my pole on one of the benches as I watch Adonis hoist and reposition the sails to get us moving again. He thinks we should reach land by nightfall.

CHAPTER TWENTY-THREE

THE GPS READS N 15°22'18.31 by W 85°42'00.59 as we prepare to dock. Adonis is on the deck while I hide in the cabin, the curtains over the portholes closed to conceal my presence. It's barely still light outside as I hear a thump against the side of the boat. I risk a small peek out of the bottom corner of the porthole. I can see Adonis silhouetted against the twilight, mooring the boat to the dock as a Hispanic-looking man approaches him.

The conversation is impossible to make out. I can only hear a few sounds and I don't read lips, but even if I did I think they're speaking Spanish, which I suck at. *I hope they let us stay here. What if they were to turn us away?* Watching the exchange between Adonis and the mystery man of the docks is making me more anxious than if I weren't able to see anything. I sink down onto the couch and stare at my fidgeting hands. *Please, please let things be okay. We need more fuel for the generator; we'll never make it to Australia if we can't get more here.*

After what feels like an eternity, I hear the lock on the hatch click, and I rush to the bottom of the ladder. The hatch opens, and Adonis beams down at me.

"Catch!"

I react before I can even think, catching a plastic bottle that he drops at me. He comes down the ladder, pulling the hatch shut behind him.

I examine the clear cold bottle with bemused interest. I can't read the Spanish writing, but it looks like some sort of soda. I haven't had soda in years! I grin up at Adonis, beyond excited.

"Cola," he says, confirming my suspicion.

"Where did you get it?" I ask, my voice filled with wonder. Soda was a very rare treat when I was growing up. *Do they just have it all over the place here?*

"Fernando sells them in his store."

I stare at him with my telltale confused look, my right eyebrow raised higher than the other, my lips scrunched together.

"The guy I paid for us to dock here for a few days," he adds, noticing my confusion.

The realization hits me suddenly that this must be a Normie area. They never sold soda out in the open in the GI part of town back home. Good thing it's dark, and he didn't see me peeking out.

"How long are we going to stay?"

The real question in my mind was, *How long can I stand being cooped up in this cabin?*

"I think that three days should be good. Long enough to rest up a bit and restock what we need. Are you okay with that?"

I dealt with prison for two months. I can do three days.

"Yeah, it's fine."

Adonis puts two cups on the little table and motions me over to him. Grabbing the soda from me, he twists the top, causing the bottle to make a hissing sound, and pours the bubbling liquid into the cups.

"To the birthday girl," he says, raising his glass in the air. "Cheers."

I mirror his gesture as he takes a sip. I quickly follow suit, indulging in the rare treat. *Damn, this is good!* I'm tempted to gulp it down, but I want to make it last. An appreciative moan escapes me, and I smack my lips after another sip.

"So . . . what do you want to do now, birthday girl?" Adonis ask, loudly placing his empty cup down on the table.

"I already told you I don't care for birthdays, Adonis," I mutter with my cup still on my lips, about to take another sip.

"What if I said I had a present for you?"

"I thought this was my present." I hold up the now empty soda bottle.

"No, no, no," he laughs. "That just happened to be available. I would have bought that if it wasn't your birthday. I mean a real present."

"You don't need to get me anything. I have all I need here with me." I take a step toward him, placing my cup on the table. "I have you."

"That you do," he murmurs as he bends to kiss my forehead.

He grasps my hand and suddenly drops to his knees in front of me. *What the hell?* I try to pull him back up, but he resists, holding my hand firmly in his.

"Adonis? What are you doing?" My voice rises in pitch from my panic. *Is his leg hurt? Why won't he stand?!*

"Giving you me—forever."

"By kneeling on the floor?"

What is he—oh no! No! My brain conjures up an ancient memory, a story my mom told me about Grandma and Grandpa. About how they used to do things in the olden days before the Cleansing. Back when more than just the elite had the ability to offer such a grand gesture to the one they love. *Is he asking me to marry him?! I think I might puke.*

"Layla Suzanne Mason, I love you more than I can say. You are my reason for living, and I don't want to spend another day in my life without you. When we get to Australia, will you do me the honor of being my wife?" he almost begs with a somber sincerity that I have never heard from him before.

SARA GROVER

I stare at him dumbstruck, my mouth hanging open like I'm trying to catch flies. I don't know what to think or feel. *Is he serious? I love him, but we've only had a few months together. Why do we even need to get married? Who cares?*

I shake my head, trying to clear the cloudiness from my brain so I can make a coherent sentence. I look down at him. His eyes are anxious and burning into mine, silently begging me for an answer.

"Adonis … I don't know what to say," I whisper breathlessly. *Yes, you do! Say yes, damn it!*

He is the only man aside from my dad that I have ever really loved. Gavin doesn't count; that fucker played with my emotions. I know Adonis loves me back, but why do we need some legal document to prove it? *Suppose they won't let us marry in Australia. Then what?*

"You could say yes." He squeezes my hand slightly and then releases it.

He digs around in his shorts pocket with his right hand and pulls out a little black box. *What in the world?* As he opens the small hinged box I gasp in shock and awe, covering my mouth with my hands as I sink to the floor, my legs no longer able to hold my weight. I've never seen anything so beautiful. *A real diamond?* I've heard the stories of how things used to be, but I never imagined I would ever have one. *A real wedding ring! Only Normies can afford such things. Well, duh, he is one, just not a normal one.* Carefully removing the sparkling sight from the box, he holds it between his thumb and index finger, offering it to me.

"You're killing me here, Layla. Will you marry me?" His voice is soft and anxious.

Tears prick the corners of my eyes. I'm overwhelmed with feelings of inadequacy and love. I love him, I really do, but he can do so much better than me. Who is to say he won't meet some beautiful, non-genetically screwed-up girl when we reach our destination and leave me? He could do so much better than me.

"Are you sure?"

"I've never been surer of anything in my life," he affirms.

"We're so young and ... and you're ... you! Look at you! You can do so much better than me."

He grabs my left hand, and I am unable and unwilling to refuse him. He is my dream come true—my happy ending. I would like nothing more than to be worthy of having such a man be mine forever, but what will happen when this fairy-tale journey ends and we have to deal with reality?

"Layla, look at me."

I comply, raising my head from my downward gaze of self-loathing to meet his.

"I. Love. You," he states emphatically, punctuating each word.

"I love you too, but—"

"No buts! I don't give a shit about this genetic garbage! I love you, and I want this more than I have ever wanted anything in my life."

His statement floors me. *He can't be in his right mind! There are millions of girls better suited for him.*

"What if you change your mind after we get there? Find someone better?" I ask, half hoping for him to say that he had never thought of that and take the ring back, rescinding his proposal. Of course, I would be utterly devastated if he did, but I always feel like I have to test him, make sure he really wants a genetically fucked-up former prostitute and drug addict. I'd rather him come to his senses now than to lead me on for years and then leave me.

"I abandoned everything I had to be with you. Do you think that little of me? That I'm that fickle? You're it for me. I wouldn't have done all of this if you weren't," he declares passionately.

"Okay," I give him a shy smile. I'm in such a state of shock and disbelief that I can't figure out anything else to say.

"Is that a yes?" he asks, his voice higher pitched than normal.

I nod in the affirmative, and his eyes and smile are so bright and alive with joy that they could light up a city.

He shakily slides the ring onto my finger. *Gosh, it's heavy!* As soon as the ring is on, he squeezes me to him in an almost suffocating hug. I can feel the joy radiating off of him, and it's infectious.

I throw my arms around his neck and smile from ear to ear as I giggle with glee. I raise my left hand up over his shoulder and hold it out so I can see my ring from where my head is nestled between his neck and shoulder. *Wow!* One large diamond on a gold band. *Simple, yet elegant.* The band fits perfectly, but the diamond looks way too big for my tiny hand.

He gently pulls me out of our embrace, interrupting my wandering thoughts. His eyes are shining as if he's about to cry, but I know it's not from sorrow. He is glowing with love and joy, and I love that I can make him feel this way.

He moves backward, taking me with him as he settles into the couch. He pulls me into his lap, my back against his abdomen, and we cuddle, my head resting on the arm of the little couch. I toy with my new ring, twirling it around on my finger as I try to get the diamond to sit precisely in the center of my finger. The large stone keeps tilting slightly to the side, probably because the stone is so massive and gravity is making it want to fall over every time that I try to set it straight. I continue this idle fidgeting for I don't know how long, mentally taking in every facet of this symbol of our love and marveling at how it sparkles so brightly even in the dim lights of the cabin. Little specks of light dance on the walls as I move it around. *I could probably blind someone with this in the sunlight.*

"So . . . do you like it?" Adonis asks apprehensively.

I grab the arm of the couch to pull myself upright. "When did you get this?"

He strokes my cheekbone lazily with his thumb. "Answer my question first."

"I love it."

He lets out a long exhale, and I can feel his body relax. "Good.

238

Your silence had me wondering there for a while."

"Okay. Now, when did you get this?" I ask again.

He laughs nervously and shakes his head. I get off of his lap and sit beside him, watching him as he fidgets.

"Well? I'm waiting," I tease.

"Layla ..." He sighs and runs his hands through his hair. "I knew I wanted to marry you the moment I saw you. I know you think I'm crazy for all that, but I can't help it."

Yes, you're crazy. Tell me something I don't know.

"Please tell me you didn't get this right after meeting me." That would just be too damn crazy. It's one thing to think you love someone right away, but to buy a ring and think of marriage? That is insanity!

"No, no, no." He closes his eyes and shakes his head.

"Okay, then when?"

"After the first time we made love," he murmurs as he stares at his twisted fingers in his lap as if he's ashamed.

Holy shit! I know I should be offended—horrified, even, that it took so little time for him to want to up and marry a girl, but I can't help but feel a little flattered. Would he have bought a ring for any girl he slept with, or just me?

"Is this the first ring you've bought for a girl?" I ask, hoping that he says yes, but mentally preparing myself for if he says no. *Please say yes.*

"Why do you think I've bought one before?" He asks, now looking at me, his eyebrows raised with suspicion.

"Just want to make sure you don't go out buying rings for every girl you slept with."

I can't even look him in the eye. I feel like such a bitch for even asking such a thing.

"No," he says flatly. "I don't."

Shit! He sounds upset.

"Why can't you just believe that there is something special about you? Just you. I can't explain it. I never feel more alive than when I'm with you. Yeah, I jumped the gun and bought a ring super early on, but I knew I wanted you forever, even then."

Why do I have a hard time believing that? I could start a list, but I'm sure I'd die of old age before I could finish it. I wish I could see myself the way that he sees me. See myself the way I see him, with love and admiration.

I shake my head a bit to shake off my self-loathing thoughts and embrace him gently. I nuzzle against his chest, and I can feel his muscles relaxing. He pulls my legs back so that they are resting beside him and my head is in his lap. He runs his hand through my hair, massaging my scalp, and it feels so good. It's a relaxing sensation, and with all that has happened today, I am unable to stop my exaggerated yawn.

"I'm sorry. This is just so new to me. I love it. I love you. It's perfect."

"Are you tired, or am I boring you?" Adonis asks playfully.

"You're never boring. I'm just sleepy. Your hands in my hair— you're going to put me to sleep in no time."

"Let's get you to bed, then."

He gently lifts my head off of his lap and scoots out from under me. I wiggle my head into the couch, too comfortable to move. Adonis gives my foot a light tug, and I pull it back and curl my legs up.

"Come on, sleepyhead. Get up," he coaxes.

I let out a loud yawn. "Just let me sleep here. I'll only be a few feet away," I mumble sleepily.

"I don't think so, baby. I'm never going to bed without you ever again."

His loving words cause a tingling warmth to spread throughout my body as if his love is a serum coursing through my veins. His love is the ultimate drug, making me feel safe and tranquil as if everything in the world is perfect when I have it, and I'm not trying to sabotage it. The feeling of serenity that he gives me makes me sleepier by the moment.

My half-conscious state is quickly interrupted. Adonis slides his arms under me, one under my head and the other behind my knees, and removes me from the couch.

"Come on, sleepyhead," he whispers again as he cradles me in his arms, his lips gently brushing my forehead in a soft kiss.

"Mmm," I groan in protest as he carries across the cabin to the bedroom.

"Oh, hush," he gently scolds as he places me on the bed.

I grab a pillow and curl up on my side, half hugging it as I bury my head in it. The bed behind me dips as Adonis gets in. He scoots over the space between us, wraps an arm around my waist, and gently pulls me toward him until my back is flush with his chest.

Can it be like this forever? Every night, sleeping in each other's arms in a state of bliss? I let out a contented sigh and wiggle my backside until it is pressed against him as well, our bodies now in full contact with each other.

The warmth of his body radiating through me is a powerful sedative. On the brink of consciousness, I am brought back by Adonis wrapping a leg over both of mine and his left hand caressing mine, gently tracing the underside of my ring.

Completely cocooned in his warmth and love, my mind soon drifts back to the brink of the peaceful nothingness of sleep.

"Forever," I barely hear Adonis whisper as the world fades away for the night.

CHAPTER TWENTY-FOUR

I RUB MY EYES AS I come out of a deep, dreamless sleep and reach out for contact with Adonis's comforting warmth, but all I feel are sheets. A sudden panic races through me and my eyes pop wide open. Pulling my legs in so I can sit up, I look wildly around our cozy little room to confirm that he's not there.

Maybe he's in the bathroom. I take a deep breath to calm myself. *He doesn't have to be next to me every time I wake up. Stop being a baby!* I scold myself. I pull the sheets off my legs and crawl to the edge of the bed by the bedroom door.

"Adonis?" I call out. "You in here?"

No answer.

I quietly walk over to the bathroom door; it's ajar, and I push it open. The room is dark and empty. I exhale loudly. In what? Relief? Relieved that some psycho or monster didn't pop out of the bathroom and kill me? I don't get why I'm so jumpy. Maybe it's the weather, but I can't shake this eerie feeling that I'm not alone, though it appears that I am.

As I quietly make my way to the kitchen, my ears are on high alert. Everything is especially loud: my breathing, my heart pounding in my ears, the rain falling outside, the water lapping against the hull. In the muted gray light, I see a paper on the table. I take in a huge gulp of air, unaware that I was holding my breath, and walk without caution to the table and pick it up.

Layla,

I didn't have the heart to wake you. You're so beautiful when you're sleeping. I went out to go shopping for food and supplies. I should be back around one. Only open the latch if you hear me knock three times. Otherwise, stay put and out of sight.

Adonis

A sigh of relief rushes from me. I clutch the note to my chest and sit down on the couch. I know that I shouldn't be so panicked all the time, but lately I just am. I can't help it. This primal fear just takes over me and all rational thought goes out the window.

The patter of the rain outside is picking up. *He's going to come back soaking wet. I hope the food will be okay if it gets wet.* Even though I know I really shouldn't, I sit up on my knees and pull the little curtain on one for the portholes to the side, just enough to watch the rain fall.

I hate having to be trapped down here, hiding. I know I told Adonis that I'd be fine—it's only for a few days—but I really can't stand it much longer. I just want to be able to stand in the rain and enjoy its cool touch on my skin, its soothing smell, and breathe the damp, rain-cooled air.

My vision blurs as I space out and stare into the distance, barely noticing the rain running down the porthole windows in little beaded tears right in front of me. I blink my eyes back into focus and check the time. The clock in the "galley" says it's after one in the afternoon, but I have no clue if that's the right time for where we are. *He should be here by now, cuddling with me as we listen to the rain.*

I turn my face back to the little window and continue my vigil, watching and waiting for his return. I'm bored out of my mind and lonely. I have nothing else to do but wait.

Finally, I see a figure in the distance running toward one of the little canopies that shelter parts of the docks. After taking a moment's rest under one, they quickly dart to another, getting closer to me each time. *It must be Adonis trying to dodge the rain.* I can't restrain my giggles. It's an act of futility trying to run through the rain and not get soaked; you might as well just walk so you don't slip and land flat on your ass.

Adonis is getting closer, though I still can't see him clearly. The rain acts like a gauze curtain, obscuring any detail. I knock on the window and wave to him to let him know that I know he's on his way in hopes that maybe he'll stop running like that. The last thing we need is for him to get hurt. Not only would it break my heart to see him in pain, but there is no way I could sail this thing on my own.

When Adonis is about twenty feet away, I realize in horror that the person I'd been watching, who I'd made noise to and waved at, is not Adonis at all! In a panic, I yank the curtain closed and run into the bedroom and close the door.

The thudding sound of feet from topside make me cower and hide under the blanket. *Why am I such a damn idiot?! He told me to stay out of sight. How could I have screwed up such a simple instruction! We're fugitives!* He can blend in with other Normies and probably not draw attention, but me, I'll stick out like a red bluebonnet.

The strange man starts pounding on the hatch door; the handle on the inside rattles violently. *Please let the lock hold! Adonis, where are you?*

A muffled, heavily accented voice fills the cabin. *"Abre ahora, señorita. Sé que estás adentro. Te veo!"*

I quiet my breathing by reducing it to tiny breaths in and out of my nose, only taking in what I need so that I don't pass out in my attempt to audibly disappear. Short, small breaths to avoid any detectable sound. All sound is amplified exponentially for me; I can hear the sound of my blood coursing through my veins like a swollen river, my heart pounding like a bass drum, the thunderous footsteps

244

from the deck, the metallic clanking of the hatch handle as the man wrestles with it. If I hear that little click that happens when it opens, I may just die from fear before he can get me.

"Abre o llamo a la policía!" the man calls out before pounding on the hatch again.

I don't know what he is saying except for *"policía"*—the cops. Escaping from prison is a surefire way to have the whole world on the lookout for you. I'm sure there is a huge prize out for my capture, and this motherfucker probably knows it.

After what seems like an eternity of attempts to get into the cabin or get me to reveal myself, the noise stops. Maybe he left to get the cops, but it could also be a trick to see if I'm dumb enough to think he left when he is just right outside, waiting for me.

Carefully, without making more than a tiny rustling noise with the fabric, I crawl out from under the covers and move silently to the bedroom door.

No matter how hard my ears strain, I can't hear anything but the slight patter of rain from outside. I need to get closer to see if I can figure out if he is still up there, waiting to ambush me. I carefully turn the knob with painful, infinite slowness, as to not cause the metal to make any clicks, and open the door slightly. Still holding the doorknob, I peek out through the small opening. All seems quiet, but I'm not convinced. It's surely a trap, but if not, I need to get out of here before the cops show up. I don't know where the hell I could run to and if I would ever see my love again, but I can't go back to prison. I'd rather die than go back to that kind of torture.

I fully open the door, my hand still holding tight to the door-knob. I slowly let it rotate back to its normal position, controlling the movement with the resistance of my wrist to prevent noise. Leaving the door open, I painstakingly walk toward the kitchen area, care-fully placing my right heel down in front of me before taking my weight to the front of my foot then repeating the movements on the left, ever so slowly moving forward, pausing between steps to listen.

As I reach the little table where we eat, noise breaks out above. Stomping and a voice coming from the docks shouting toward the boat mixed with the patter of rain and the small waves sloshing against the boat. The sneaky bastard above shouts something back in rapid Spanish that I can't make out.

The sudden activity causes me to draw in a loud gasp or air and I drop to the floor, instinctively taking cover under the little table like a stupid kid, as if hiding here could keep me safe!

The second voice, also speaking Spanish but not as fluently, I recognize as Adonis's.

My stupidity has put him in danger yet again. *What did he ever see in me? I told him he should have stayed away. His life would be so much easier if he had never met me.* He would be home in his huge house right now, enjoying comfortable living and plenty of food instead of rationing beans and rice and having to constantly be on alert.

There are four loud thuds on the deck above as if heavy objects have been dropped or fallen hard on it accompanied by less intense Spanish chatter. If I had been allowed to go to school, I would have learned Spanish properly. Not knowing what they're saying is driving me crazy with curiosity and anxiety. The only words I can make out are simple common words that, out of the context of the rest of the conversation, mean nothing.

"Cinco millones?!" I hear Adonis say in a raised voice.

That much I can understand. *Five million. Five million what?* Is this asshole asking to be paid off with that kind of price? We don't have that kind of money on us. Adonis left almost everything he had with my family except for what we would need for supplies and a bit for when we reach our destination, assuming our money is any good there.

"Si. Cinco millones o llamo a la policía."

"¡Estás loco! No tengo esa cantidad de dinero!" Adonis objects.

"¡Qué pena! La recompensa por usted es sólo un millón," the

stranger laughs.

His laughter is quickly cut off with a loud thud. The squeaking of shoes against the wet deck caused by quick-moving feet precedes the sickening thumps of flesh beating flesh and bodies slamming into the deck with loud crashes. Muffled grunts and curses accompany the other noises in a cacophony of testosterone-infused rage.

It's all my fault. This happened because I was stupid enough to be seen; now Adonis is probably hurt badly from trying to protect me. The guilt I feel for my stupid carelessness is crushing. I feel so small as I curl up under the table, but not small enough. I wish I could shrink into nothingness or go back in time and not be such an idiot.

I'm stunned out of my pity party by a sudden lack of noise. *Where did they go? Are they alive? Is Adonis alive? Is he hurt?* Maybe they knocked each other out. If something horrible happened to him, I'd never forgive myself, ever. It should be me instead of him in harm's way.

Taking a deep breath to try to steady my shaking body, I slowly start to crawl from my spot under the table to the ladder below the hatch. It's so deadly quiet up there that I can only hear myself breathing and a high-pitched ringing in my ears.

Pushing up the front on my body from my crawling position, I hear a loud thud on the hatch and fall backward in my panic. *No! That bastard can't still be here! Adonis!*

In a flash, I scramble to my feet and make a run for the bedroom. A second thud comes harder as I reach the door, and a third quickly follows as I slam the door behind me.

"Layla!" a weak, raspy voice calls out. "Open … the … fucking hatch!"

"Adonis?" I ask, my voice barely a nervous squeak. *He's okay!*

I fumble with the doorknob of the bedroom, my hands still shaking and slick with sweat from the adrenaline coursing through my body. After four failed attempts of my hands slipping off, unable to get a firm hold, my logic comes back to me. I grab the bottom of my shirt with my hand and use the fabric to create enough friction to keep my sweaty palms from slipping, and I yank the door open faster than I can move out of its way, smashing the tips of my toes on my left foot.

"Fucking shit!" I growl through clenched teeth, breathing in and out quickly to keep myself from screaming.

Another thud comes from the hatch, though with less force than the others. "Layla ... please."

His voice is weak and choppy. I hobble through the cabin as quickly as possible as Adonis repeatedly slaps the hatch door with little conviction, as if he's given up on everything.

Grimacing through the deep ache in my foot, I climb the ladder just enough to turn the lock. I give the hatch as strong of a push as I can muster, but it won't move.

"Adonis! It's unlocked now. You have to move so you can—"

Before I can finish stating the obvious, the hatch jerks open. I fall back in surprise as his rain-soaked sneakers drop to the second rung of the ladder, falling at least three feet and resulting in a surging literal pain in my ass.

Rain falls through the open hatch, creating a large wet spot on the floor in the cabin. When he turns from the ladder to walk, it's as if the Earth starts spinning slower or stops entirely. Time moves in slow motion, making every detail all the more striking and painful.

He looks at me on the floor, his left eye almost swollen shut, but even then I can see the disappointment and emotional distance he is trying to create. The bleeding gash on his cheek is nothing compared to the look in his eyes. I know that look. I've been guilty of it for most of my life. The look of someone who has emotionally walled themselves off to the world. Walling off the huge void they feel inside, preferring it stay empty and painless rather than risk letting anything painful fill it in.

In a matter of minutes, though it felt like an eternity, Adonis became a one-man fort, and it's my fault. Yes, he's alive, thank goodness, but will I ever be able to bring him out of this emotional solitary confinement? Will I ever be able to fix this massive mistake on my part, again, or will I lose him before we make it to Australia?

CHAPTER TWENTY-FIVE

ONLY A FEW INTERMINABLE MINUTES pass in the time between Adonis locking himself in the bathroom and coming back out, but it might as well be forever. The sounds of the sink and the toilet are all normal noises, but the situation is anything but. I feel like I should offer to patch him up, but come on—he's an actual doctor. I can't do any better than he can do for himself, assuming he would even take my help.

His face is a bit bloody, but nothing that looked too bad other than his eye. As I lean my head toward the door to listen, just to make sure he's okay—or at least that is what I want to tell myself—the door swings open. Caught off guard, I freeze in my awkward crouched-down leaning position and offer up a weak smile.

He regards me without emotion, just standing there, waiting for me to get out of his way. I straighten my posture and step back so he can pass me.

Striding stiffly toward the hatch and without even looking back or pausing a beat, he says, "Why don't you stop being useless and help bring the shit I bought down here and put it away?"

Not a shred of the love that was in his voice last night comes through now. *He has never spoken to me like that! And the way he did it, with indifference, as if he were relaying patient vitals to a nurse, all matter-of-fact and nothing else to it ...*

He drops the hatch shut behind him as I stand here with a blooming chill that feels like it originates in my bones.

He hates me. He's finally had enough of me. The urge to go to the bedroom and curl up into a ball and die is overwhelming, but I can't. *I can't let him get to me like this!* After everything I have lived through, I'll be damned if I let him be what takes me down. *I won't allow it! I survived just fine before meeting him. Hell, I was better off before I met him.*

I stop reflexively rubbing my arms; it won't warm this coldness. *Pull it together, Layla!* Determined, I straighten my arms at my sides and clench my hands as I make my way topside to do what needs to be done to survive—until I can get off this fucking boat once and for all. *Just get the supplies, put things where they need to be, and then I can just ignore him until he decides he wants to apologize for being such an asshole.* Yeah, I screwed up, again, but I tried to warn him to stay away, but he refused to listen. *It's his own damn fault.*

The wind has picked up, or maybe it has been this way for a while. I haven't been outside in ages. I close my eyes and let the light rain caress my face as the wind kisses it, giving me pleasant chills that flow through my veins. I feel cleansed and refreshed as I take in deep purifying breaths through my nose, reveling in the sweet smell of the fresh rain mixed with the salty sea.

It's amazing how the simple act of standing out in the rain can bring such internal peace. In spite of all the shit in my life, I still have the ability to take a moment and just feel the world around me. I am still here, against all the odds, to indulge in life's simple pleasures. Moments like this are the eye of the hurricane that is my life, an ephemeral calm before all hell breaks loose again.

A sudden jerk of the boat ends my serenity. Adonis is at the stern and has just shoved us away from the dock. He hunches over with an odd gait as he goes to start the outboard motor. In a few quick pulls, it starts, and he moves with smooth efficiency toward the helm. Now I can see why he was standing so strangely. The hum of the motor does nothing to drown out my scream of terror.

Adonis moves swiftly, grabbing me from behind, roughly clasping his hand over my mouth. I try to wriggle away from him, but his grip tightens, one arm around my waist, the other almost suffocating me. My struggling and screaming are futile. He is no longer the man I knew. He must no longer care if he hurts me, because his hold only gets tighter; my only choice is to comply.

I cease my screams against his hard hands. It's a pointless waste of energy. *Who would hear me? Do I even want anyone to hear me? No. To be heard would be the end of us both.* I just want to scream for the sake of it, to let out my pain, fear, and frustration at the world. I want to scream into the void until I exhaust myself, but I can't.

I feel sick and weak. I let my arms and legs to go limp, and as Adonis lets me slip from his hold, I sink to the floor like a stone in a pond. Hugging my knees to my chest while resting my forehead on my knees, I let loose hot, silent tears. Tears for the sweet man I once knew—the man who used to save lives instead of taking them.

Most of my tears are for myself. I'm a selfish bitch deep inside. I'm angry with myself. The overwhelming feelings of guilt and self-hatred feel as if they physically weigh me down. As if my veins are full of lead, a heavy, sluggish sensation spreads through my body. *I caused all of this. I didn't do as I was told. I let that man see me, and now he is dead because of it.*

Awash in cold, heavy guilt, I stare at the prone figure at the stern. Wet ebony hair is plastered to his face by the rain. His complexion, once dark, though probably bright at the same time, is now a dull brown hue, like clay in the sun. Maroon blotches mar his hands, evidence of the heated exchange that took his life.

I'm vaguely aware of Adonis working on the sails in the periphery of my vision. The sound of the outboard motor, the whipping of the sails, and the ocean meld together to create the perfect white-noise soundtrack for my surreal state of existence. The constant drone, along with the sound of my pulse in my ears, helps me to detach. As I stare unfocused at the body on the deck, my trance is broken by a figure standing over the man and the sudden absence of the droning of the motor.

My attention shifts to Adonis; clothes drenched by the rain, they cling tightly to his skin. The muscles in his arms and back are clearly defined by the semi-transparent fabric that hugs them as he adjusts the mainsail. He ties the ropes off with flawless grace and precision and shifts his left shoulder back slightly. Knowing he is about to turn around and see me watching him, I drop my gaze to my lap, hoping he didn't notice.

I don't know how to talk to him right now. What could he possibly say? What could I say? *"I feel as if someone punched a hole in my chest, leaving me hollow and broken. I want to love you, but you're no longer the man I fell in love with."* I'm sure that would go over real well, assuming I could even find my voice to say the words.

Though I can hear his footsteps, and feel them getting closer from the increased vibrations of the deck, I refuse to lift my head, even when I know he is standing right next to me. I can't see him, but I can feel his proximity.

He lets out a long sigh, and I feel the heat of his hand on my shoulder. In contrast with how physically cold I am and the coldness that radiates from my core, his hand is like fire. I shrink away from his touch, stunned by the drastic change in sensory input.

I hear his knee pop as he crouches down in front of me and replaces his hand on my shoulder, this time holding it with a firm grip so that I cannot pull away unless I muster the will to move more than a few inches.

"Go inside," he says with a gentleness I was never expecting to hear from him again.

It's as if he reversed time to before today's events, returning to the sweet, gentle man that I love. *How can he switch from being so hostile to this in such a short span of time?* He's the most capricious person I've ever known.

I don't respond or move; I don't have the strength to do either. All that has transpired today has left me drained of energy and my body heavy and immobile. Like a rock, I just exist, staying where I am. I have no will to be the proverbial rolling stone; I'd rather stagnate here and gather moss than be broken into pebbles when the hill terminates in a cliff.

His other hand presses under my chin. Lacking the strength to fight it, I allow him to lift my head so that I can see him through my soaked bangs. His gaze is gentle, warm, and full of sorrow. "Get warmed up. I'll take care of the other stuff," he coaxes.

Still, I do not move. If a statue could have feeling, I bet this is how it would feel—heavy, stiff, and cold to the core. I feel like the weight of the world is pressing down on me like Atlas. I drop my chin, but Adonis gently coaxes it back up, eyeing me pleadingly. I wonder if he can see it, my "soul, through the resignation in my eyes, the emptiness, the heartache.

He must see something, as he pulls my body into his, wrapping his arms around me and rubbing my back quickly but with care, creating heat from the friction of his movements. The comforting warmth spreads from my back to my core and limbs, bringing a sense of peace and safety with it. The safety of his arms. After all the crap, I still feel a sense of home and belonging when he's holding me like this.

"I'm sorry for snapping at you. It wasn't your fault," he says softly, like he really means it. But how could he?

I choke back a sob and shudder as I'm reminded of how much it truly is my fault. "Yes, it is!" The tears won't stay in my eyes, and I can't stop them. How can he be so forgiving? "I let someone see me," I confess. "I didn't listen! I'm sorry; so sorry!"

"There's a reward out for our capture and a description of the boat. Fernando thought he could threaten us and cash in, piece of shit." His voice is filled with immense disgust at the mention of Fernando. "I had no choice; I had to protect you. I lashed out at you, and I'm sorry."

A rush of intense relief, guilt, sorrow, and love wash away my best attempt at being controlled and stoic, and I can't do it anymore. Without my emotional walls to protect me, a heaving sob escapes me and the floodgates breach. My fingers grip the back of his shirt, clinging on as if my life depends on keeping him right where he is. He pulls me closer, resting my head on his shoulder, and gently sways me side to side while simultaneously rubbing my back and shushing me like you would a baby.

I feel calm and safe, but only for a moment. The movement of the boat combined with the swaying of his arms and the stress of today hits me like a rogue wave without warning. With an energy I didn't know I had, I break from Adonis's hold and scramble to the edge of the boat. My body shudders as I vomit violently into the sea.

I repeatedly hurl until I have nothing left, and then I rest my head on the boat's edge. I try to take a deep, cleansing breath in through my nose, but it causes me to gag on my snot and dry heave again. My nose and eyes are running like a faucet, and my lungs yearn for a deep, relaxed breathing pattern. I blow my nose in my hand to clear my airway and try again. Taking a deep breath in through my nose, my lungs fill, and I hold it for a few moments before blowing it out slowly through my mouth. I repeat the slow, deep breaths three more times. My rapid heartbeat slows as my whole body receives the oxygen it so badly needed but couldn't get when I was expelling the contents of my stomach into the ocean.

Exhausted from the ordeal that my body just put me through, to-day's insanity, and my seesawing emotions, I close my eyes, let out a long exhale, and roll over toward the safety of the center of the boat.

Adonis sighs loudly, though I can tell it's not one with the purpose to get my attention but one that sounds full of guilt and dejection. I open my heavy eyelids just enough to see him sitting on the edge of the bench, his elbows on his knees and head in his hands, as he stares at me with a forlorn expression.

Noticing my eyes open, he lifts his head, straightening his posture, and lowers himself to the floor. He scoots himself along the floor until he is right in front of me and sits with his legs crossed.

"We should get you inside, baby," he says as he lifts my head slightly and rests it in his lap.

I want to go inside, but I'm too tired and comfortable to move. The warmth of his body envelops me in a cozy invisible blanket as he runs his fingers through my wet hair in long, slow strokes, his fingernails lightly grazing my scalp.

"Mmm," a moan of relaxed pleasure escapes me.

"You like that?" he chuckles slightly.

I nod and nudge his hand, which, to my displeasure, has stopped, coaxing him to continue.

"How about this? I'll play with your hair all you want later …"

I nudge him again and sigh, making my disappointment as obvious as I can without words.

"Later. After you've had some proper rest, I'll pet you till your heart's content. Okay, my little kitten?"

I make a puckish, low growling noise. Adonis lets out a hearty laugh and ruffles my hair.

The tone of his voice and the playfulness of our rapport eases me. *I haven't lost him. I could never lose him.* He's my guiding light. Sometimes the light may flicker in the wind, threatening to go out, but it's an eternal flame, and it will always lead me home—to him.

CHAPTER TWENTY-SIX

FOR THE LAST THREE MONTHS, the seas have been fair. Little storms pop up on occasion, but nothing that my expert captain can't handle. The ocean has been kind to us, for if it were to turn violent, we'd have no place to seek safe harbor. There's nothing but open ocean in every direction for as far as the eye can see, and it has been that way for what seems like forever. The water is just a never-ending rippling mirror that seems determined to burn my skin with its reflection whenever I venture out onto the deck for more than an hour.

I spend most of my time in the cabin now, trying to read some of the books that Adonis has onboard. Mostly it's just medical crap that I'll never understand with words that are impossible to pronounce, but some of the pictures are interesting to stare at and think about for a while. I mean, which other organs in our bodies know about themselves except the brain? We use our brain to know what it looks like and how it works; imagine if the heart were self-aware. Sometimes it feels like it is, trying to persuade the brain to follow its lead, but I can't help but wonder how different we would be if our hearts were aware of their existence and able to wonder about their purpose.

Maybe I could have been some sort of doctor, too, if I'd had the chance to get an education when I was growing up. But that time in my life is gone, and I can never get it back. *What will I be when we reach land? Just a wife and mother?* It seems so inconsequential to be just those things. I admire my mother and all that she did for me and still does for my siblings, but I feel like I need more than just that. After everything that I've had to deal with in my short life, I don't want to die without having done something memorable. Maybe I'm just selfish, but I want the world to remember me when I'm gone, not be forgotten like all the others in the GI community. It's not that I'm not happy having Adonis or our future child; I just feel like there is more out there for me.

Maybe I'm just whiny, but what else can I do with all the spare time that I have on my hands but think about such existential problems? The only other things I can do are cook when it's time for meals and bask in his attention when I can get it. Adonis bought a lot of good stuff at the market on that wild day that we last saw land, including exotic spices to experiment with and meats. Lately, I haven't been able to stomach the spicy stuff, which sucks because it smells so good. Almost everything but crackers gives me heartburn or makes me puke at this point. So, I mostly just cook for him, my mouth watering the whole time while I wish I could eat it. It's pure torture.

When I do get the pleasure of his undivided attention, it's only a few hours in the early morning and late at night. We talk about the sorts of things I guess "normal" people would when dating or whatever, things like: What's your favorite color? What's your favorite food? Do you think aliens exist?

"My favorite color is blue," Adonis answered when I asked him that trivial question. I couldn't help but laugh at him.

"You must be loving it out here. You see nothing but blue all the time!" I teased.

"Not ocean blue, bluebonnet blue. Spring is my favorite time of year, or at least it was. Not like we will see a sight like that in Australia. What yours, huh? Pink? A girly little color that wishes it were red?" he returned.

"No! Purple, like the twilight, just before it gets totally dark after sunset. I also look good in it because of my being extremely pale and my hair color. Pink! Psssh!" I retorted. I like our little bickering; it's lighthearted and amusing.

He's been sailing later into the night lately, wanting to get to our destination as soon as possible, which leaves me feeling exceptionally lonely. I go up on deck for short visits during the day, but he's keenly focused on navigating the seas or whatever else is on his mind that our conversations are brief, but I use them to pry into his mind to relieve my curiosity and boredom.

"What's with your name? I mean, Adonis? How could your parents have known you would've turned out to be so damn sexy?" I tease.

"My mom had a thing for Greek mythology. She just thought I was perfect. At least to her." That revelation pulls at my heart. His mother must have loved him dearly. If only he had been able to grow up with all that love.

"Didn't they ever call you by a nickname? Donnie? Addy?" I pry, half joking and also wanting to get off the somber subject of his deceased mother.

"No!" he laughs. "Those would be horrible. Don't ever call me that," he warns me playfully.

"I don't know; it might slip out in bed one of these days. Three syllables are quite a mouthful when in the throes of passion."

He puts a clamp on the helm and sits by me on the bench. "Don't you dare," he states with mock severity, facing me directly, our noses touching. "Now you need to get back inside. All this sun is bad for your porcelain skin. I can't make love to you if you're sunburnt." He kisses me on the nose, and I know the discussion is over.

As I sit down at the little table to bore myself with a game of solitaire, I get a nasty pinching pain in my lower back. This early pregnancy stuff is bullshit. I thought you had to be a lot further along than this to start having aches and pains. I take a look at the little calendar by the sink, which Adonis has been ritually marking off every damn day since I missed my period, starting from when he thinks I conceived. Today is December 31. 94 days pregnant, according to Adonis's calculations. It is also four days until Mom's thirty-ninth birthday, and I have no way of telling her she is going to be a grandmother.

I'm sure she would be more excited than I am about it all. She would probably go on and on with tips and advice and start knitting blankets, booties, and the whole lot. I do want to be happy about the whole baby thing, but at the same time it doesn't even feel real. When I do think about it being real, I feel as if I'm trapped. Once you have a child, that's it; you have to be there for them for life. With a baby, there will be no more adventures or excitement. I know my "exciting life" has been difficult and chaotic, and downright deadly at times, but I don't think I can handle routine and boring for the rest of my life and not go crazy.

I could always go back to sleep; that is always an easy way to pass the time. Though I am not at all tired, I figure that maybe I can do something exciting in my dreams to waste the day away. Lying in bed, I stare at the ceiling, zoning out in hopes that it will make me sleepy. With unfocused eyes, I stare and I stare until it all disappears and I am elsewhere.

I'm in a house, a big house. It's not Adonis's house, though it's strange how familiar and new it feels at the same time. In front of me is a rickety ladder that goes up to a landing, but on my left is an elaborate staircase that leads to a landing parallel to the one I am looking up at. Though the stairs look safe and unsuspecting, I am compelled to climb the ladder.

I place my hands on the dusty rungs. The dust is gritty under my palms. I tug down on the rung to test it; it squeaks a bit but holds tight. A nervous sweat starts to collect on my upper lip, but I steel my nerves and place my right foot on the bottom rung and slowly raise my left foot up until all of my weight is being held by this dusty piece of wood.

I let out a long exhale, relieved in the structural soundness of the ladder, and begin climbing. The ten feet or so to the top are easier than I thought they would be; the hard part is that there isn't anything for me to hold to help me over the edge of the landing. The floor is wooden, surprisingly clean, and well waxed. Not at all what I would expect to see after the appearance of the ladder, but then I could have taken the stairs.

With the floor at eye level, I climb two more rungs until I have nothing left of the ladder to hold on to with my hands. I brace my hands on the floor, palms flat, and push down and forward, sliding my body onto the floor like a seal gliding onto a dock after jumping out of the water. My heartbeat pounds frantically as I feel that my feet are still dangling over the edge. Moving my hands out from under my torso, I quickly throw my arms forward and scoot further away from the edge until the floor completely supports me.

As I stand to look around, I'm in awe. This place is beautiful, yet simple. Laid out before me is a huge bedroom with plush rugs, a large four-poster bed made of what looks like maple wood, a matching armoire, dresser, vanity, nightstands, and a full-length gilded mirror. The image in the mirror makes me gasp. I look down at my stomach to see if what I see if real, but I'm still the same.

Looking back in the mirror, the other me is huge! She is stroking her very pregnant belly and smiling from ear to ear. My mirror version is mouthing something while looking down as if she's talking to the baby. *What is she saying? What am I saying?* I step closer to the mirror and she—I mean, me—stares back at me and says it again, staring me in the face.

"I can't hear you! What? What are you saying?" I plead with my other self.

She just stares me straight in the eyes. It's the eeriest, most unsettling feeling. It's as if my own self, yet also a stranger, is trying to peer into my soul. My eyes burn as I try to keep them open, trying to see what she knows through her—no, my eyes. "Tell me!" I say in my head, willing her to talk or write it down or something.

Unable to hold my gaze with the mirror me any longer, I blink hard, holding my eyes shut for a few seconds to relieve the burning. Suddenly, as if the version of me in the mirror were inside my head and controlling my body ...

"Cordelia," I whisper, opening my eyes.

"Who's Cordelia?" Adonis asks. He's sitting on the bed beside me, leaning over me with one hand next to my arm, propping him up.

"I ... I don't know," I stammer, blinking my eyes hard, trying to clear my head.

"If you say so," he says with a shrug, planting a kiss on my forehead. "I was wondering when you were going to wake up, sleepyhead."

"Why? What's wrong?"

I just fell asleep—what could be so urgent?

He must notice my concerned look, because he quickly gives me a sly smirk and his eyes have that humorous twinkle in them.

"I'm starving. Are you going to make me dinner or what, little woman?" he says in a deadpan voice.

Rolling my eyes, I grab my pillow. "Men!" I say with an exaggerated groan, tossing my pillow at him before I get up to make dinner.

"Just right there. You see it?" Adonis asks as he jabs his finger at a spot on the horizon with violent intensity, as if he were trying to stab it. "That little dark spot right there!"

I squint my eyes hard, trying to focus on what he sees. He must be seeing mirages, or I'm blind as a bat. "I just see the ocean and the damn sun reflecting off of it. I'm sorry."

He gives an exasperated sigh while making a gesture like he is trying to throw some imaginary object before running down the ladder into the cabin. I take my eyes from the horizon and sit down on the bench beside the helm. Shutting my eyes tight, I still can't get rid of the blazing image of the sun, a flashing white spot that I still see with my eyes closed. *I can't stand this boat much longer.* My ankles are starting to swell when I stand up too long, and I'm starting to get a bump. Who knows how long before my fat ass won't fit through the hatch?

Adonis comes bounding out of the hatch with binoculars in hand. "I didn't know we had those," I declare. I haven't seen them before, and I have been through everything in this boat simply for lack of anything better to do.

"You might want to consider getting glasses when we get there; I think you're blind," he chuckles. "They were with the flashlights and such. Now come here." He stands on the deck, binoculars to his face, beckoning me forward with his right hand.

"You know, maybe my supposed 'horrible vision' is a good thing for you. Who knows? Maybe if I could see better, I would find you hideous," I tease as I come up beside him.

"Maybe …" He hums. "And maybe you might just die of a heart attack from how hot I really am—now look!" He thrusts the binoculars toward me. Scoffing, I grab the binoculars firmly and jerk them out of his hands, showing my disapproval of his arrogance. I squint through the lenses and focus in on the object. *Holy shit!*

"Oh my god, Adonis! It's a boat! We must be nearly there!" I squeal with excitement.

"A ship," he quips as I bounce on my heels in excitement.

"Same thing!"

"Technically …"

"Oh, will you just shut up and not correct me, please? Honestly! Now, shouldn't we send them a signal? Radio—do we have a flare gun?"

"It's too bright out; they probably wouldn't see a flare. I can try the radio—and hope that they're Australian and not from somewhere in Asia."

We've been at sea for too long.

"I don't know how much more ocean I can take! We're much closer to Australia than South America or Asia at this point. Who else would be all the way out here in the middle of nowhere?" I almost shout. Grabbing onto his firm forearms, I stare pleadingly into the gorgeous eyes that brightly contrast against his overly tanned and wind burned face like emeralds shining in the wet sand.

Static hisses and pops as Adonis scans the frequencies.

"pssssshhhzzz — vess—hissss"

"Turn it back, turn it back!" I whine! "I heard a voice." Adonis turns the dial back to the left a tad and the voice returns.

"Stabad, fifteen degrees north-north-east, oveh," a husky voice drawls in a strange accent over the signal.

"Roga. Proceed wid caution," a second voice replies back. Adonis's face goes slack and pale. "What is it? What's wrong?" I badger him, shaking his shoulder when he doesn't respond. "Adonis?" Without a glance at me, he picks up the transmitter and depresses the button on the right side.

"This is Uniform Sierra Tango X-ray four-one-one-six-one-four-five, we are unarmed. Do you copy? Over," he says with a calm that contrasts with his face and clammy hands. I grab his left hand and ease his clenched fist open and give him a reassuring squeeze.

Do they think we're dangerous? That's crazy!

"Copy Tango X-ray, this is the Alpha November Pyxis. State your intentions."

"We are civilians seeking asylum. We've been at sea for months. Over," he calmly answers the strange-sounding man over the radio.

Will they help us? Are they friend or foe? What the hell does Alpha November mean? I have too many questions, but I don't want to interrupt. Adonis has adopted a very stoic expression as we wait for a response. I can tell that he probably has just as many thoughts running through his head as I do from the way his brow is furrowing deep in thought.

After what seems like an eternity, the man with the strange accent is back. "State your passenger manifest. Over."

"Myself, Adonis Caraway, and my fiancé, Layla Mason. Over," he responds before releasing the button. The hiss of the radio returns as the only sound in the cabin.

Fiancé! I lift my left hand a bit so I can admire the ring with its way-too-big-for-my-little-hand diamond. Being at sea for all of this time has rendered the word practically meaningless; all we have out here is each other. Such labels have no purpose, but if or when we get to land, it will be the word that defines what we are to each other in the eyes of the law, that says I will be his wife very soon—and the mother of his child.

I'm suddenly a bit dizzy, which happens more frequently lately, realizing that our lives are going to be changing drastically. Whether that change is good or bad, I don't know, but our little bubble that we've been living in for these past four months or so is about to be burst. I grip his hand a little tighter to keep myself balanced.

"Stand by, Tango X-ray, and breathe easy. You're in safe harbor now. We're coming to you. Over."

Adonis turns to me, and his face blooms into a smile as bright as the summer sun. Still gazing at me, blinding me with his radiant light, he speaks into the receiver, "Roger that! Thank you, sir!"

He lets the receiver drop to the floor, and without a moment to respond his lips are on mine as he gently cradles my face in his hands. When his mouth breaks its sensual hold on mine, I'm breathless and filled with love and joy. Resting his forehead against mine, we hold each other, gazing into each other's eyes. "We're finally going home, baby."

CHAPTER TWENTY-SEVEN

LIEUTENANT AVERY BAKER BOARDS OUR little sailboat after coming up in a small inflatable motorboat called a dingy. She's very formal looking. Her bun of scarlet hair, which contrasts strangely with her caramel skin tone, is perfectly intact after all the wind she endured speeding over to us. Her soft voice betrays the strict facade she wears.

"You two are from the US, huh?" she queries. We both nod. "Well, no worries about us sending you back. You made it this damn far—no going back now."

Never going back. It's final—I'll never see my family again. I know I can't go back—I'll be executed—but hearing it's certain still hurts a bit.

"How far out are we?" Adonis inquires.

"About a hundred thirty-five kilometers. We'll hitch you up with a tow rope—much faster that way. Then you can just relax till we get to port. We can sort out all the legalities when we get there. I don't foresee any problems with letting you in. You said you're a doctor—is that right?"

"Yes. Mostly emergency medicine," Adonis answers.

"Have your certificates with you, by any chance?"

"Do you want me to get them?"

"No, no. It can wait—just checking."

I've been standing here like a prop this entire conversation. It's starting to get a bit annoying. It's like Adonis has ceased to acknowledge my existence since she came on board. I can't help but feel a bit jealous, like he's checking her out or something. I want to say something at least, damn it.

"What port are we heading to?" I pipe in.

"Brisbane, of course! I'm sure you'll love it there," she beams. "Alright, day's a-wastin', so if you can get that spinny up and head toward the ship, we'll get you hitched up and ready to go."

Without faltering in the least, Lieutenant Baker gets back into her "dingy," casts off, fires up her outboard motor, and speeds across the water toward the ship.

With Miss Prim and Proper out of sight, Adonis finally looks at me. I have my arms crossed firmly, hoping he gets the hint.

"What?"

"Oh! I exist now!" I mock.

"That was an important conversation. In case you've forgotten, we haven't seen anyone other than each other in months," he admonishes me.

"You sure saw her, alright," I say sarcastically.

"Are you jealous?" His voice rises in pitch with surprise.

"No," I lie. "I just hate being ignored. It's like you were the only person on this boat—like I wasn't coming, too, and didn't matter."

"Don't be jealous. She's not my type."

"I'm not. And what is your type? I'll need to be sure to keep those kinds of women away from you."

"My type is pregnant, moody, and going to be my wife soon. Now, stop your pouting. You need a nap with a mood like that. This baby is about to go fast, and I don't need you falling overboard, so shoo." He waves his hand at me like he is swatting a fly.

"I'll go, but only because I have to pee, not because you said so," I remark stubbornly. I swat his butt after I've opened the hatch and escape down it before he can reciprocate. "You better behave, mister. I've got my eye on you," I call out before shutting the hatch.

With our boat hitched to the ship, we can now relax for the next few hours and enjoy our time alone together. We should be getting into port sometime in the night. Finally, the sun will set on our journey of getting here, and tomorrow it will rise on a new one—our future. Tomorrow will not just be a new day, but a whole new life. Tomorrow we'll have to deal with all sorts of legalities, and I don't know what else. How should I know what to expect when you run away to the other side of the world and actually make it? I don't think they make a how-to book on that. What I do know is that I'm happy to have Adonis to myself during the daytime. He doesn't have to do any work with the sails and can just sit back and relax with me.

"Are you as nervous as I am?" Adonis mutters, staring at the ceiling of our little floating bedroom.

I roll onto my side and prop myself up on my elbow to look at his face. He's scrunching his eyebrows, appearing deep in thought. "Of course I'm nervous. It's going to be way different than our lives back home and here. I don't know if I'll remember how to walk on solid ground," I giggle.

He gives me a warm little smile and lets out a contented sigh. I think I've alleviated some of his anxiety by pretending I have none of my own. I do, though—a lot of it. *Where are we going to live? If they have him working, what will I do with myself all day? What's the food like? What if Adonis meets someone else and leaves me?* I've hated having to be on this boat for so long, but I'm going to miss our private little world.

"Well, I know one thing we're going to do as soon as we can,"

Adonis chimes in, bursting my negative thought bubble.

"What?"

"Ask a judge to marry us."

Oh! I stare down at my ring. *Get married. Mrs. Caraway.* I suddenly feel ill and have to shake my head to expel the unpleasant feeling. I can't take that name—not the same name as that bastard father of his. No way!

Adonis sits up and starts to softly stroke my back. "You okay? You looked like you were going to throw up for a second there." His voice filled with concern.

I clear my throat. "I'm fine. It's just—about getting married ..." I hesitate. I don't know how to say this in a way that won't hurt him.

"Are you saying you don't want to?" he asks softly but panicked.

My words fly out as verbal vomit. "No, no, no—not no I don't want to marry you, but no I don't *not* want to marry you—it's the name thing." I stop before I bite my tongue off and try to gauge his reaction. He doesn't look mad—at least I don't think he does. Confused, maybe.

"What about the name thing?"

"I can't be Mrs. Caraway." He has his mouth open like he is about to say something in objection. "No. Let me finish," I chastise him. "It's not that I'm ashamed of you. The name just makes me think of your asshole father and your bitch stepmother. I can't live with that or have our child live with that."

"I was going to say, before you so rudely cut me off, that I was thinking the same thing."

"What?" I exclaim in shocked bemusement. "Really?" He nods at me. "Oh, thank fuck! I thought we were going to end up fighting about this." I breathe a huge sigh of relief.

"No arguments from me. I get it. I hate my name too," he muses.

"So, I keep my last name and the baby gets mine too?"

"Yep. One other thing, though."

"Okay," I say suspiciously. "What?"

"I want to change my last name to Mason. That way, we can all have the same name, leaving no room for anyone to question that we're married and a little family of our own."

Loud groaning noises and what sounds like a crack of thunder wakes me in a panic. Sitting up, I look around frantically in the dark. Adonis is sound asleep next to me, his mouth slightly open as he snores ever so softly. He appears completely undisturbed from the monstrous noises; on top of that, it doesn't feel like we are moving, either. *Why have we stopped, and what in the hell is that awful noise?*

"Adonis!" I whisper loudly as I lightly shake his shoulder. "Wake up! Can't you hear that?!"

He stirs and groggily rolls to his side. "Huh? What? Go back to sleep, baby."

He flops onto his back and falls back to sleep instantly like he had never even heard me. More deep groaning sounds ring out, only they seem much closer this time. The sound is chilling and ominous, and I swear I can feel them vibrating through my blood. I pull his pillow out from under his head and smack him, "Wake up! Don't you hear that?" I say through gritted teeth to keep myself from yelling at him.

This time he sits up with a jolt, breathing rapidly. "What? What? What's wrong?" he mumbles.

"Now you're awake!" I scold. "Stop breathing so loud and listen."

A few minutes of stifling silence pass before a loud bang startles us, followed by the sounds of rushing water and a persistent low-pitched groan. "What is that?! Are we sinking? Why aren't we moving?" I ask rapidly in a whispered panic.

"We're not sinking, but let's find out what's going on." Adonis throws back the sheets and makes for the door. He pauses a beat and gives me one of those "come here" hand signals; I shake my head with a clear "no" implied. *In fact, make that a hell no!* Whatever is out there sounds terrifying enough from in here. He's supposed to do all the checking on scary noises duties. He's the man in this relationship, damn it!

He comes back to the bed and grabs my hand and pulls me to my feet, trailing me behind him as he moves through the cabin to the ladder. "Come on!" It takes every bit of courage in me to not lean back on my heels and fall to the floor like a tantrum-throwing toddler in order to keep him from making me follow him, though he would probably just drag me along anyway. He lets go of me to open the hatch and I'm tempted to run back to the bed, but I'm as curious as I am scared out of my mind.

Adonis opens the hatch, and the noises are even more monstrous. Resounding cracks and bangs mixed with what sounds like someone filling an enormous bathtub pound my ears as I watch him climb the ladder to the deck. After what seems like an agonizing eternity of waiting, his hand appears through the hatch, giving me a thumbs up.

Okay, he's alive, he says it's okay to come up. Breathe, Layla, breathe. I take several deep breaths, trying to steel my nerves, but fail miserably. My palms are sweating and my hands shaking as I slowly climb, each ladder rung vibrating with the cacophony that is so deafening I can barely make out Adonis shouting "It's okay, come on!" as he grabs my right hand as it nears the top.

I stumble into his embrace as I try to get my footing on deck. I'm shaking from head to toe. There is a thick mist in the air and all around us is darkness, and not just from it being nighttime. There appear to be titanic walls all around us, the stars only appearing as misty blurs directly overhead and nowhere else on the horizon.

I wrap my arms firmly around him, holding him for dear life. "How is this okay?!" I shout. He begins to rub my back as he holds me tightly and lowers his head so he doesn't have to yell. I hear him

272

exclaim in my left ear, "It's amazing! They're locks!" with a child-like excitement.

What? Locks are what you have on doors; this is a monster! He's lost his fucking mind. I break the comforting contact of my face with his chest in order to give a reply in his ear. "What are you talking about?"

"A series of walls to let ships in and out without allowing the sea level to rise near shore. An excellent defense system, too. I thought they were just a rumor, but then why would they tell us the truth?" he answers with way too much certainty in his voice. *So, the place we're heading to never flooded? Who wouldn't tell us the truth?* I have too many questions.

"I don't want to be out here anymore, Adonis. Please, I'm scared." I want to go back inside and hide and have him hold me there, not out here. The blackish gray all around us and the mist are chilling me to my core; though I'm sure it isn't even actually cold out, it's all in my mind.

"Don't worry, baby, we're safe. We can go inside." He lightly coaxes me to turn around and drapes his arm over my shoulder as he guides us steadily to hatch.

Back inside, the noises are still noticeable but become less frequent and more distant. We are moving slowly now, but Adonis assures me that we will probably go through the process a few more times before the night is over and to try to sleep. I'm exhausted from the emotional gymnastics caused by these walls or whatever and would love more than anything to sleep, but the noises keep me on edge.

Adonis is cuddling against my back, and I envy how easily he can sleep. I start to drift off as I listen to his steady breathing when another loud bang causes me to shudder, waking Adonis. *I'm going to have a heart attack before daybreak at this rate.* As soon as I start to get calm, BOOM—another noise has to come and rattle me.

Adonis goes into his soothing mode with me, draping his arm over me and pulling me close while he shushes me like I'm an overgrown baby. "Shhhhh, it's okay. I've got you," he murmurs against my neck. If I weren't so hyperalert and anxious, it would probably tickle, but I can't feel anything but anxiety right now.

After taking in a deep breath, I let out a loud sigh and try to relax, but I can't. My muscles are tense and in fight-or-flight mode. "I can't sleep. All the noises make it impossible! As soon as I get close to sleeping, something else goes bump in the night."

"How about I sing you to sleep?" he whispers.

I can't help it; a slight smile pulls at the left side of my mouth. *He's so sweet, always thinking about me. Probably more than I think about him.* Well, I think about him all the time, but I need to think about him in a non-self-serving way, like how I can do things for him to make him happy. I'm going to work on that when we get settled—on making him happy every day just because.

"Well?" he croaks, his voice is groggy. "You didn't answer me."

Lost in my thoughts about how such a simple suggestion from this sweet man of mine makes me feel, I left him hanging. "Sure. I've never heard you sing before. I'd like that."

"Yes, you have, baby, you just don't remember," he says softly, his voice sounding wistful yet sad.

"When?" I feel horrible. How could he have sung to me before and I not remember? My mind races through all of our time together, searching for that moment, but I can't find it.

"When you were sleeping, my beautiful girl. Now be quiet, and I'll help you sleep again."

A soulful melody in a captivating voice comes from his lips; it's about me, by name. It's sweet, yet sad, saying I have him on his knees and turned his world upside-down. I want to ask him if he made this up and if he feels that way or if he heard it somewhere. I would ask him, but his voice is so beautiful and soothing, I don't want to inter-rupt. The horrible noises outside fade into the background as I listen to him, not only enjoying the sound of his voice but also the rhyth-mic vibration of his chest against my back as he sings.

CHAPTER TWENTY-EIGHT

"HAPPY NEW YEAR!" ADONIS WHISPERS excitedly in my ear, waking me much too early for my liking. He has the curtain in front of our cabin porthole pulled back, and the sky is just barely getting that tinge of pale pink and lavender, indicating the sunrise is approaching.

Yawning, I stretch my arms to the side, giving him a shove. "The sun isn't even up yet," I mumble sleepily.

"I couldn't sleep any longer. Today is the day!" He is radiating excitement, and his smile is contagious. I can't help but give him a sleepy smile, though my eyes are still puffy and squinty in the near darkness.

Yes, today is THE day! The day we finally leave our little floating home. We pulled into port last night and moored at a small dock in the Navy Yard. It was so late when we got in that they decided to have us stay on our sailboat for the night and figure out housing and all the legalities in the morning. As much as I've hated being cooped up in what at times felt like a buoyant jail cell for so long, my eyes well up at the thought of leaving it. Yeah, at times it was claustrophobic—and the fact that I'm getting fat didn't help either—but it has been home. Our home, our safe place in an endless watery abyss.

Getting out of bed means the beginning of another new life for us. I'm excited about it but scared at the same time, not wanting to move for fear of the change. That's the crazy thing about change; you want it so bad sometimes, but when it arrives you want to hold on to the way things are, afraid that the future may not be all it promised to be.

"Come on, Layla! I made breakfast. Get up and get dressed, gorgeous. Today I make you my ball and chain forever," he laughs. *Ball and chain! What a little shit!* I sit up and give him a light kiss, then nip his bottom lip.

"Ouch!" He feigns a frown but fails horribly.

"Better watch it, mister," I chuckle. "I'm more like a cannonball."

"True. You blow me away."

My heart swells. He's such a sweetheart and a stinker at the same time. I want to spend forever in our little bubble on this boat, but I know that time has to go on, and I have to get up and go on with it.

"More dehydrated eggs?" I ask dryly with a smirk, knowing the answer already. We don't have anything else left.

"Only the best for my baby and littler baby," he states with sarcasm and gives me a wink as he heads out of our room and into the kitchen.

"Oh, I can't wait for real food!" I declare. *Forget my earlier hesitation; I'm all for the future now. A floor that doesn't move under my feet and real food await!* I quickly divest myself of my—correction, Adonis's T-shirt I was sleeping in and slip into a sundress, heading to the kitchen for my last bland breakfast in our micro-paradise.

After eating, I go to "the head" and take a quick shower and get dressed. As I'm brushing out my hair, Adonis enters our room with a box.

"Where did that come from?" We don't have any boxes in here; there isn't any room for such useless things.

"It's time to go, baby. Lieutenant Baker is on deck. She brought a couple of boxes for us to collect our personal effects."

What's with that woman? Is she the official welcoming committee or what? I roll my eyes in irritation before asking the obvious nagging question. "And where are we supposed to take our things that you want me to put in boxes? We don't have a home. This is our home," I emphasize, pointing at the floor.

"They are going to put us up in a small apartment within walking distance of a hospital so that I can work. We won't be coming back here," Adonis explains, sounding dejected and staring at the floor now.

Never coming back? Why the hell not? It's our boat, isn't it? Well, it was his father's, but fuck him. He isn't here, and it's not like we're going to return it.

"Why aren't we coming back?" I demand.

"The government is seizing it as an asset and will sell it to help pay for our housing and basic needs until I start getting paid."

I know I shouldn't be so upset about the boat. It seems logical enough—we have to pay our way somehow—but I can't help feeling violated, and a bit pissed off. "What the hell would they do with us if we just washed up on a log?" I hiss. *How dare they take this from us!* I know we won't have much use for it anymore, as I don't plan on going on any more sea adventures. *But still, it's ours!*

He runs his hands through his hair, clearly frustrated or confused or both. "We took this boat in order to get here; it was a means to an end, not a permanent living arrangement. I'm going to miss her too—the boat. I have a lot of good memories thanks to this girl." He absentmindedly rubs his hand along the bulkhead as if he were petting a dog. "Some great times before I met you as well as our time together on her, but it's time to let it go. We aren't sailing off into the sunset again; we made it. It's only fair to sell it. If we didn't have this, we would probably end up in a homeless shelter until I start making an income. We're lucky."

I hate that he has to make it make so much damn sense. Sighing with resignation, I take the box from him. "Fine. This apartment better be worth it," I pout as I turn to head to our room and gather my clothes and few personal belongings.

With my box of clothes, a few personal items (my pictures, the letter Daisy wrote to me, and the seashells), and my hygiene products, I make my way to the ladder. Putting the box at my feet, I reach up and open the hatch. The brightness of the early morning consumes the rectangular hole above my head and a sea breeze snakes its way in, fluttering a few strands of around my face. Closing my eyes, I take in a deep cleansing breath and try to steel myself for the day to come and the permanent departure from my small but cozy floating abode.

I lift the box above my head and, using one ladder rung to give me the necessary height, I push it out onto the deck. As I reach my hand out to the ladder rung, I can't help but hesitate. Stepping back down, I turn to give the cabin one last look, trying to commit it all to memory with every detail possible. Our little table and bench, the kitchenette with its single stove coil—our room.

"Are you coming up or not?" Adonis calls from topside.

"Just give me a minute," I call back, almost absentmindedly. I walk toward our room, or what *was* our room. I gently open the door, feeling the need to be as quiet as possible, as if what I'm doing is somehow wrong. Doting on the past, I'm afraid to disturb the memories this room holds. The brown comforter is bunched up at the foot of the bed, and the deep-blue sheets are crooked and wrinkled as if someone still lives here and had just jumped out of bed to take a shower before coming back to make the bed. The thought of making the bed crosses my mind briefly, but I swat the thought away like an annoying fly. *This is how it should always stay.* To alter this space in any way seems sacrilegious, like vandalizing a grave or an ancient temple. I wish that this bed, where we laid many nights as a reunited and stronger couple, could stay as it is forever, but I know that it won't. Someday, someone else will call this place their own and make love in this very bed. That knowledge is painful and repulsive.

My memories are all that I'll have of this place, and for me, smell is something I remember longer than visions. I can hardly recall what my grandmother looked like anymore, as she passed when I was only three years old, but I will always remember how she smelled. It's hard to describe, but there were hints of lavender and talc that always accompanied her presence.

As I gently sit on the edge of the bed, I steady myself with one hand and stroke the sheets gingerly with the other. A sudden feeling of loss and grief overcomes me, and as hard as I try, I can't keep the lump growing in my throat from coming out in a sharp, abrupt sob, which I quickly stifle as I gather the sheet in my hands and pull it to my face. Taking a deep inhale as I close my eyes, I calm my trembling breaths and try to center myself. When all of my crystal-clear memories fade from my mind's eye over time, I will still remember the smell of these sheets. Nothing can take that away from me or what our time here has meant to me—to us.

Lieutenant Baker greets me cheerily as I exit the cabin. "Morning! Ready to go?"

I nod my head and give her a weak smile. "I guess. It's just so early," I finish with a yawn.

The sky is becoming brighter, but the sun is still below the horizon. The navy yard looks bleak with gray ships moored on gray concrete piers. Our little sailboat is a shock of blue and white in a colorless pallet. Lieutenant Baker has made her way to solid ground as I hesitate, lost in my thoughts while I gaze at the brightening spot where the ocean meets the sky. This is it. The end, the beginning.

Adonis's hand touches my shoulder, "Time to go. You okay?" he asks gently, bringing me back to the here and now.

Placing my hand over his on my shoulder, I give him a gentle squeeze. "Yeah, I'm okay. I just want to see the sunrise from the boat one more time. Can we wait just a few more minutes? It's almost there." Just one more sunrise, one more new day welcomed from a place I know and feel safe. I can't really understand why. Maybe it's closure, or perhaps opening a new experience, but I just need that last sunrise before I go.

"Yeah, sure. We can have one more sunrise," Adonis agrees as he lets go of my shoulder. He wraps his arms around me from behind as we silently watch the sun seemingly rise from the ocean and usher in the first day of the New Year and our new life.

CHAPTER TWENTY-NINE

AS WE RIDE THROUGH THE streets of Brisbane, I stare idly out the window while holding Adonis's hand in the back seat of the plain black car, its windows darkly tinted. The buildings closest to the navy yard are short and drab in appearance, but as we approach the city center they reach for the sky, similar to those of Old Houston. Lieutenant Baker points out the courthouse we will need to go to tomorrow to sort out immigration paperwork; she already booked us an appointment. But as for today, we are to get settled, much to Adonis's disappointment, as he had his heart set on us getting married today.

"Sorry, mate, but it's unfortunately not going to be able to happen that quickly," she starts to explain. Adonis squeezes my hand as if trying to reassure me, but in all honesty, I am a bit relieved. There's too much going on: a new home, having to start all over with almost nothing, Adonis having to start working again, leaving me alone for the first time in months. It would be nice to slow things down if we can. It's overwhelming.

"Typical citizens have to declare their intent to marry at least a month before they tie the knot. You two, being immigrants, will have to apply for a special marriage permit on top of needing to sort out all the paperwork to become citizens," she continues on, but she stops as she looks in her rear-view mirror and spots the disappointed look that is Adonis's slight frown. "Cheer up! A month will pass before you know it. Besides, you will be plenty busy, I'm sure, making yourselves at home, exploring the area. We have lovely parks, and there's the zoo. Good stuff."

Adonis gives my hand another squeeze and perks up a bit, offering the lieutenant a smile. "No worries. Just can't wait to make it official, that's all," he reveals.

Aw! I sit up tall and reach my face up to kiss his cheek. "I'm not going anywhere, so there's no rush." He beams down at me and nuzzles his nose against mine before kissing the tip of it. With his worries seemingly banished, I lean into him, our hands still clasped as we wait for our destination.

"What in the hell?" I hear Lieutenant Baker say to herself as she pushes the brakes suddenly.

The flow of traffic has almost halted, and there are flashing lights and a crowd of people jamming the sidewalks on the way to our new home, a small apartment near the University of Queensland. The location was chosen for us because it's relatively cheap and has a lot of public transportation so that Adonis can start working at a nearby hospital as soon as he's cleared with immigration for a work permit.

"What's wrong?" People are starting to crowd around our car, and it's disturbing.

"Someone must have leaked it. Goddamn it! When I find out—" Lieutenant Baker starts to rant.

"What the hell is going on?" Adonis demands, cutting her off.

"Someone must have leaked your housing location to the press."

"The press?" I ask. "What the hell is 'the press'?"

"The news reporters. You two are big news. We haven't had anyone make it here from the Americas in over fifty years! It's not an easy journey, as you already know."

Lieutenant Baker holds down the car horn as people flashing

bright lights start knocking on the windows and push their faces up against them trying to see us through the dark glass. It's a disturbing spectacle. I shrink down, trying to hide, though it seems they can't see us, try as they might, and nuzzle my head into Adonis's lap for comfort.

"What do they want?!" I whine.

"They want to know about you, but they could have waited for a press conference. Showing up here is just tasteless. A bunch of damn looky-loos! Scum!" she seethes, disgust dripping from her words.

Rapidly hitting the horn, making a series of short, loud bursts, Lieutenant Baker slowly moves through the crowd inch by agonizing inch until we hear a strange "whoop" sound, and I see a red and blue flashing light come through the front windshield. My blood turns to ice as I realize what that means. *The police!*

"No, no, no!" I mumble as I hold on to Adonis for dear life. "How did they find us?!" I whisper.

"Oi! Calm down!" Lieutenant Baker shouts back at me. "They're here to help us. This isn't where you came from."

Oh! I'm so used to being afraid of the police that I forgot. Any time police were around back home, it wasn't good, but I'm not there anymore. I'll probably always have anxiety around authority figures, but I know in the logical part of my mind that I don't need to be afraid. It will be a constant battle of instinct and logic, but one I am determined to win. I have to learn to cope; no more haze, and now, no more kava. I have a baby inside me that I have to care for, and I need to deal with my anxieties on my own. I sit up, shake my head, and take in a huge breath, trying to calm my pulse, which is going a mile a minute.

"We're safe here, remember?" Adonis reminds me, flashing a teasing grin.

"Sorry." A sheepish grin adorns my face. Feeling foolish like this would usually be too much for my pride to handle and I'd get angry to hide it, but I can't help but laugh. I heave a big sigh of relief and giggle at myself. "Old habits die hard, I guess?" I muse.

Rather quickly, the crowds start to recede. Police officers are directing them away from the vehicle and we start moving at a normal pace again. People still line the streets along the sidewalks but are no longer on the road as we travel four more blocks before stopping in front of a wooden barricade. Lieutenant Baker rolls down her window to talk to an officer who is standing by the barricade.

"Lieutenant Baker?" the officer asks as he peers behind her, eyeing Adonis and me suspiciously before giving us a friendly smile.

"Yes, sir. Is the perimeter secure?"

"All tenants are either not home or secluded to their residences until further notice. No one's entering or exiting," the officer relays to our escort. The officer gives a hand signal to another officer behind the barricade, and the obstacle is moved out of our way.

Lieutenant Baker gives the officer a salute and slowly drives us into a sectioned-off area on the other side of the barricade, shielding us from the throngs of people trying to get as close as they can.

She puts the car in park and turns to us. "Well, it's been a pleasure meeting you two. Welcome home." Her tone is very official, but I can tell that she means it; I can spot a fake smile a mile away. I know I didn't care for her much at first; being used to having Adonis's attention all to myself spoiled me some, and I've never been big with socializing, but she's okay.

An officer approaches the car and opens the door on Adonis's side, and the comfortable silence gets sucked out of the car. Hundreds of people are shouting unintelligibly, and my anxiety kicks back in. Adonis unbuckles his seatbelt and puts his left leg out the door before I grab his hand and give it a firm tug, letting him know I don't want to get out, that I'm frightened. My hand is sweating, and my hand easily slips when he pulls back at me.

"It's okay; they're just curious. Besides, they're back there." He nods his head, toward the barricade, which looks to be a hundred feet or so away.

I give him a wide-eyed stare to drive home the point of how terrified I am. My heart is pounding, and I'm perspiring everywhere—my hands, upper lip, armpits, etc. "When I get out, I'll stand right there"—he points to right outside the door—"and put my back to the crowd so you can get out and I'll block their view, okay?" I nod in acceptance, unbuckle myself, and take his hand again as he steps out of the car.

I quickly follow him out. With his back turned toward the crowd, he covers his face with his left arm while draping his right over my head as an officer whisks us quickly to the apartment building door. The officer holds a card in front of the door handle, and it opens. When the door closes, I am relieved by the noise reduction and breathe deeply, having unconsciously been holding my breath as we rushed from the car to the little lobby where we now stand.

The air in here is much colder than outside. My arms are covered in goosebumps as my body hair stands on end. It's not cold, cold; it's refreshing, but my body can't help but react to the combination of cooler air and my shot nerves from all the commotion.

The lobby is small but cozy. The walls are a calming shade of light green and the lighting is subtle yet sufficient. On the wall adjacent to the front door are dozens of little mailboxes, a corkboard with papers pinned to it, and a small counter where a middle-aged woman with a slight frame is sitting with a polite smile when our eyes meet.

"Good morning!" the woman greets us in a high-pitched cheery voice.

Adonis casually approaches the counter, gives his usual dashing smile, and introduces us.

"Pleased to meet you. I'm so thrilled that you will be staying here. The name's Madison, and if you ever, and I mean *ever,* need anything, don't hesitate to give me a ring or drop by. I know it must be overwhelming with everything you've got going on, but no worries here. Welcome home!" Madison blurts out rather rapidly while gesticulating with her hands. She is a very animated, high-energy person; I like her.

"Thank you, Madison. It's a pleasure to meet you too. We will definitely be talking later, as I'm sure I'll have a million questions, but at the moment I'm just really tired," I relay.

"Oh! Of course! You must be, you poor things. Right!" Madison stammers. She turns to a cupboard on the wall, unlocks it with a key, and reveals rows of keys on numbered hooks. She scans her finger along the numbers, mumbling to herself, before grabbing a key and closing the cupboard. "Here you go." She holds out the key to Adonis. He catches it in his hand as she drops it to him.

"You will be in number 415, one of our furnished units. Fourth floor, third door on your left. Can't miss it."

"Thank you!" I smile at Madison and give her a small wave before grabbing Adonis by the arm and heading up the stairs.

www.ingramcontent.com/pod-product-compliance
Lightning Source LLC
Chambersburg PA
CBHW051144030726
47504CB00004B/1039